GEPT

全民英檢聽力測驗

So Easy 中級篇

實踐大學副教授 李普生 編著

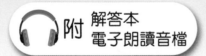

附 解答本
電子朗讀音檔

最逼真！模擬試題提升應試能力
最精闢！範例分析傾授高分技巧

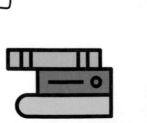

三民書局

國家圖書館出版品預行編目資料

全民英檢聽力測驗SO EASY(中級篇) ／ 李普生編
著.——初版八刷.——臺北市：三民，2019
面； 公分

4712780663295
1. 英語 2. 考試指南 3. 試題

805.1892   97003720

© 全民英檢聽力測驗SO EASY(中級篇)

編 著 者	李普生
發 行 人	劉振強
著作財產權人	三民書局股份有限公司
發 行 所	三民書局股份有限公司
	地址　臺北市復興北路386號
	電話　(02)25006600
	郵撥帳號　0009998–5
門 市 部	(復北店)臺北市復興北路386號
	(重南店)臺北市重慶南路一段61號
出版日期	初版一刷　2008年3月
	初版八刷　2019年8月
編　　號	S 807380

行政院新聞局登記證局版臺業字第○二○○號

有著作權 · 不准侵害

4712780663295

給讀者的話

在國際化、全球化的趨勢引導下，「全民英語能力分級檢定測驗」(General English Proficiency Test, GEPT) 已成為學校公民營機關單位用來測試學生成員英語能力的主要工具。姑且不論這種以考試來決定受測者語言能力的做法是否合宜、理論是否站的住腳、而功效是否真的可以作為與國際接軌及與世界同步的證明，「全民英檢」已是現今畢業升遷的主要憑藉已是不爭的事實；與其研究它的公信力，倒不如思考如何做才能打敗制度奪取高分！

根據全民英檢的主辦單位——財團法人語言訓練測驗中心所公佈的資料，全民英檢的對象是以在校學生及一般社會人士為主，其題型與命題則依各階段學習者的特質分為五級，且不拘限於特定領域或教材，測驗內容則是聽說讀寫四技並重，考生只要通過所報考級數即可取得該級的及格證書。該中心亦指出因此項測驗主在對本地學生社青的英語能力提供一個公平客觀且可信度高的評估，所以其本質與目的實與 TOEFL 或 IELTS 有所不同；只要能參考國內各級英語教學之課程大綱及本土生命經驗與特色相關的資訊，無須特別準備應可輕鬆過關。惟因國內英語教學素以讀寫為主，加強聽說練習將對受測者有所幫助。換句話說，「平常心」和「實力」應是通過英檢的關鍵。

編者一向以為英語文學習之道無它，唯勤而已。當然事前的準備和練習的確有助於考試的過關；所謂「臨陣磨槍，不快也光」亦即如此，但日常實力的累積，語言四技的均衡使用，及持之有恆的態度和做法更是成功的不二法門！

在我們開始進一步研究解析之前，希望這番「老生常談」能對正要參加或準備參加全民英檢的考生有所啟發。

全民英檢中級聽力測驗簡介

通過「全民英語能力分級檢定測驗」中級測驗者，英語能力相當於高中畢業的程度，具有使用簡單英語進行日常生活溝通的能力。如能聽懂在日常情境中的一般會話、公共場所廣播，氣象報告及廣告等；在工作情境中，通過中級檢定者能聽懂簡易的產品介紹與操作說明及大致聽懂外籍人士的談話及詢問。

換句話說，for those who pass the Intermediate and/or High-Intermediate level of tests, he/she should be able to understand or to do the following:

—talk more about abstract ideas and express her/his opinion

—participate in discussions and be able to politely interrupt, and take turns in communicating; agree or disagree with other people's opinion

—give a logical argument to support a view and express his/her feeling and general emotions

—converse with relative ease in everyday social situations and use conventional social language, both formal and informal, in greeting and welcoming people

—help people with problems by making suggestions and giving advices, talk and speculate about hypothetical situations in the past and present

—listen to natural speech and conversation and begin to understand nuances, subtleties, and details

（編註：若讀者能看懂上述的英文說明，恭禧您！您已經通過中／中高級英檢中的閱讀能力測驗單元並獲得滿分）

全民英檢聽力測驗中級題型分三部分：

Ⅰ：看圖辨義一共十五題。每題聽光碟播出題目和四個英語句子之後，選出與所看到的圖畫相符的答案。每題只播出一次。

Ⅱ：問答一共十五題。每題聽光碟播出的英語句子（疑問句或直述句），再從試題中的四個答案中選出最適合的答案。每題只播放一次。

III：簡短對話一共十五題。每題聽光碟播放的一段對話和一個相關的問題，再從試題中四個選項中，選出一個最恰當的答案。每段對話和問題只播出一次。

▶測驗分數換算：

初試：聽力及閱讀能力測驗

複試：口說及寫作能力測驗

聽力測驗和閱讀能力測驗成績總合達 160 分，且其中任一項成績不低於 72 分始得通過初試。複試則需寫作和口說能力測驗皆達 80 分始得通過。初試及複試皆通過者，發給合格證書。成績紀錄自測驗日期起保存兩年。

	聽力	閱讀	寫作	口說
通過標準	兩項測驗成績總和達 160 分，且其中任一項成績不低於 72 分。		80	80
滿分	120	120	100	100

現在我們已知道中級聽力測驗的標準、題型和分數換算方式，讓我們正式開始練習。

電子朗讀音檔下載教學

1. 前往「https://reurl.cc/jK7lp」下載電子朗讀音檔。

2. 將檔案解壓縮，密碼為 TEST 3 第 2 題圖片房號。

（請留意英文大小寫、標點符號是否輸入正確。）

3. 待解壓縮完成後，即可使用。

＊若解壓縮後發現檔案缺漏，請再次解壓縮即可。

＊若仍無法順利進行下載，歡迎前往「Sanmin English – 三民英語編輯小組」臉書粉絲專頁私訊詢問。將有專人為你服務，謝謝。

「Sanmin English – 三民英語編輯小組」臉書粉絲專頁：

https://www.facebook.com/SanminEnglishEditor/

全民英檢 So Easy 聽力測驗（中級篇）

CONTENTS

CONTENTS

聽力測驗試題
範例分析

不論是接受型 (receptive) 能力的聽讀，或生產型 (productive) 的說寫，英語四技的基礎，不分初、中、中高或高級，不外乎音、字、句型和片語。以音為例，若不知母音子音之分為何，不知音節為何，不知重音為何，不知語調為何，不知在何種前提下前音和後音之間會有何種現象或改變，不知哪些音必須仔細分辨，否則聽起來都是一樣，那聽力不可能提升而成績更不可能增加。同樣地，若字無法分辨同義反義，不知何為同音異義或同形異音異義，就算是背熟整本字典，成績可能依然平平。因此，想要在聽力測驗上拿高分，光是了解題型還不夠；知音辨音及知字辨字才能選出正確答案。

　　所以在本單元中，我們不僅要熟悉題型，我們更要能將複雜的音字句型片語規律化；一看見固定題型就能找尋固定答案，看到關鍵字就能掌握題意。更要配合所講述的題型佐以相關的音字詞規則。使所有考生能再最短的時間內不僅通過英檢取得高分，更能將英語文相關的規則做複習一併提升自我英語文能力。

看圖辨義

　　題目問，受測者則看圖作答；簡潔扼要規格固定所以模糊空間不大，除非自己大意不小心，實在沒有拿不到高分的理由！在此部分中，所提問題不外乎可明確辨識的主題現象場合活動 (overview, general impression) 或詳實細微的描述和差異 (specific information, details) 或從已知事實對未知或未來做推測 (guessing, inference) 等，而問題形式除了 "yes/no" 問題 (closed questions) 外就是 Wh- 問題 (open questions)；前者除 yes/no 外別無選擇，後者則須仔細參閱圖示找出答案。例：

⑴ "Is this man singing?" "Yes, he is." Or, "No, he isn't."

⑵ "Does he look happy?" "Yes, he does. He wears a big smile on his face." Or, "No, he doesn't. He looks troubled."

⑶ "What is the man doing?" "The man is singing."

⑷ "How does the man look?" "He looks as if he had something in mind."

Question 1

 TRACK 01

A

For Question number 1, please look at picture A.

Question number 1:

Are these people soldiers?

(A) Yes, they are. They are soldiers.

(B) Yes, they are. They are police officers.

(C) No, they aren't. They are students from a local university.

(D) Many soldiers were wounded in the war.

翻　譯　這些人是士兵嗎？

(A) 是的，他們是。他們是士兵。

(B) 是的，他們是。他們是警察。

(C) 不，他們不是，他們是當地大學的學生。

(D) 很多士兵在戰爭中受傷。

答　案　A

提　示　本題是以 be 動詞為主的疑問句。本類型題目要注意：以 be 動詞或助動詞 (do, does, did, shall/should, will/would, have must, need...) 等開頭的問句，所謂的封閉式問句，習以 yes/no 回答

Question 2

For Question number 2, please look at picture B.

Question number 2:
Doesn't John smoke?

(A) No, he does.

(B) Yes, he doesn't.

(C) Yes, he does.

(D) No, he smokes only when he wants to.

翻 譯　約翰沒有抽菸嗎？

(A) 不，他有。

(B) 是的，他沒有。

(C) 是的，他有。

(D) 不，他只有在他想抽煙的時候才抽。

答 案　**C**

提 示　本題以否定問句的形式出現。作答時不要管 not，其他考量與回答肯定敘述句時相同，也屬於封閉式題型。

Question 3

For Question number 3, please look at picture C.

Question number 3:

Mary looks very happy, doesn't she?

⒜ Yes, she doesn't.
⒝ Yes, she does.
⒞ No, she does.
⒟ No, she doesn't.

翻 譯 瑪莉看起來很快樂,不是嗎?
⒜ 是的,她不是。
⒝ 是的,她是。
⒞ 不,她是。
⒟ 不,她不是。

答 案 B

提 示 本題是以附加問句的形式出現:
⑴ 附加問句是用來徵詢對方贊成或反對的看法。
⑵ 附加問句的主詞和動詞必須與前面敘述句的主詞和動詞一致。
⑶ 若期待對方回答,附加問句的讀法與 yes/no 問句讀法一樣,語調要上揚,
否則要下降。因回答時只有 yes/no 兩種選擇,也屬於封閉式問句題型。

Question 4

For Question number 4, please look at picture D.

Question number 4:

Have you ever been to Disneyland in California ?

(A) Yes, I have been there once.

(B) Yes, I have gone to Hong Kong .

(C) No, I have never been to the U.S.

(D) No, I have never been to Disney World.

翻 譯 你曾經去過加州的迪士尼樂園嗎？

(A) 是的，我曾經去過一次。

(B) 是的，我曾經去過香港。

(C) 不，我不曾去美國。

(D) 不，我從未去過迪士尼世界。

答 案 A

提 示 本題是以現在完成式的句型出現；因以助動詞 have 開頭，所以也是封閉式題型。以現在完成式的時態來表現過往經驗時，通常與下列副詞連用：
never（一次也沒有）、ever（曾經）、once（一次）、twice（兩次）、three times（三次）、how many times?（有幾次…？）

Question 5

For Question number 5, please look at picture E.

Question number 5:
Who is that man?

(A) He is my father.

(B) He is our basketball coach.

(C) He is just a passer-by.

(D) He is nobody.

 那個男人是誰？

⒜ 他是我爸爸。

⒝ 他是我籃球教練。

⒞ 他只是一個路人。

⒟ 他只是個小人物。

答 案 A

提 示 ⑴ 本題是以疑問代名詞 who 開頭的疑問句。因以疑問詞開頭的問句，往往
會給回答者較大的回答空間，所以又稱為開放式問句。

⑵ who 用來問人與人之間關係，所以在回答時多以與親屬關係相關的名詞
為主。

Question 6

For Question number 6, please look at picture F.

Question number 6:
What is that man?

(A) He is my uncle.

(B) He is a teacher.

(C) He is an old friend of mine.

(D) He is a stranger.

翻 譯　那個男人是做什麼的？
(A) 他是我叔叔。
(B) 他是一位老師。
(C) 他是我的一個老朋友。
(D) 他是一個陌生人。

答 案　**B**

提 示　本題是以疑問代名詞 what 開頭的問句；通常這類問句不外乎詢問職業身份，當然它也可能單純的問「何物」。例：What are you thinking about? 多記一些與職業有關的名詞會對本類型題目有幫助。

Question 7

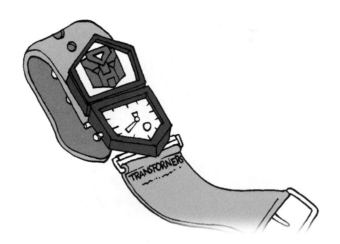

For Question number 7, please look at picture G.

Question number 7:
Do you have the time?

(A) Twenty minutes to one.
(B) I like the one with a cartoon character on it.
(C) No, I don't have.
(D) It's about nine o'clock.

翻　譯　現在幾點？
　　　　(A) 十二點四十。
　　　　(B) 我喜歡上面有卡通圖案的那個。
　　　　(C) 不，我沒有。
　　　　(D) 現在大約九點。

答　案　A

提　示　"have" 當主動詞用時，意思是「有、吃」，但在此題中的 have 則解為「知道」；「你知道現在幾點嗎？」所以參考圖示後答案為 A。

Question 8

For Question number 8, please look at picture H.

Question number 8:

Where is Jack?

⒜ He is in an amusement park.

⒝ He is in a library.

⒞ He is exercising in the gym.

⒟ He is talking to someone on the street.

翻 譯 傑克在哪？

⒜ 他在遊樂園。

⒝ 他在圖書館。

⒞ 他在健身房運動。

⒟ 他在街上和人說話。

答 案 C

提 示 當題型以疑問副詞 (when, where, why, how) 為主時，其句型可能為：

⑴ 疑問副詞 + be V/ 助動詞。例：How did you come to school every day?

⑵ 疑問副詞 + 副詞。例：How fast were you driving when the policeman stopped you?

⑶ 疑問副詞 + 形容詞。例：How many people are present?

第二部分
問 答

　　和第一部分的「看圖辨義」相比，本部分因少了圖示而使得影響答案的可能變多。題本上可以看到四個答案選項似乎給受測者些優勢，但仔細一想，受測者也很可能因這些額外的資訊而受到誤導。看看下面的範例：

What's happening?

(A) Nothing much, how about you?

(B) It all happened at nine last night.

(C) I have no idea.

(D) It seemed that someone had set fire on the old house.

似乎四個答案都有可能：「變化不大，你呢？」、「昨晚九點發生的。」、「不知道。」、「似乎有人縱火燒掉那棟老房子。」

　　當然，這題的答案是 A，因為這是一種口語式的寒暄應酬話。除非受測者能充分且確實掌握到不同領域的不同表達，這組看似容易但陷阱不少的題目還真會構成威脅。也正因此，回答時要先將所呈現出的答案在心中做一分類，看看答案相互間的關係和彼此的性質，以及和其他任何可以觀察到的線索做一比較。

　　在本部分中，題型不外乎以敘述句的形式來求得他人的贊成或反對，來徵求他人的附和或反駁，來提出反證或補述；或以問句的形式來取得資料說明或相關訊息。不同情境會有不同的表達，而對不同表達的認識越多，取得高分的機會就越高。當然，就如同「看圖辨義」一樣，對同音異義字分辨的能力依然扮演重要的角色。

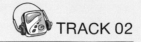 **TRACK 02**

Q1 | What is your name?

(A) Her name is Ann.

(B) My name is Ms. Mary

(C) My name is Mary Jean Smith.

(D) I didn't give my name.

翻 譯　你叫什麼名字？

(A) 他的名字叫安。

(B) 我叫瑪麗小姐。

(C) 我的名字叫瑪麗‧珍‧史密斯。

(D) 我沒有給你我的名字。

答 案　**C**

提 示　本題型為以疑問詞開頭的開放式疑問句，主在查詢個人基本資料，如姓名、住址、電話、手機或電子信箱等。當別人詢問名字時，習慣上我們會報上全名；Mary 是名 (given name/first name)，Smith 是姓 (last/family name)，而 Jean 則是中間名 (middle name/Christian name)。類似的問法還有：

—Who's she? And what's her name?

　She is my sister and her name is Linda.

—Do you have Mary's phone number? If not, how about her cell?

　I don't have her phone number but her cell number is 0900-123-456

—What's your ID number?

　My ID number is A100200300.

—Where do you live/What's your address?

　I live at No. 65, on Chung Hsiao E. Road, Sec. 3, Taipei.

—What do you usually do over the weekend?

　I usually do the laundry, clean the house, and go grocery shopping on Sunday morning.

Q2　How about going to the movies tonight?

(A) Not that I want to.
(B) I'm sorry, we are fully booked.
(C) I like to see the action movie.
(D) Sounds good to me.

翻　譯　今天晚上和我去看電影如何？
(A) 我並不是說我想去。
(B) 很抱歉我們已經客滿了。
(C) 我喜歡看動作片。
(D) 聽起來不錯。

答　案　**D**

提　示　本題型也是疑問詞開頭的開放式問句，主在徵詢對方意見看法、提出請求或詢問可能性。它的答案不外乎好或不好，但在用詞遣字上就會有不同的意境和表達了。例如表達接受的方式有：

I love to.

I'll be glad to.

I am thrilled/flattered!

That's a deal/You got yourself a deal.

See you at six.

上述的回答似乎都沒有明確的指出去或不去，但這些都可視為接受的同義。由本範例中，我們也可以看出並不是一定要說 "yes" 才代表好而 "no" 才是不！這點隨著受測級數的增高和題目內容的漸趨複雜，更該謹記在心。拒絕的方式有很多種。例：

I'll be busy tonight.

I have a previous engagement.（事先有約）

I have other plans.

I'll take a rain check.（緩期）

同樣地，雖不見 "no" 但就是不要、沒空或無法接受。在這類型的題目中，它的重點固然可以放在發問的方式如「正式」或「非正式」上。例：

I was wondering if you would like to go to the movies with me tonight?
（正式）

Want to go to the movies with me tonight?（非正式）
而它們的答案也可以相當制式：
Yes, I'll go to the movies with you tonight.
No, I will not/can not go to the movies with you tonight.
但，根據編者的揣測，制式化的問答應不是英檢的本意。

Q3 **Oh, hi, Jack, haven't seen you for a while. How's going?**

(A) Well, pretty much the same. How about yourself?
(B) Well, nice to see you, too.
(C) Well, I just finished my finals.
(D) Well, I have to run now.

翻譯 嗨，傑克！好久沒看到你了，最近好嗎？
(A) 嗯，幾乎差不多。那你呢？
(B) 嗯，我也很高興見到你。
(C) 嗯，我剛考完期末考。
(D) 嗯，我現在必須離開了。

答案 A

提示 本題型是典型問候寒暄語；因用 how，所以是開放式問句。選項 B 及 C，乍看下並無不當，但本題主在問對方近況如何，B 和 C 都沒有直接回答出問題核心。A 除了告知最近情形外，還一併回問對方，所以選 A 是最恰當的。

Q4 **How about those Yankees last night?**

(A) I think they were great!
(B) I think they lost the game.
(C) I think they will have a great comeback next year.
(D) I think they will have a new coach next year.

翻譯 洋基隊昨天打的怎樣？
(A) 我覺得他們打的很棒！

(B) 我覺得他們輸球了。

(C) 我覺得他們明年會重整旗鼓。

(D) 我覺得他們明年會有新教練。

答案 A

提示
(1) 一聽到 "how about..." 或 "what about..." 時，受測者就應該連想到這種題型的目的是在問看法或表達意見。選項 B 是敘述事實，而選項 C 及 D 則是對未來表現的看法；只有 A 明確的告知自己的看法。類似的回答還有：

They were phenomenal!（嘆為觀止）

They were terrible. They sucked!（糟透了）

(2) 若句尾中沒有問號，而句尾則語調升高，"How about those Yankees last night!" 則視為肯定句，表對洋基隊昨晚的表現滿意。

Q5 Could you help me with my homework?

(A) Yes, I'd be honored.

(B) Yes, but you will have to wait till I finish my study first.

(C) Yes, what seems to be the problem?

(D) Yes, that's a deal.

翻譯
你可以幫忙我的家庭作業嗎？

(A) 當然，我很榮幸。

(B) 當然，不過你要等我寫完論文。

(C) 當然，出什麼問題？

(D) 當然，一言為定。

答案 B

提示
本題的關鍵在 "could," 而問題的用意在徵詢對方幫忙的可能。選項 A 與題意有出入；「榮幸」與能否助人應無直接關係。選項 C 若用在修車廠或服務中心會更恰當，D 則適用在回應他人邀請時。B 則因答應且加以適度說明故為正確答案。

Q6 That skirt looks great on you; it matches your blouse perfectly.

(A) Well, I made a terrible mistake.

(B) Well, it only cost me one hundred dollars.

(C) Well, I was looking for a red one.

(D) Well, thank you.

翻 譯　你穿這條裙子很好看，它和你的襯衫很搭

(A) 噢，我犯了一個可怕的錯誤。

(B) 噢，我只花了一百元。

(C) 噢，我在找一件紅色的。

(D) 噢，謝謝。

答 案　**D**

提 示　本題為敘述句，旨在稱讚。既非問價錢也非問是否有任何憾事；D 雖簡單但卻能充分表達對對方讚美的謝意。兩物之間的搭配貼切也可以用：

A matches B perfectly.

A goes well with B.

A fits B well.

Q7 Thank you so much for helping me with all those boxes.

(A) That's a lot of stuff you have there.

(B) Just put it over there.

(C) You are perfectly welcome.

(D) Say no more.

翻 譯　非常謝謝你幫我搬這些箱子。

(A) 你那兒有很多東西。

(B) 把它放在那就好。

(C) 不用客氣。

(D) 不用再說了。

答 案 C

提 示 又是敘述句，只不過在表達感激。選項 A 聽起來像抱怨，選項 B 和回應別人的感謝沒有關係，而選項 D 意思是「不用再說了」，又過於粗魯，所以 C 是唯一選擇。

Q8 I am sorry for not being able to go to your birthday party last night.

(A) The party was put off.
(B) We all had fun last night.
(C) That's all right.
(D) It's only a small party.

翻 譯 昨晚不能去你的生日派對我感到很抱歉。
(A) 派對延期了。
(B) 我們昨晚玩的很盡興。
(C) 沒有關係。
(D) 他只不過是個小派對。

答 案 C

提 示 C 選項以「沒有關係」回應別人的道歉非常適合，但 A 選項「派對延期」、C 選項「我們昨晚玩的很高興」和 D 選項「那只是個小派對」和題目都沒有關係，所以 C 是最適合的答案

Q9 You look pale. What happened to you?

(A) It was much more difficult than I thought.
(B) I think I had a cold.
(C) I had a flat tire.
(D) I think I am too thin.

翻 譯 你的臉色很蒼白。怎麼了嗎？

(A) 它比我想像中的難多了。

(B) 我覺得我感冒了。

(C) 我的輪胎漏氣了。

(D) 我覺得我太瘦了。

答　案　**B**

提　示　這型題目主在查詢對方的身心狀況；A、C 及 D 皆答非所問，只能選 A。

簡短對話

　　此部分的題目主要根據一段四到六句不等的對話在四個答案中找出最恰當的一個。通常對話內容不會提及所討論的內容或方向,但透過其中的一些關鍵字,受測者要找出正確的答案並非難事。也因題目內容及長度較前兩部分來的長,確實且仔細聽且聽懂題目更是致勝的不二法門。本部分的題目若為問句通常是以疑問詞為主:誰在何時、何地、為何原因、做何事及如何做 (who, when, where, for what purpose, what, and how)。就像寫文章一樣,能抓住對話的主題,了解內文細節及參與對話者之間的關係,這個部分就至少有一半以上的勝算了!當然,並不是每個問題都會讓受測者在文字間找答案;也許最單純的 yes/no 問題也會出現,果真如此,別懷疑,有時最簡單的答案往往就是最恰當的答案!

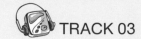 TRACK 03

Q1

M: What do you think about the movie we just saw? I personally think it's great!

W: Well, to be honest with you, I wasn't really that crazy about it.

M: Why's that?

W: I thought the leading actor should act better than he did in the movie.

Question: What does the woman think about the movie?

(A) She doesn't like the plot.

(B) She doesn't think the ticket price is reasonable.

(C) She doesn't like the popcorn from the snack bar.

(D) She doesn't like the acting.

翻 譯　男：妳覺得我們剛看的電影如何？我個人覺得它棒透了！

女：老實說，我並不覺得它有多好。

男：為什麼？

女：男主角在電影中的演技可以再好些。

問題：下列答案中何者為最可能的選擇？

選項：(A) 她不喜歡它的情節。

(B) 她覺得票價太貴了。

(C) 她不喜歡販賣部賣的爆米花。

(D) 她不喜歡他的演技。

答 案　D

提 示　本題的關鍵字在 "to be honest"，一般當我們使用如 however、yet、although、while、on the other hand、on the contrary、to the contrary、in spite of、for all that、nevertheless、nonetheless、still 等轉換字時，我們實際的意思往往會和所敘述的情狀相反；A、B 及 C 是對電影以外事物的不滿，所以 D 才是正確的答案。

Q2

W: The apartment is just what we need; small yet cozy enough for just two of us.

M: But where are we going to put all our stuff?

W: I don't mind to have them all thrown away and get some new ones.

M: But can we afford to do that with the mortgage?

Question: What are they talking about?

⒜ Buying a house.

⒝ Renting a car.

⒞ Staying at their friend's house.

⒟ Finding a hotel.

翻　譯

女：這正是我們需要的公寓！對我們兩個人來說，雖小但溫馨。

男：我們要將所有的東西放哪呢？

女：我倒不介意把它們扔了再重買。

男：加上貸款，我們負擔得起嗎？

問題：他們在談什麼？

選項：⒜ 買房子

　　　⒝ 租車子

　　　⒞ 住到朋友家

　　　⒟ 找間旅館

答　案 A

提　示　⑴ 本題的關鍵字是 "mortgage"（抵押借款），其他的字如 "cozy"、"get some new ones(furniture)" 等都不過是障眼法。回答類似問題時，不要老是想美好的事物；生活的現實面還是要顧到的。若在下列的選項中，你又會選那個答案呢？

Q：What do you think these couple will do eventually?

⒜ Give up buying the house.

⒝ Borrow money from everyone they know to buy the house.

⒞ Ask help from their parents.

⒟ Have their friends chip in for them.

若依歐美文化，正確答案會是 A，但如以中國人的角度來看，B、C 或 D 很可能會是正確的答案；文化差異使然。

(2) 另外，"yet" 除了「（迄今）…尚未」，還有「但是」的意思。我們所熟知的 "but" 不可和 "though/although" 連用，但 "yet" 可以。例：

Though he is young, he has lots of experiences.

Though he is young, yet he has lots of experiences.

Q3

M: Mary, What happened to your mid-term? You failed in almost every course you took!

W: Dad, I'd tried really hard, but I just didn't seem to have enough time.

M: What about the fact that you always sit in front of that machine and talk to your friends?

W: That's a mistake on my part. I will do better the next time, I promise you.

Question: What kind of machine is the father talking about?

(A) A television.

(B) A computer.

(C) A cellular phone.

(D) A video game.

翻　譯　男：瑪莉，你期中考是怎麼回事？你幾乎每一科都考砸了

女：爸，我真的努力了，但我似乎總是時間不夠。

男：那你總是坐在那機器前和朋友聊天的那件事又怎麼說？

女：那是我不對。我答應你我下次一定考好。

問題：父親所說的「那機器」是什麼？

選項：(A) 電視。

(B) 電腦。

(C) 行動電話。

(D) 電動玩具。

答　案　B

提　示　本題的答案選項並不難；四個生字應該都是大家所熟悉的。但對話中的用字，若不仔細聽或不了解，很可能就找不到答案甚至於不知答案為何。所以光是靠找線索背題型，但卻不能從最基本的背誦字彙和片語著手，還是過不了關。本題若是能了解 "talk to your friends"（和朋友聊天），便可知道對話中的 machine 指的是 computer。

Q4

W: When is the camping trip going to be?

M: It will be on the 5th and 6th of October. But, I also heard that there's going to be a super typhoon on its way here then.

W: Are we going to cancel the trip for good if there is really a super typhoon?

M: I don't think so; we will probably postpone it for a week.

Question: If the typhoon does come, when will the camping trip be held?

(A) 10th and 11th of October.

(B) 11th and 12th of October.

(C) 12th and 13th of October.

(D) 13th and 14th of October.

翻　譯　女：露營將在什麼時候？
男：十月五號和六號。但我聽說那時可能有個超級強颱要來。
女：那我們要取消露營嘍？
男：我覺得應該不會這樣。我們可能延後一周吧。
問題：如果颱風真的來了，露營將在何時舉行？
選項：(A) 十月十號及十一號。
　　　(B) 十月十一號及十二號。
　　　(C) 十月十二號及十三號。
　　　(D) 十月十三號及十四號。

答　案　C

提　示　(1) 本題說穿了只不過是簡易的加法問題；十月五號六號延後一周，答案加一加就出來了。既非植樹問題也不是雞兔同籠，問題是「聽懂了嗎？」國外考試，不論是托福 (TOEFL) 或大學 / 高中學術性向測驗 (SAT/SSAT)，尤其是數理項目，重在觀念而非繁瑣的計算；懂得基本理論和加減乘除、大於、小於、等於及倍數、因數的英文名稱，就可迎刃而解。切莫自尋煩惱找些艱澀的題目來打擊自己的信心。

(2) 「加」的說法有 add、plus、and，「減」則為 subtract、minus，「乘」是 multiply、times，「除」是 divide。

Q5

W: Jack, you look great! What happened to you?

M: I try to come here at least twice a week to keep fit.

W: I can see that you've really done a tremendous job!

M: And I feel great, too.

Question: Where do you think this conversation is most likely to take place?

(A) In a bar.

(B) In a diet center.

(C) In a gym.

(D) In a fitness center.

翻 譯　女：傑克，你看起來棒透了！怎麼回事？
男：我試著每週最少來這裡兩次來保持健康。
女：看來你還真的下工夫了。
男：我的感覺也很棒呢！
問題：這段對話最可能發生在何處？
選項：(A) 酒吧。
(B) 減肥中心。
(C) 健身房。
(D) 減肥中心。

答 案　C

提 示　本題為典型問地方的題目，而關鍵字則為 "keep fit" 除了解釋為「合適合宜」外，fit 也可解釋為健康的、強健的。英文字好玩及討厭的地方就在一字多解，下面列出 fit 在不同情境下的意思及用法：
The new dress fits her well.（搭配合宜）
I found it hard to fit in when in a new environment.（融合、融入）
The house is not fit for you to live in.（適合）
Is he fit for the job?（可以勝任）

Q6

M: I just went to the hospital to see John. He looks terrible.

W: What happened to him?

M: He said that he was hit by a reckless driver while walking on the street.

W: That's too bad. Hope he would get well soon.

Question: What happened to John?

(A) He drove carelessly.

(B) He drove after drinking a lot

(C) His driver license was expired.

(D) He had a car accident.

翻　譯　男：我剛去醫院看約翰。他看起來糟透了。
女：他怎麼了？
男：他說他被一名魯莽的駕駛撞到了。
女：太不幸了。希望他早日復原。
問題：約翰怎麼了？
選項：(A) 他開車很不小心。
(B) 他酒後開車。
(C) 他的駕照過期了。
(D) 他發生車禍。

答　案　D

提　示　本題的重點在於對話中的 "he was hit by a reckless driver"，意思是「他被一個魯莽的駕駛撞到了」，也就是發生車禍的意思。

Q7

W: Give me a reason, Mr. Smith, why I should hire you.

M: Well, I am willing to learn and eager to improve.

W: That sounds good enough for me. You are hired.

M: When should I report for duty?

Question: Why do you think Mr. Smith got hired?

⑷ He is a sweet talker

⒝ He is honest and sincere in convincing people

⒞ He is a good-looking man

⒟ He is really good at words

翻　譯

女：告訴我，史密斯先生，為何我該雇用你？

男：嗯，我願意去學習，而且我樂於自我提升。

女：這對我而言就夠了。你被雇用了。

男：我該何時報到呢？

問題：你覺得為何史密斯先生被雇用？

選項：⑷ 他是個甜言蜜語的傢伙。

　　　⒝ 他在說服他人時誠實真摯。

　　　⒞ 他長的很好看。

　　　⒟ 他是個能言善道的人。

答　案　B

提　示　"why" 主在問原因，而原因有些是顯明易見，而其他則須花些時間來推理體會。或許這類題型出現的機率不高，但它真的能測驗出受測者的實力。如果編者是出題者，在十題的簡短對話部分中，我至少會出一兩題如此性質的題目！

Q8

M: I am a big fan of yours, Ms. Chen.

W: Oh, really?

M: Yes. I have the whole collection of your works. Can I have your autograph?

W: I'll be glad to. Where do you want me to sign it?

Question: What is Ms. Chen's profession?

(A) A singer

(B) A writer

(C) A dancer

(D) A cook

翻譯

男：陳小姐，我是您的崇拜者。

女：哦，真的嗎？

男：是的。我有您作品的全集。我能請您幫我簽名嗎？

女：我非常樂意。你要我簽在哪？

問題：陳小姐的職業為何？

選項：(A) 歌手。

(B) 作家。

(C) 舞者。

(D) 廚師。

答案 B

提示 與上題範例類似，本題多少也有些推理的成分在內。"work" 這個字當複數時和原本意思不同：

iron works（鐵工廠）、works by Monet（莫內的作品）

有些字彙單複數之間意義不同：

(1) 同形義不同。例 "family"：

1. a family：一個家庭

2. family：家人（們）

(2) 不同形不同義。例 "staff"：

1. staffs：職員、幕僚

2. staves：棒、杖

(3) 不同形同義。例 "person"：

1. person：人

2. people：人們

而拼法則可能是同音異義 (homonym)。如 air/heir。或同拼法但異音異義 (heteronym)。如 record：(n.) 唱片，(v.) 記載登錄。

Note

聽力測驗
實戰練習

本單元包含八回聽力測驗，提供讀者真實的模擬練習，增加實戰經驗。

聽力測驗（中級篇）

本測驗分三部分，全為四選一之選擇題，每部分各 15 題，共 45 題。

TEST 1

第一部分	**看圖辨義**
第二部分	**問　答**
第三部分	**簡短對話**

TRACK 04

第一部分： 看圖辨義

第一部分有 15 題，為第 1 題至第 15 題，試題中有數幅圖畫，每一圖畫有 1～2 個描述該題之題目，每題請聽 CD 播出題目以及 A、B、C、D 四個英語敘述之後，選出與所看到的圖畫最相符的答案，每題只播出一遍。

Question 1　　　　　　Ans. _____

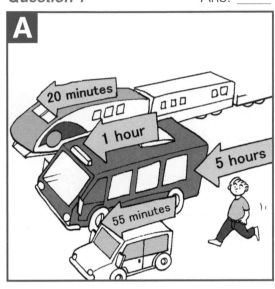

Question 2　　　　　　Ans. _____

Question 3　　　　　　Ans. _____

Question 4　　　　　　Ans. _____

Question 5 Ans. _____

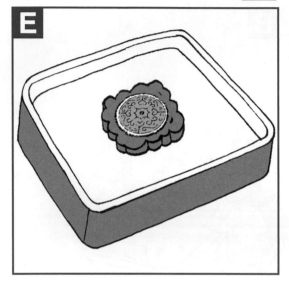

Question 6 Ans. _____

Question 7 Ans. _____

Question 8 Ans. _____

Question 9   Ans. _____

Question 10   Ans. _____

Question 11   Ans. _____

Question 12   Ans. _____

Question 13   Ans. _____

Question 14   Ans. _____

Question 15   Ans. _____

TRACK 05

第二部分：問　答

第二部分共有 15 題，為第 16 題至 30 題，每題請聽 CD 播出一個英語問句或直述句之後，從 A、B、C、D 四個回答或回應中，選出一個最適合者作答。每題只播出一遍。

16. (A) It treats me unfairly.
    (B) It's terrible!
    (C) How are you?
    (D) I have been traveled around the world.

17. (A) Yeah! It's a small world, isn't it?
    (B) Let me know when you'll be here next time.
    (C) We should stop doing that!
    (D) Something is bound to happen.

18. (A) I don't think I have the pleasure.
    (B) Whom are you talking about?
    (C) It doesn't ring a bell.
    (D) Do I have to?

19. (A) Not a chance.
    (B) You bet I would.
    (C) We'll see.
    (D) I don't think so.

20. (A) Wish you were there.
    (B) I used to play games on weekends.
    (C) It's the worst I have ever seen.
    (D) All my family like to play computer games.

21. (A) Don't mention it.
    (B) Buy me a present.
    (C) Try to return me a favor next time.
    (D) You could if you try.

22. (A) You can give me your address again.

(B) You want me to give you a map?

(C) There is an information desk over there.

(D) You want me to repeat it again?

23. (A) My watch says 11:30.

(B) I have the slightest idea.

(C) It's way pass your bed time.

(D) I am already late for my work.

24. (A) How unfortunate!

(B) Couldn't be better!

(C) Things could be worse.

(D) There will be heavy rain tomorrow.

25. (A) You're welcome.

(B) The fake one would be cheaper.

(C) Well, thank you. That's a present for my birthday.

(D) The necklaces and earrings are all on sale now.

26. (A) On the contrary, I know exactly what I am doing.

(B) Yes. Do you know where I can find it?

(C) No. I am just looking.

(D) Yes, but I have no choice.

27. (A) I bought a new one at home.

(B) I'll see if I can get some.

(C) I'll call the serviceman.

(D) The machine doesn't work.

28. (A) I can't wait to go to the new school.

(B) It was absolutely the best place.

(C) We decide to transfer him to a new office.

(D) I am not happy with the environment here.

_____ 29. (A) When will the next shipment come in?

(B) When is it due?

(C) When will you have more?

(D) The new product has come on to the market.

_____ 30. (A) There is something wrong with my nose.

(B) I don't like the smell of the flowers.

(C) I think something is burning.

(D) Mm...the soup smells delicious.

TRACK 06

第三部分：簡短對話

第三部分共有 15 題，為第 31 題至 45 題，每題請聽 CD 播出一段對話及一個相關問題之後，從 A、B、C、D 四個選項中選出一個最適合者作答。每題只播出一遍。

_____ 31. (A) Husband and wife.
(B) Father and daughter.
(C) Boyfriend and girlfriend.
(D) Classmates.

_____ 32. (A) She is happy with her co-worker.
(B) She is in bad terms with her co-worker.
(C) The man is her boss' son-in-law.
(D) The man is having a crush on her.

_____ 33. (A) The woman used to work before she gave birth to her son.
(B) The woman is in the job market for the first time.
(C) The woman is trying to find a job.
(D) The man is trying to give the woman a job.

_____ 34. (A) They are not sure.
(B) They are certain.
(C) They are positive about it.
(D) They are angry with it.

_____ 35. (A) Quit her school.
(B) Give up learning completely.
(C) Try really hard to improve herself.
(D) Try really hard to ignore other students.

_____ 36. (A) He was grounded by his father.
(B) It's going to rain.
(C) He doesn't feel like to.
(D) He is going to stay home and catch some sleep.

37. (A) Yes, but the firefighters put it out.
    (B) Yes, a fire did break out in the concert last night.
    (C) Yes, and everyone's fingers had been crossed.
    (D) No, it was only his imagination.

38. (A) It means days, months, years, and so on.
    (B) It means the minutes and seconds.
    (C) It means the period of time that people are in.
    (D) It means the days, the months, and the years when people were born.

39. (A) Everyone was busy using power point.
    (B) Everyone was busy blaming each other.
    (C) Everyone was busy snapping his fingers.
    (D) Everyone was busy playing games with his fingers.

40. (A) A friend in need is a friend indeed.
    (B) A dog is man's best friend.
    (C) With a friend like him, who needs enemies.
    (D) One for all and all for one.

41. (A) She thinks that's unbelievable.
    (B) She thinks that's very courageous of him.
    (C) She thinks that's impossible for him to do a good job.
    (D) She thinks that's stupid.

42. (A) A traffic ticket for double-parking.
    (B) A traffic ticket for turning right on red light.
    (C) A traffic ticket for buying the lotto.
    (D) A traffic ticket for not fastening seat belt.

43. (A) Yes, she believes in the man completely.
    (B) Yes, but with some reservations.
    (C) No, she doesn't believe a word of what he said.
    (D) No, and she made sure that the man knew it too.

44. (A) He doesn't want to talk to the woman.

(B) He doesn't want to come near to the woman.

(C) He is still angry with the woman.

(D) He is thinking about something else.

45. (A) No, she is about to lose her temper with all these questions.

(B) No, she is disappointed with all these questions.

(C) Yes, and she answered all these questions.

(D) Yes, she is quite happy with all these questions.

聽力測驗（中級篇）

本測驗分三部分，全為四選一之選擇題，每部分各 15 題，共 45 題。

TEST 2

第一部分 **看圖辨義**

第二部分 **問　答**

第三部分 **簡短對話**

 TRACK 07

第一部分： 看圖辨義

第一部分有 15 題，為第 1 題至第 15 題，試題中有數幅圖畫，每一圖畫有 1～2 個描述該題之題目，每題請聽 CD 播出題目以及 A、B、C、D 四個英語敘述之後，選出與所看到的圖畫最相符的答案，每題只播出一遍。

Question 1 Ans. _____

Question 2 Ans. _____

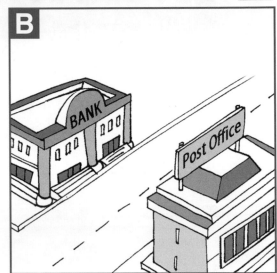

Question 3 Ans. _____

Question 4 Ans. _____

Question 5   Ans. _____

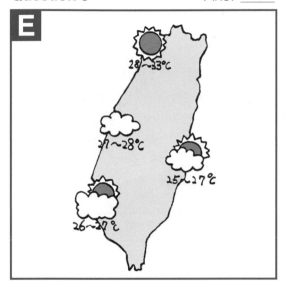

Question 6   Ans. _____

Question 7   Ans. _____

Question 8   Ans. _____

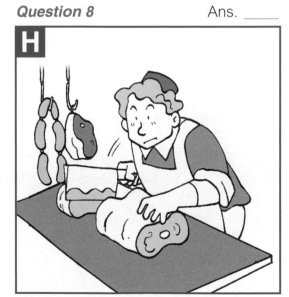

Question 9　　　　　Ans. ＿＿＿

Question 10　　　　　Ans. ＿＿＿

Question 11　　　　　Ans. ＿＿＿

Question 12　　　　　Ans. ＿＿＿

Question 13 Ans. _____

Question 14 Ans. _____

8:10-9:00	**Math**
9:10-10:00	**History**
10:10-11:00	**Geography**
11:10-12:00	**English**

Question 15 Ans. _____

 TRACK 08

第二部分：問答

第二部分共有 15 題，為第 16 題至 30 題，每題請聽 CD 播出一個英語問句或直述句之後，從 A、B、C、D 四個回答或回應中，選出一個最適合者作答。每題只播出一遍。

16. (A) I don't know, but I do know that it's only August now.
    (B) It should cool off pretty soon.
    (C) Thanks to global warming.
    (D) Yesterday was better.

17. (A) I am freezing.
    (B) Sure. No Problem.
    (C) What for?
    (D) Are you too cold?

18. (A) I don't know what to say.
    (B) My heart goes with you.
    (C) He is bad news.
    (D) You can say that again.

19. (A) Sorry, but life is short.
    (B) OK. What about tomorrow?
    (C) Sure. What do you have in mind?
    (D) It's a piece of cake.

20. (A) That's not a good day for me.
    (B) Something suddenly came up.
    (C) How about a cup of tea?
    (D) When on Saturday?

21. (A) I'll be probably about fifteen minutes late.
    (B) The movie theater is around the corner.
    (C) It starts at five o'clock.
    (D) What's the name of the movie?

_____ 22. (A) I had good time last weekend.
    (B) Please show me the way.
    (C) The food there is great.
    (D) Did you talk to your parents first?

_____ 23. (A) It's OK. Traffic is usually bad during this hour.
    (B) That's a lousy excuse!
    (C) Perhaps you need more exercise.
    (D) You should at least have a good reason.

_____ 24. (A) Who cooked the meal?
    (B) Oh, I'm surviving.
    (C) Medium-rare, please.
    (D) It's delicious

_____ 25. (A) I just can't figure him out.
    (B) Sure. What's about?
    (C) I didn't mean it.
    (D) I don't feel like to go with you.

_____ 26. (A) We never close.
    (B) I'll give you a lift home if you like.
    (C) The business hours are from 11 am to 10 pm.
    (D) There is a nice restaurant over there.

_____ 27. (A) Sure. Here are the application forms.
    (B) Do you have enough money?
    (C) I am sorry, but we are fully booked.
    (D) It opens at two o'clock in the afternoon.

_____ 28. (A) How about trimming a bit on the sides?
    (B) The shampoo is especially for greasy hair.
    (C) I don't like my new hairstyle.
    (D) It is half price now.

_____ 29. (A) The garlic has a strong flavor.
　　　　　　(B) Yes, but I can have that exchanged right away.
　　　　　　(C) That's too much!
　　　　　　(D) It is free after eight o'clock.

_____ 30. (A) Medium rare, please.
　　　　　　(B) The meat is still raw.
　　　　　　(C) How about some salad on the side?
　　　　　　(D) Can I have another drink?

第三部分：簡短對話

第三部分共有 15 題，為第 31 題至 45 題，每題請聽 CD 播出一段對話及一個相關問題之後，從 A、B、C、D 四個選項中選出一個最適合者作答。每題只播出一遍。

31. (A) Yes, she will.
　　(B) No, she won't.
　　(C) It's hard to tell.
　　(D) I love it.

32. (A) 7 to 9 a .m.
　　(B) 5 to 8 p.m.
　　(C) 11 am to 1 p.m.
　　(D) 11 pm to 12 midnight.

33. (A) The man was playing things by the book.
　　(B) The man was taking his chances.
　　(C) The man was pretty sure that he would be lucky.
　　(D) The man had no idea what the loading and unloading zone mean.

34. (A) Some spoiled food.
　　(B) Some spicy food.
　　(C) Some greasy food.
　　(D) Some plain food.

35. (A) The woman was trying to lose weight.
　　(B) The woman was trying to gain a few pounds.
　　(C) The woman was getting a facelift.
　　(D) The woman was under some special medication.

36. (A) He is on medication in the hospital.
　　(B) He is having a routine physical check-up.
　　(C) He is working at home.
　　(D) He is devoting himself to his business.

_____ 37. (A) Easy and pleasant.
　　　　　(B) Enjoyable but challenging.
　　　　　(C) Difficult and boring.
　　　　　(D) Carefree and happy.

_____ 38. (A) Yes, he doesn't want to drive anymore.
　　　　　(B) No, he doesn't have driver's license.
　　　　　(C) Yes, he has driven for miles and is tired.
　　　　　(D) No, he just tried to scare the woman away.

_____ 39. (A) No, he is not. He is just making jokes on the woman.
　　　　　(B) Yes, he is. He is jealous of the woman.
　　　　　(C) No, he is not, he is just wondering when she will take a shower.
　　　　　(D) Yes, he is. He hates the woman for coming up with a wonderful idea.

_____ 40. (A) They both feel time passes fast.
　　　　　(B) The woman likes the man better when he was young.
　　　　　(C) Both of them would like to be kids again.
　　　　　(D) They both enjoy being grown-ups.

_____ 41. (A) She is going abroad for fun.
　　　　　(B) She is going abroad for business.
　　　　　(C) She is taking her daughter to the summer camp.
　　　　　(D) She is joining the summer camp overseas.

_____ 42. (A) He just had a plastic surgery.
　　　　　(B) He just had a heart transplant.
　　　　　(C) He just had a mole removed.
　　　　　(D) He just had a spa.

_____ 43. (A) Because George always makes a fool of himself by saying something stupid.
　　　　　(B) Because George acts like a clown in front of everyone.
　　　　　(C) Because George sings terribly, yet he loves to sing in front of

everyone.

(D) Because George loves to show off in front of everyone.

_____ 44. (A) They don't have enough hands.

(B) They are short of waiters.

(C) They are running out of food.

(D) They really don't care that much about the woman and her friend.

_____ 45. (A) Jean and her friends had a wild party.

(B) Jean and her friends had a study session.

(C) Jean and her friends had a quiet discussion.

(D) Jean and her friends tore the house apart.

聽力測驗（中級篇）

本測驗分三部分，全為四選一之選擇題，每部分各 15 題，共 45 題。

TEST 3

 TRACK 10

第一部分: 看圖辨義

第一部分有 15 題，為第 1 題至第 15 題，試題中有數幅圖畫，每一圖畫有 1～2 個描述該題之題目，每題請聽 CD 播出題目以及 A、B、C、D 四個英語敘述之後，選出與所看到的圖畫最相符的答案，每題只播出一遍。

Question 1　　　　　Ans. _____

Question 2　　　　　Ans. _____

Sanmin Hotel
Room 709

CHECK IN: 4 P.M.
CHECK OUT: 12 NOON
PLEASE DO NOT SMOKE.

Question 3　　　　　Ans. _____

Question 4　　　　　Ans. _____

Question 5   Ans. _____

E

Shopping List

1. milk   6. cabbage
2. fruit   7. batteries
3. tissue
4. rice
5. sugar

Question 6   Ans. _____

F

You are invited to
a reception honoring
Jerry White
as the new president
of Sanmin University

Saturday, January 26.
6:30 p.m.~9:30 p.m.
MCA Center

Question 7   Ans. _____

G

Question 8   Ans. _____

H

Question 9   Ans. _____

Question 10   Ans. _____

Question 11   Ans. _____

Question 12   Ans. _____

Question 13   Ans. _____

Question 14   Ans. _____

Question 15   Ans. _____

 TRACK 11

第二部分共有 15 題，為第 16 題至 30 題，每題請聽 CD 播出一個英語問句或直述句之後，從 A、B、C、D 四個回答或回應中，選出一個最適合者作答。每題只播出一遍。

16. (A) No, I have been there many times.
    (B) Yes, I go there on a daily basis.
    (C) We went to a downtown restaurant yesterday.
    (D) The food is terrible there.

17. (A) No problem. I'll pick you up at seven.
    (B) Going there by plane is much quicker.
    (C) I wish I could go with you.
    (D) I ride the bus to work.

18. (A) Pass the butter, please.
    (B) There's some leftover vegetables.
    (C) I can't. I am full already.
    (D) Sure. Go ahead.

19. (A) I know. The test is not so easy.
    (B) He is hard to get along with.
    (C) Yes, I think yellow color is better for you.
    (D) I can't seem to get this idea through to Jack.

20. (A) You can throw them in the garbage can.
    (B) The garbage collector comes every Monday evening.
    (C) Sounds great! We have to catch up on many things.
    (D) I am going on a vacation tomorrow.

21. (A) Don't worry! It's my treat.
    (B) You don't have to. It's not your fault.
    (C) I would be happy to help you clean the apartment.
    (D) That's OK. I don't mind waiting here in line.

_____ 22. (A) I prefer tea to coffee.

(B) Medium rare, please.

(C) The service is terrible here.

(D) Eating less meat makes you healthier.

_____ 23. (A) I thought she has just bought a new sofa last week.

(B) I'll meet you at the supermarket after dinner.

(C) I have got the flu.

(D) I don't have the slightest idea.

_____ 24. (A) I go to school by train.

(B) I got up late and missed my bus.

(C) I was punished for being late again.

(D) The teacher asked me to follow the rules.

_____ 25. (A) Sure, no problem.

(B) Yes, I have been there twice.

(C) There is one just around the corner.

(D) The bank lend money at a high interest rate.

_____ 26. (A) Really? What about your family?

(B) That serves you right!

(C) I visited old buildings there.

(D) I prefer travelling to Taipei.

_____ 27. (A) No, thanks.

(B) Drinking coffee is not good for your health.

(C) That will be 100 NT dollars.

(D) Sure. How would you like it?

_____ 28. (A) You are having second thought, aren't you?

(B) I failed the test.

(C) Have you tried taking exercise?

(D) Oh, really? I don't mind the challenge.

_____ 29. (A) Yes, I am. I am used to it already.

(B) It's far away from my home.

(C) We have a new principal this semester.

(D) Yes, he is a friendly person.

_____ 30. (A) Wow! I can't believe the deadline is tomorrow.

(B) The paper is due this Friday.

(C) I'm taking a course in chemistry.

(D) Mine is ready.

TRACK 12

第三部分：簡短對話

第三部分共有 15 題，為第 31 題至 45 題，每題請聽 CD 播出一段對話及一個相關問題之後，從 A、B、C、D 四個選項中選出一個最適合者作答。每題只播出一遍。

31. (A) Yes, he will.
    (B) Yes, he will but he will insist on switching to another one.
    (C) No, he will leave immediately.
    (D) No, he will file a complaint to the manager.

32. (A) She is offering to take the message.
    (B) She is offering to have John return the call ASAP.
    (C) She is offering to have John run to school right away.
    (D) She is offering to have John go to see the caller.

33. (A) In a department store.
    (B) In a duty-free shop.
    (C) In a hospital.
    (D) In a second-hand store.

34. (A) Finding another job or not.
    (B) Turning down the job offer or not.
    (C) Going for a job interview or not.
    (D) Accepting the job offer or not.

35. (A) Husband and wife.
    (B) Mother and son.
    (C) Roommates.
    (D) Father and daughter.

36. (A) To see a dentist.
    (B) To see a plastic surgeon.
    (C) To see a construction worker.
    (D) To see a psychiatrist.

_____ 37. (A) At the immigration check point in an airport.
(B) At the reception desk in a hotel.
(C) At the information center in downtown city.
(D) In a welcome party.

_____ 38. (A) The new boss is an easy-going man.
(B) The new boss has a very pleasant personality.
(C) The new boss does everything by the book.
(D) The new boss is hard on everyone.

_____ 39. (A) They are planning a trip.
(B) They are planning a party.
(C) They are planning a meeting.
(D) They are planning a school reunion.

_____ 40. (A) She fell and broke her arm while skiing.
(B) She fell and broke her arm while watching other skiing.
(C) She fell and broke her arm while someone ran into her.
(D) She fell and broke her arm while climbing ladder.

_____ 41. (A) He is just being polite.
(B) He is too full to have any.
(C) He doesn't really like it.
(D) He is on diet.

_____ 42. (A) He is thinking of asking the woman out for a drink.
(B) He doesn't really like to walk in the park.
(C) He only walks with women.
(D) He doesn't like to walk alone.

_____ 43. (A) He can't speak.
(B) He will tell the first person he meets.
(C) He will keep secrets.
(D) He doesn't really want to know anything.

_____ 44. (A) It's no where to be found.
   (B) Right next to where they stand.
   (C) Across the street from where they stand.
   (D) They have no idea.

_____ 45. (A) She wants to have a chat with him.
   (B) She wants him to do something for her.
   (C) She needs him to help her take care of her child.
   (D) She is just asking.

聽力測驗（中級篇）

本測驗分三部分，全為四選一之選擇題，每部分各 15 題，共 45 題。

TEST 4

TRACK 13

第一部分： 看圖辨義

第一部分有 15 題，為第 1 題至第 15 題，試題中有數幅圖畫，每一圖畫有 1～2 個描述該題之題目，每題請聽 CD 播出題目以及 A、B、C、D 四個英語敘述之後，選出與所看到的圖畫最相符的答案，每題只播出一遍。

Question 1   Ans. _____

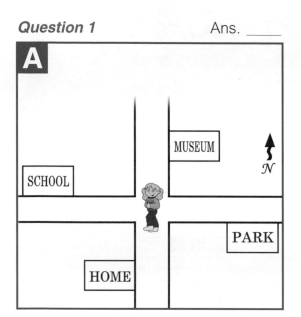

Question 2   Ans. _____

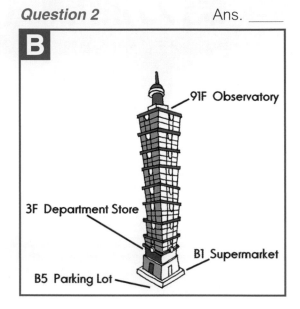

Question 3   Ans. _____

Question 4   Ans. _____

Question 5   Ans. _____

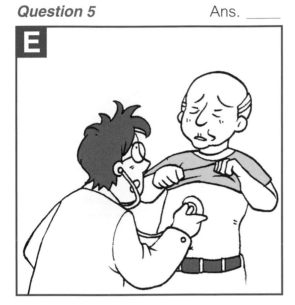

Question 6   Ans. _____

Question 7   Ans. _____

Question 8   Ans. _____

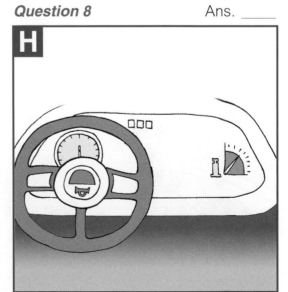

Question 9   Ans. _____

Question 10   Ans. _____

Question 11   Ans. _____

Question 12   Ans. _____

Question 13   Ans. _____

Question 14   Ans. _____

Question 15   Ans. _____

TRACK 14

第二部分：問答

第二部分共有 15 題，為第 16 題至 30 題，每題請聽 CD 播出一個英語問句或直述句之後，從 A、B、C、D 四個回答或回應中，選出一個最適合者作答。每題只播出一遍。

16. (A) Business English and Elementary Japanese.
    (B) I know you like me.
    (C) I only go there once a week.
    (D) I am trying to be smarter.

17. (A) I am a senior.
    (B) I was born in 1981.
    (C) It's been four year since I moved here.
    (D) I am eighteen years old.

18. (A) No, I am between jobs.
    (B) I am a good doctor.
    (C) I work in Sanmin Bookstore.
    (D) I love my job.

19. (A) Fine, thank you.
    (B) Yes, it's a peak season.
    (C) Well, nothing much.
    (D) Good for you!

20. (A) I will not vote for you.
    (B) I will vote tomorrow.
    (C) I need to calm down.
    (D) No, I don't like him.

21. (A) It depends.
    (B) I hope not.
    (C) Whatever you say.
    (D) It looks like rain.

_____ 22. (A) It's very good.

(B) Tell me more about it.

(C) That's enough!

(D) I'm not listening.

_____ 23. (A) No, I am not interested at all.

(B) No, it is exciting.

(C) Yes, let me tell you more about it.

(D) Yes, I'd like to have some more.

_____ 24. (A) Don't ask.

(B) I think you'll be busy then.

(C) Give me a break!

(D) I feel sorry for you.

_____ 25. (A) I don't agree with you.

(B) I'd like to do that very much.

(C) Never heard of it.

(D) I don't smoke.

_____ 26. (A) I am sorry.

(B) It's not possible.

(C) Smoking is bad for you.

(D) You are kidding me.

_____ 27. (A) The new movie is coming soon.

(B) Yes, I know, and I am well prepared.

(C) Bless you!

(D) It's just the beginning.

_____ 28. (A) Nothing is impossible.

(B) You'll have to wait.

(C) I have an idea.

(D) I am a person who gets up very early.

_____ 29. (A) I am talking to Mr. Jones.

(B) Yes, speaking.

(C) Mr. Smith is not talking to you.

(D) Is Mr. Smith there?

_____ 30. (A) There is a parking lot across the street.

(B) We can't afford that.

(C) How about taking a taxi?

(D) I never take the bus.

第三部分： 簡短對話

第三部分共有 15 題，為第 31 題至 45 題，每題請聽 CD 播出一段對話及一個相關問題之後，從 A、B、C、D 四個選項中選出一個最適合者作答。每題只播出一遍。

31. (A) They are setting up the dinner table.
    (B) They are having a cooking class.
    (C) They are eating in a restaurant.
    (D) They are buying some plates and spoons.

32. (A) They are going to the supermarket.
    (B) They are going to the toy store.
    (C) They are going to the museum.
    (D) They are going to the park.

33. (A) The woman is thinking of renting a house.
    (B) The man wants to rent an apartment.
    (C) The man is selling a house.
    (D) The man wants to buy a car.

34. (A) In a hospital.
    (B) In a school.
    (C) In a factory.
    (D) In a bank.

35. (A) No, they will probably do that some other time.
    (B) No, but the woman writes a check for that.
    (C) Yes, because the man is angry.
    (D) Yes, they will meet each other in an hour.

36. (A) Yes, he has already turned things around.
    (B) Yes, he is confident that things will definitely be better.
    (C) No, but he hopes that things will become better finally.
    (D) No, but he will go to the church and pray.

37. (A) She was sick.

(B) She lost her job.

(C) She is going to be a nurse.

(D) She didn't want to go to a doctor.

38. (A) She walks to places where are far away for exercising.

(B) She eats healthily and exercise regularly.

(C) She only eats some fruit every day.

(D) She doesn't know what to do.

39. (A) If the woman wants, she can still find time to keep in touch with her classmates.

(B) He understands that the woman is too busy for anything.

(C) He believes that the woman does not want to be with her classmates.

(D) He believes that the woman does not miss her classmates at all.

40. (A) Perhaps she will, but she needs to make some arrangements first.

(B) Yes, she will help him immediately.

(C) Yes, but the man will have to wait for a long time.

(D) No, she's too busy, so the man will find someone else to help.

41. (A) He probably goes to bed too late.

(B) He can't sleep well at night.

(C) He has a lot of work to do.

(D) He tries to ask help from the woman.

42. (A) She thinks that Judy is not mad at the man.

(B) She encourages the man to talk to Judy.

(C) She will go and cheer Judy up herself.

(D) She thinks Judy might want to be left alone.

43. (A) It's her birthday.

(B) She's got a baby.

(C) He's got a new credit card.

(D) She wants to have dinner.

44. (A) The man does.
    (B) The woman does.
    (C) Both of them like her.
    (D) Both of them don't like her.

45. (A) She likes the man.
    (B) She has no choice.
    (C) It's his birthday today.
    (D) They are not friends.

聽力測驗（中級篇）

本測驗分三部分，全為四選一之選擇題，每部分各 15 題，共 45 題。

TEST 5

 TRACK 16

第一部分有 15 題，為第 1 題至第 15 題，試題中有數幅圖畫，每一圖畫有 1～2 個描述該題之題目，每題請聽 CD 播出題目以及 A、B、C、D 四個英語敘述之後，選出與所看到的圖畫最相符的答案，每題只播出一遍。

Question 1   Ans. _____

Question 2   Ans. _____

Question 3   Ans. _____

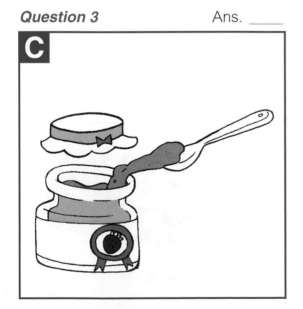

Question 4   Ans. _____

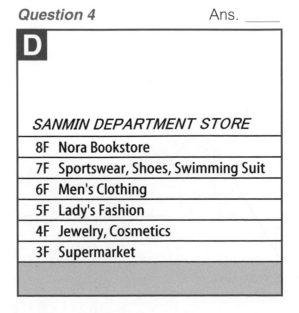

SANMIN DEPARTMENT STORE

8F	Nora Bookstore
7F	Sportswear, Shoes, Swimming Suit
6F	Men's Clothing
5F	Lady's Fashion
4F	Jewelry, Cosmetics
3F	Supermarket

Question 5   Ans. _____

Question 6   Ans. _____

Question 7   Ans. _____

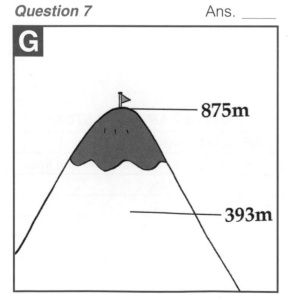

875m

393m

Question 8   Ans. _____

Question 9 Ans. _____

Time	No.	Destination	Status
13:30	609	TAICHUNG	ON TIME
13:45	53	TAINAN	ON TIME
14:00	271	TAIPEI	DELAYED
14:15	7	KAOHSIUNG	ON TIME
14:30	611	TAOYUAN	ON TIME

Question 10 Ans. _____

Question 11 Ans. _____

Question 12 Ans. _____

Question 13   Ans. _____

Question 14   Ans. _____

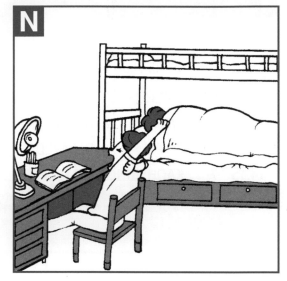

Question 15   Ans. _____

第二部分：問答

第二部分共有 15 題，為第 16 題至 30 題，每題請聽 CD 播出一個英語問句或直述句之後，從 A、B、C、D 四個回答或回應中，選出一個最適合者作答。每題只播出一遍。

_____ 16. (A) You can say that again!

(B) You are right on the money!

(C) You came up with a wonderful idea.

(D) You are dead wrong about that!

_____ 17. (A) We need a Chinese-English dictionary.

(B) We need milk and some bread.

(C) We need some flowers for the living room.

(D) We need to get four chairs and a table.

_____ 18. (A) I want to buy a new computer.

(B) Dancing classes help improve your social life.

(C) I really need to talk to you now.

(D) I am too busy to have any spare time to socialize.

_____ 19. (A) I put your number down in my notebook but I lost it.

(B) May I talk to John, please.

(C) I dial the number, but no one answered it.

(D) You dial a wrong number.

_____ 20. (A) Anyway, time is running out.

(B) I dislike talking this matter here.

(C) OK, how about this weekend?

(D) I prefer cats to dogs.

_____ 21. (A) Did you take any message?

(B) Who is that handsome guy?

(C) Did he say when?

(D) Too bad, you should have called him.

22. (A) I am about to tell you what happened.
    (B) It takes me a lot of time to answer the question.
    (C) How about this Wednesday?
    (D) I will go out with Sue today.

23. (A) No, on second thought, I'll buy a new one.
    (B) It's making a lot of noise.
    (C) Sure. No problem.
    (D) I need to turn on the radio now.

24. (A) What for? I am not going anywhere.
    (B) Really? When did it happen?
    (C) I don't like books anyway.
    (D) Yes, I was going to ask you about that myself.

25. (A) It's not as good as I think.
    (B) It has so many big stars.
    (C) It's a musical, isn't it?
    (D) It has beautiful scenery.

26. (A) I am just going to check out.
    (B) Well, I am looking for a birthday present.
    (C) I will pack this present before his birthday.
    (D) I am just leaving.

27. (A) The second shelf to your right.
    (B) You can get the prescription filled here.
    (C) You need to take the cough medicine right now.
    (D) Why don't you try the new medicine?

28. (A) You have to check out at noon.
    (B) We close at eleven o'clock.
    (C) May I know what the trouble is?
    (D) The manager is off today.

29. (A) To my room if that's OK with you.
(B) I don't think so.
(C) I'm going to take a shower first.
(D) To the park.

30. (A) Sorry, I can't. I have an exam tomorrow.
(B) I am always on your side!
(C) As a matter of fact, I don't like it.
(D) I receive high salary. I can't complain.

 TRACK 18

第三部分： 簡短對話

第三部分共有 15 題，為第 31 題至 45 題，每題請聽 CD 播出一段對話及一個相關問題之後，從 A、B、C、D 四個選項中選出一個最適合者作答。每題只播出一遍。

31. (A) It will probably be a movie.
    (B) It will probably be a TV cooking show.
    (C) It will probably be a football game.
    (D) It will probably be a variety show.

32. (A) Since 1989.
    (B) About ten years.
    (C) About two years.
    (D) About twenty meters.

33. (A) He is a teacher.
    (B) He is a writer.
    (C) He is a painter.
    (D) He is a musician.

34. (A) Taking taxi to the airport is the cheapest way.
    (B) Taking taxi to the airport is the easiest way.
    (C) Taking taxi to the airport is the most expensive way.
    (D) Taking taxi to the airport is the quickest way.

35. (A) The shopping center.
    (B) The street vendors.
    (C) The convenient store.
    (D) The toys store.

36. (A) A social gathering.
    (B) A TV game show.
    (C) An academic competition.
    (D) A sport event.

37. (A) Yes, but with some conditions.
    (B) No, he will not.
    (C) Yes, he will.
    (D) No, he has his own problem to worry about.

38. (A) To put the papers in the trash.
    (B) To take out the garbage when he goes.
    (C) To separate everything according to their weight.
    (D) To separate garbage according to their categories.

39. (A) She will try to leave at ten.
    (B) She is leaving at ten thirty.
    (C) She won't leave for a while.
    (D) She is not leaving at all.

40. (A) To call her when he arrives.
    (B) To send her an e-mail when he gets there.
    (C) To write her when he gets to the destination.
    (D) To buy her a thread when he sees the special one.

41. (A) He was well prepared.
    (B) He wasn't quite well prepared as he thought he would be.
    (C) He wasn't sure.
    (D) He just didn't study at all.

42. (A) That Mary and John might get married someday.
    (B) That Mary and John will split up soon.
    (C) That Mary and John remains to be good friends forever.
    (D) That Mary and John will have bad days in the future.

43. (A) To take bus to the bookstore.
    (B) He dials a wrong number.
    (C) To take MRT to the bookstore.
    (D) The bookstore opens at nine o'clock.

44. (A) They are having different views on family.
    (B) They are having a pleasant discussion on family.
    (C) They are having a conversation on how important the family is.
    (D) They are having a quarrel about family.

45. (A) A physician.
    (B) A surgeon.
    (C) A psychiatrist.
    (D) A dentist.

聽力測驗（中級篇）

本測驗分三部分，全為四選一之選擇題，每部分各 15 題，共 45 題。

TEST 6

 TRACK 19

第一部分： 看圖辨義

第一部分有 15 題，為第 1 題至第 15 題，試題中有數幅圖畫，每一圖畫有 1～2 個描述該題之題目，每題請聽 CD 播出題目以及 A、B、C、D 四個英語敘述之後，選出與所看到的圖畫最相符的答案，每題只播出一遍。

Question 1　　　　　　Ans. _____

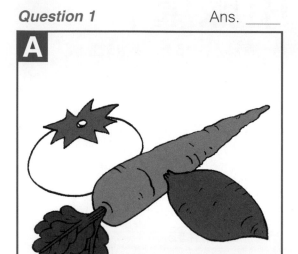

Question 2　　　　　　Ans. _____

Question 3　　　　　　Ans. _____

Question 4　　　　　　Ans. _____

Question 5   Ans. _____

Question 6   Ans. _____

Question 7   Ans. _____

Question 8   Ans. _____

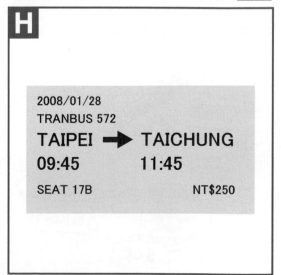

2008/01/28
TRANBUS 572
TAIPEI ➡ **TAICHUNG**
09:45   **11:45**
SEAT 17B   NT$250

Question 9 Ans. _____

Question 10 Ans. _____

Question 11–12 Ans. _____

Question 13 Ans. _____

Question 14   Ans. _____

Question 15   Ans. _____

TRACK 20

第二部分：問答

第二部分共有 15 題，為第 16 題至 30 題，每題請聽 CD 播出一個英語問句或直述句之後，從 A、B、C、D 四個回答或回應中，選出一個最適合者作答。每題只播出一遍。

16. (A) She just went to a dentist last week.
    (B) Yeah, she loves to eat anything that is sweet.
    (C) Actually, she is a very sweet girl.
    (D) As I know, she is really into making candies.

17. (A) Honestly, I don't have enough money.
    (B) Sorry, I didn't order this.
    (C) I'd like something sweet.
    (D) I can't. I am too full.

18. (A) That's why I need some time to sleep on it.
    (B) That's why I need to take a shower.
    (C) That's why I need to take a nap.
    (D) That's why I need to come back to Taiwan.

19. (A) That's beyond my comprehension.
    (B) That's out of the question.
    (C) That's absolutely ridiculous.
    (D) That's terrific!

20. (A) How would you like your steak?
    (B) That would be USD155.
    (C) Anything else?
    (D) I am sorry. I will have it replaced at once.

21. (A) Smoking is not allowed here.
    (B) Mind your own business!
    (C) No. Please go outside.
    (D) Yes. I'll smoke a cigarette too.

_____ 22. (A) I get up early in summer.

(B) I collect stamps.

(C) I want a cup of black coffee.

(D) I love to wear anything red.

_____ 23. (A) No wonder you got black and blue all over you.

(B) No wonder you have everything in black and white.

(C) I can see blood in your eyes.

(D) No wonder you got red eyes.

_____ 24. (A) At least he didn't suffer.

(B) I am glad to hear that.

(C) I wonder when he'll be back.

(D) He died from a serious car accident.

_____ 25. (A) A man is running after me.

(B) We need a mechanic to fix the car.

(C) We need to stop at the nearest gas station.

(D) Get off the car right away!

_____ 26. (A) Yeah, why not? Baseball is my favorite sport.

(B) Sure. I'll beat you this time.

(C) It's my treat this time.

(D) How about eating Chinese food?

_____ 27. (A) The tea is too hot.

(B) What do you have for dessert?

(C) Check, please.

(D) Coffee is fine.

_____ 28. (A) I am having a headache.

(B) To the cafeteria. Want to come along?

(C) The ship headed north.

(D) Turn right at the corner and you will see it.

_____ 29. (A) My pet cat died last night.

(B) I won the first prize in a speech contest.

(C) Don't worry, be happy.

(D) I'm sorry for your loss.

_____ 30. (A) Let me check for your foot.

(B) You want some pain killers?

(C) I'll call the eye doctor.

(D) Killing yourself is not the only solution.

第三部分：簡短對話

第三部分共有 15 題，為第 31 題至 45 題，每題請聽 CD 播出一段對話及一個相關問題之後，從 A、B、C、D 四個選項中選出一個最適合者作答。每題只播出一遍。

_____ 31. (A) An old friend whom they haven't seen for a while.
　　　　　(B) An old friend whom they have kept constant contact with.
　　　　　(C) An old friend whom they don't like.
　　　　　(D) An old friend whom they tried so hard to forget.

_____ 32. (A) A movie.
　　　　　(B) A live show.
　　　　　(C) A game.
　　　　　(D) A sale

_____ 33. (A) It's a win-win situation.
　　　　　(B) It's a no-win situation.
　　　　　(C) It's a win-loss situation.
　　　　　(D) It's a loss-loss situation.

_____ 34. (A) They are going to give Jack a credit card.
　　　　　(B) They recognized Jack's efforts in trying to pass the exam.
　　　　　(C) They felt sorry for Jack since he would never pass the exam.
　　　　　(D) They will offer after-school lessons for Jack.

_____ 35. (A) No, the woman got it on sale.
　　　　　(B) Yes, the woman got it at the original price.
　　　　　(C) Yes, the woman got it at a very high price.
　　　　　(D) No, the woman paid nothing for the dress.

_____ 36. (A) She needs to sign his name on the receipt.
　　　　　(B) She needs to show the receipt of perchasing the book.
　　　　　(C) She needs to show both his credit card the the receipt.
　　　　　(D) She needs to use another credit card to pay the book.

37. (A) She wanted to save money.
    (B) She didn't have any money.
    (C) She had little money left.
    (D) She didn't want to have dinner with the man.

38. (A) John called first before he showed up at the woman's door.
    (B) John showed up at the door without telling the woman in advance.
    (C) The woman knew that John was going to visit her.
    (D) The woman was surprised to see John because she was not ready to see him.

39. (A) A part-time job.
    (B) A difficult job.
    (C) A highly-paid job.
    (D) A temporary job.

40. (A) A waitress and a customer.
    (B) A hostess and a guest.
    (C) A mother and a son.
    (D) A daughter and a father.

41. (A) If the woman receives good grades, she will have the present she deserves.
    (B) Whether the woman receives good grades or not, she will get the present.
    (C) The man doesn't want to keep his promise.
    (D) The woman won't get any present whether she receives good grades or not.

42. (A) A tomato.
    (B) Cheese.
    (C) Onion.
    (D) Diet Coke.

43. (A) He was thinking of telling Mr. Smith the truth.

(B) He was thinking of some excuses for not handing in his report on time.

(C) He was thinking of having the woman help him out.

(D) He was thinking of having the woman go to see Mr. Smith with him.

___ 44. (A) In a classroom.

(B) In a concert hall.

(C) In an online shop.

(D) In an office.

___ 45. (A) In a hotel.

(B) In a restaurant.

(C) In a department store.

(D) In a hospital.

聽力測驗（中級篇）

本測驗分三部分，全為四選一之選擇題，每部分各 15 題，共 45 題。

TEST 7

 TRACK 22

第一部分：看圖辨義

第一部分有 15 題，為第 1 題至第 15 題，試題中有數幅圖畫，每一圖畫有 1～2 個描述該題之題目，每題請聽 CD 播出題目以及 A、B、C、D 四個英語敘述之後，選出與所看到的圖畫最相符的答案，每題只播出一遍。

Question 1   Ans. _____

Question 2   Ans. _____

Question 3–4   Ans. _____

Question 5   Ans. _____

Question 6　　　　　　　Ans. _____

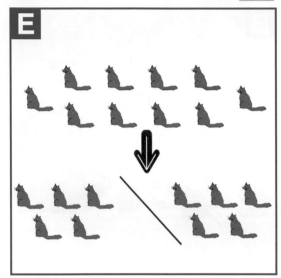

Question 7　　　　　　　Ans. _____

Question 8　　　　　　　Ans. _____

Question 9　　　　　　　Ans. _____

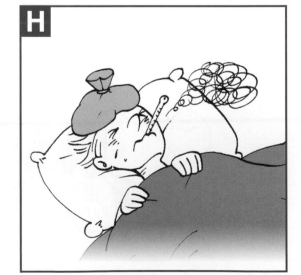

Question 10   Ans. _____

Question 11   Ans. _____

Question 12   Ans. _____

Question 13   Ans. _____

Question 14   Ans. _____

Question 15   Ans. _____

TRACK 23

第二部分：問答

第二部分共有 15 題，為第 16 題至 30 題，每題請聽 CD 播出一個英語問句或直述句之後，從 A、B、C、D 四個回答或回應中，選出一個最適合者作答。每題只播出一遍。

16. (A) I am all ears.
    (B) I am all eyes.
    (C) I am all hearts.
    (D) I am all by myself.

17. (A) Don't do that again!
    (B) That's my grandmother.
    (C) Hey! What are you doing now?
    (D) Wow! It's so beautiful!

18. (A) I'm not that strong.
    (B) I don't agree with that.
    (C) Have you been there before?
    (D) That would be fine.

19. (A) We are all students.
    (B) I'm a doctor, and she's a nurse.
    (C) Yes, sir.
    (D) That's Mr. Smith. He is the manager here.

20. (A) I am really glad about the news.
    (B) That's a bad idea.
    (C) I hope thing will turn out to be better.
    (D) Let's pray everything will be just fine.

21. (A) Why do you like ice cream?
    (B) Yes, sure. Coke is my favorite.
    (C) No, I only drink milk.
    (D) No, thanks. Just water will be fine.

_____ 22. (A) What's wrong with him?

(B) He must be falling in love with the chair.

(C) He is looking for his cat everywhere.

(D) Maybe we should call him Jerry.

_____ 23. (A) Are you sure? My name is Jason.

(B) Really? I'll sit here all night.

(C) Oops, I'm sorry.

(D) You can't do this to me!

_____ 24. (A) Let's find out.

(B) My father does.

(C) You're the boss.

(D) We usually eat out.

_____ 25. (A) That's why he is so crazy.

(B) That's why he is so clever.

(C) That's why he is so popular.

(D) That's why he is so weak.

_____ 26. (A) Finally!

(B) Great, now I can watch TV.

(C) It's just about time to have dinner.

(D) Is there any gas station nearby?

_____ 27. (A) Do you have the time?

(B) How many people in your party?

(C) From 6:30 to 10:00 a.m.

(D) It's a Japanese restaurant.

_____ 28. (A) Sure, we only take cash.

(B) No problem.

(C) That's a question!

(D) It's your own business.

29. (A) I can give you the list of all expenses.
    (B) Yes, it's very cheap.
    (C) Seven hundred and thirty thousand dollars..
    (D) That's a good trip.

30. (A) Stay away from me! I am afraid of blood.
    (B) I know CPR. Let me try.
    (C) Who is that guy?
    (D) Watch out! The car is coming!

TRACK 24

第三部分： 簡短對話

第三部分共有 15 題，為第 31 題至 45 題，每題請聽 CD 播出一段對話及一個相關問題之後，從 A、B、C、D 四個選項中選出一個最適合者作答。每題只播出一遍。

_____ 31. (A) She liked neither of them
   (B) She liked both of them.
   (C) She liked one more than the other.
   (D) She needed more time to think about it.

_____ 32. (A) He speaks French and Germany.
   (B) He is a professor.
   (C) It is his line of work.
   (D) He knows almost everything.

_____ 33. (A) Yes, because she has plenty of time.
   (B) Yes, and she is very interested.
   (C) No, and she is not home.
   (D) No, and she makes an excuse.

_____ 34. (A) Terrible.
   (B) Excellent.
   (C) So-so.
   (D) Perfect.

_____ 35. (A) She doesn't like pizza.
   (B) She always have fried chicken for dinner.
   (C) She decides to have pizza.
   (D) She usually eats healthy and light.

_____ 36. (A) He is a high school student.
   (B) His name is Mark.
   (C) His name is Jonathan.
   (D) He is wearing a black T-shirt.

37. (A) It was a good news.

    (B) It was long and boring.

    (C) It was great.

    (D) It was talking about tea.

38. (A) He is happy to pay his share when going out with his friends.

    (B) He is always trying to get away from paying the bill.

    (C) He loves to play hide-and-seek.

    (D) He is always short of money.

39. (A) A talk with Jean.

    (B) A performance for Jean.

    (C) A trip to the United States with Jean.

    (D) A secret farewell party for Jean.

40. (A) A convenience store.

    (B) A ticket office.

    (C) A police station.

    (D) A bus stop.

41. (A) Because she is very rude.

    (B) Because she is a very serious person.

    (C) Because she doesn't like the man.

    (D) Because she loves those photos very much.

42. (A) To change her boss right away.

    (B) To get a new job immediately.

    (C) To talk to her boss before making any decision.

    (D) To keep quiet.

43. (A) Yes, and she is going to return the table.

    (B) Yes, and she has already figured out what she's going to be about it.

    (C) No, but she thinks it's pretty cheap.

    (D) No, but she'll buy the table and the tablecloth as well.

44. (A) No right turn.
    (B) Beware children.
    (C) No smoking.
    (D) Stop and go.

45. (A) No, because he can't afford that.
    (B) No, because the hotel doesn't have any twin room.
    (C) Yes, because the hotel can make some necessary arrangements.
    (D) Yes, because he can move the bed by himself.

聽力測驗（中級篇）

本測驗分三部分，全為四選一之選擇題，每部分各 15 題，共 45 題。

TEST 8

 TRACK 25

第一部分： 看圖辨義

第一部分有 15 題，為第 1 題至第 15 題，試題中有數幅圖畫，每一圖畫有 1～2 個描述該題之題目，每題請聽 CD 播出題目以及 A、B、C、D 四個英語敘述之後，選出與所看到的圖畫最相符的答案，每題只播出一遍。

Question 1   Ans. ____

Question 2   Ans. ____

Question 3   Ans. ____

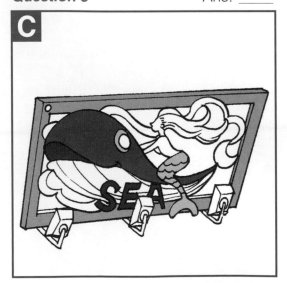

Question 4   Ans. ____

Question 5   Ans. _____

Question 6   Ans. _____

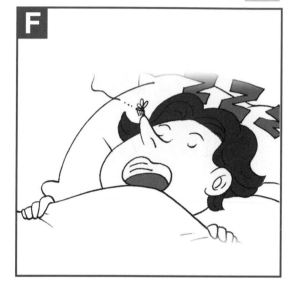

Question 7   Ans. _____

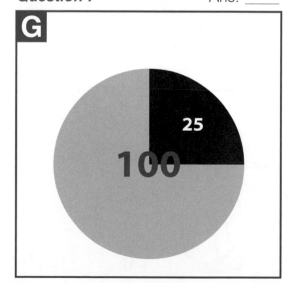

Question 8   Ans. _____

Question 9   Ans. _____

Question 10   Ans. _____

Question 11   Ans. _____

Question 12   Ans. _____

Question 13   Ans. _____

Question 14   Ans. _____

Question 15   Ans. _____

TRACK 26

第二部分：問答

第二部分共有 15 題，為第 16 題至 30 題，每題請聽 CD 播出一個英語問句或直述句之後，從 A、B、C、D 四個回答或回應中，選出一個最適合者作答。每題只播出一遍。

_____ 16. (A) I am sorry to hear that.
(B) Really? What brand is it?
(C) Really? How old is it?
(D) How about taking a taxi?

_____ 17. (A) It's one of my hobbies.
(B) It will begin at 7:30 p.m.
(C) It's on my desk. You can take it anytime.
(D) It's terrible! I can't believe we came all the way for that.

_____ 18. (A) No excuse. I won't let this happen again.
(B) This is the first time I came late.
(C) I know it's too early to have dinner.
(D) Wake me up if you have time.

_____ 19. (A) I'll have chocolate cake.
(B) I'll have a glass of wine.
(C) I'll have some ice cream.
(D) I'll have the beef.

_____ 20. (A) I don't like Japan.
(B) I'll probably go to the library.
(C) I'll definitely go there.
(D) I'll probably go to Taiwan.

_____ 21. (A) That's very nice of you.
(B) You are so mean.
(C) What a nice shot!
(D) What are you trying to do?

22. (A) Great, I'll go find him.
    (B) Who will help me with the work?
    (C) I feel exactly the same.
    (D) To work hard is necessary.

23. (A) No. I lied to you.
    (B) Yes. But only because I didn't want you to get hurt.
    (C) No. And I'll keep this for good.
    (D) Yes. I found it in the backyard.

24. (A) You can find it everywhere.
    (B) He is not my type of person.
    (C) The visitor center is over there.
    (D) Just turn left at the corner.

25. (A) I could earn NTD 100 a month.
    (B) Enough to pay the rent.
    (C) I'm five feet and six inches tall.
    (D) I don't need any cash.

26. (A) No. I am a big fan of Jazz.
    (B) Yes, I play video games all the time.
    (C) Let's get into the action!
    (D) Why don't you hit it hard?

27. (A) I am working for my college degree.
    (B) I can't tell you why.
    (C) I am still a kid.
    (D) I will try to get one.

28. (A) Don't yell at me like that!
    (B) Yeah, I saw her steal your money.
    (C) She will lose this game.
    (D) She is what you think she is.

_____ 29. (A) What's the count?

(B) Are you Mr. Wang?

(C) Where am I?

(D) Do you like peaches?

_____ 30. (A) That will be fine.

(B) I don't like orange juice.

(C) It's up to you.

(D) No problem.

 TRACK 27

第三部分: 簡短對話

第三部分共有 15 題,為第 31 題至 45 題,每題請聽 CD 播出一段對話及一個相關問題之後,從 A、B、C、D 四個選項中選出一個最適合者作答。每題只播出一遍。

_____ 31. (A) A father and a daughter.
(B) A mother and her son.
(C) A boss and his employee.
(D) Two strangers.

_____ 32. (A) No, she will not stop using instant messages.
(B) No, and she will take advantage of others.
(C) Yes, and she will ask others to do the same.
(D) Yes, unless she knows who is sending her messages.

_____ 33. (A) Yes, he thinks she is hungry.
(B) Yes, and he wants more.
(C) No, he thinks that she is having too much.
(D) No, he doesn't want her to have anything.

_____ 34. (A) Because her neighbor doesn't love her.
(B) Because her neighbor is always making noises.
(C) Because her neighbor keeps calling her.
(D) Because her neighbor is cheating on her.

_____ 35. (A) She wants to kill herself.
(B) She is complaining about herself.
(C) She thinks she is perfect.
(D) She is looking for a way to live.

_____ 36. (A) The woman's new boyfriend.
(B) The woman's father.
(C) The woman's teacher.
(D) The woman's younger brother.

37. (A) Leaving the TV on without watching it.
    (B) Buying some things he doesn't need.
    (C) Driving his car in the downtown area.
    (D) Watching movies without buying his ticket.

38. (A) That's something she should be proud of.
    (B) That's something she should be more careful about.
    (C) That's something she should stop.
    (D) That's something she should learn to do.

39. (A) Take the red one.
    (B) Take the blue one.
    (C) Take them both.
    (D) Don't take any of them.

40. (A) How could the woman be so stupid?
    (B) How could the woman send the money without telling him?
    (C) How could the woman force others to do something wrong?
    (D) How could the woman be so generous?

41. (A) The man will finish her homework and then clean up her room.
    (B) The woman will ask the man to clean his room.
    (C) The woman will clean the man's room herself.
    (D) The man will finish his homework and then meet his friends.

42. (A) They are in a bank.
    (B) They are in a park.
    (C) They are in a bookstore.
    (D) They are in a train station.

43. (A) Three altogether.
    (B) Six altogether.
    (C) Nine altogether.
    (D) Twelve altogether.

_____ 44. (A) She is going to perform in school's play.

(B) She is going to play in her school's basketball team.

(C) She is going to watch school's play.

(D) She is going to sell tickets for school's play.

_____ 45. (A) He will be fired.

(B) He will get more pay.

(C) He will leave the company soon.

(D) He will employ the woman.

ANSWER KEY

Test 1

1	2	3	4	5	6	7	8	9	10	11	12	13	14	15
B	B	A	C	A	B	D	C	B	A	A	A	D	B	A
16	**17**	**18**	**19**	**20**	**21**	**22**	**23**	**24**	**25**	**26**	**27**	**28**	**29**	**30**
B	A	A	B	C	A	D	A	C	C	A	B	D	A	C
31	**32**	**33**	**34**	**35**	**36**	**37**	**38**	**39**	**40**	**41**	**42**	**43**	**44**	**45**
C	B	A	A	C	A	D	C	B	A	C	A	B	C	A

Test 2

1	2	3	4	5	6	7	8	9	10	11	12	13	14	15
B	D	B	A	B	C	A	C	D	A	B	C	B	C	B
16	**17**	**18**	**19**	**20**	**21**	**22**	**23**	**24**	**25**	**26**	**27**	**28**	**29**	**30**
A	B	A	C	A	A	D	A	D	B	C	A	A	B	A
31	**32**	**33**	**34**	**35**	**36**	**37**	**38**	**39**	**40**	**41**	**42**	**43**	**44**	**45**
A	D	B	B	A	A	B	D	A	A	C	A	A	B	A

Test 3

1	2	3	4	5	6	7	8	9	10	11	12	13	14	15
A	A	B	C	D	A	B	B	C	B	B	A	A	A	B
16	**17**	**18**	**19**	**20**	**21**	**22**	**23**	**24**	**25**	**26**	**27**	**28**	**29**	**30**
B	A	C	D	A	B	A	D	B	C	A	D	D	A	B
31	**32**	**33**	**34**	**35**	**36**	**37**	**38**	**39**	**40**	**41**	**42**	**43**	**44**	**45**
A	B	C	D	A	A	A	D	B	A	B	D	C	C	B

Test 4

1	2	3	4	5	6	7	8	9	10	11	12	13	14	15
A	D	B	A	B	A	C	B	C	B	C	C	A	A	B
16	**17**	**18**	**19**	**20**	**21**	**22**	**23**	**24**	**25**	**26**	**27**	**28**	**29**	**30**
A	A	C	B	D	A	C	A	C	B	A	B	A	B	B
31	**32**	**33**	**34**	**35**	**36**	**37**	**38**	**39**	**40**	**41**	**42**	**43**	**44**	**45**
A	A	B	D	A	C	A	C	A	A	A	D	C	A	C

Test 5

1	2	3	4	5	6	7	8	9	10	11	12	13	14	15
A	D	B	C	A	D	D	C	B	A	C	B	B	D	A
16	**17**	**18**	**19**	**20**	**21**	**22**	**23**	**24**	**25**	**26**	**27**	**28**	**29**	**30**
A	B	D	A	C	A	C	C	D	A	B	A	C	A	B
31	**32**	**33**	**34**	**35**	**36**	**37**	**38**	**39**	**40**	**41**	**42**	**43**	**44**	**45**
A	A	A	B	B	D	C	D	A	C	B	A	C	A	D

Test 6

1	2	3	4	5	6	7	8	9	10	11	12	13	14	15
D	D	A	D	C	A	B	C	B	C	D	B	A	D	C
16	**17**	**18**	**19**	**20**	**21**	**22**	**23**	**24**	**25**	**26**	**27**	**28**	**29**	**30**
B	D	A	A	D	A	B	D	A	C	B	D	B	A	B
31	**32**	**33**	**34**	**35**	**36**	**37**	**38**	**39**	**40**	**41**	**42**	**43**	**44**	**45**
A	A	D	B	A	B	B	B	A	C	A	C	B	D	A

Test 7

1	2	3	4	5	6	7	8	9	10	11	12	13	14	15
B	A	B	D	C	A	A	C	A	C	A	B	D	C	A
16	**17**	**18**	**19**	**20**	**21**	**22**	**23**	**24**	**25**	**26**	**27**	**28**	**29**	**30**
A	D	B	D	A	D	A	C	B	C	D	C	B	A	B
31	**32**	**33**	**34**	**35**	**36**	**37**	**38**	**39**	**40**	**41**	**42**	**43**	**44**	**45**
A	C	D	A	D	C	B	B	D	B	D	C	B	C	C

Test 8

1	2	3	4	5	6	7	8	9	10	11	12	13	14	15
A	D	D	A	A	C	A	B	D	A	C	D	C	B	A
16	**17**	**18**	**19**	**20**	**21**	**22**	**23**	**24**	**25**	**26**	**27**	**28**	**29**	**30**
B	D	A	D	D	A	C	B	D	B	A	A	D	A	D
31	**32**	**33**	**34**	**35**	**36**	**37**	**38**	**39**	**40**	**41**	**42**	**43**	**44**	**45**
B	A	C	B	B	A	A	B	A	A	D	C	B	A	B

全民英檢中級模擬試題

Barbara Kuo／編著

必勝秘訣

☑ **秘訣 1** 初試複試內容 all in one！

完整收錄初試及複試的測驗內容，輕鬆熟悉英檢中級所有考題。

☑ **秘訣2** 掌握必考的聽力情境！

聽力試題強調日常生活情境用語，立即融入情境、了解語意。

☑ **秘訣3** 熟悉測驗模式，不陌生，不怯場！

反覆練習閱讀寫作及口說能力，轉眼就能妙筆生花、對答如流。

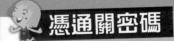

GEPT

全民英檢聽力測驗
So Easy 中級篇

實踐大學副教授 李普生　編著　解答本

最逼真！模擬試題提升應試能力
最精闢！範例分析傾授高分技巧

三民書局

CONTENTS

聽力測驗腳本與解析

Test ①

第一部份：看圖辨義

1. For question number 1, please look at picture A.

   Question number 1: What is the most economic way to travel to Taichung?

   (A) By bus.

   (B) By train.

   (C) By car.

   (D) On foot

   問題：到台中最省時的方法為何？

   選項：(A) 搭巴士

   　　　(B) 搭火車

   　　　(C) 搭汽車

   　　　(D) 步行

   提示："economic" 可當「省時」也可當「省錢」。

2. For question number 2, please look at picture B.

   Question number 2: Where do you think this interaction is most likely to happen?

   (A) In a hotel

   (B) In a restaurant.

   (C) In a car rental company.

   (D) In an amusement park.

   問題：下列互動最可能發生的場所為何？

   選項：(A) 旅館

   　　　(B) 餐廳

   　　　(C) 租車公司

   　　　(D) 遊樂園

3. For question number 3, please look at picture C.

   Question number 3: How do you think the boy is feeling today?

   (A) Happy.

   (B) Sad.

   (C) Business as usual.

   (D) Mad

問題：你覺得這男孩今天感覺如何？

選項：(A) 快樂

　　　(B) 悲傷

　　　(C) 沒有特別感覺

　　　(D) 憤怒

提示：前三題所用的都是疑問詞：what, where, how，疑問詞開頭的問句又稱開放式問句，回答多為文字說明。

4. For question number 4, please look at picture D.

   Question number 4: Is the girl going to the school?

   (A) She is running for something urgent.

   (B) No, she is on the way to school.

   (C) Yes. She is. She is going to the school.

   (D) She gets up early every day.

   問題：這女孩正往學校去嗎？

   選項：(A) 她正跑去處理某件緊急事情。

   　　　(B) 不，她正往學校的路上。

   　　　(C) 是的。她正往學校去。

   　　　(D) 她每天早上很早起床。

   提示：本題係以 be 動詞 "is" 開頭的問句；以 be 動詞 (am, are, is, was, were) 或助動詞 (do, does, did, have, has, had) 開頭的疑問句，它的答案多以 "yes" 或 "no" 為主。

5. For question number 5, please look at picture E.

   Question number 5: What is it?

   (A) It's a moon cake.

   (B) It's ginger.

   (C) It's fried chicken.

   (D) It's watermelon.

   問題：圖示中為何物？

   選項：(A) 月餅。

   　　　(B) 薑。

   　　　(C) 炸雞。

(D) 西瓜。

6. For question number 6, please look at picture F.

Question number 6: Which season of the year is it in the picture?

(A) Spring.

(B) Summer.

(C) Autumn.

(D) Winter.

問題：圖片是一年四季中的那個季節？

選項：(A) 春季

　　　(B) 夏季

　　　(C) 秋季

　　　(D) 冬季

提示："which" 可同時為疑問詞及關係代名詞：

　　　Which do you prefer, coffee or tea？（疑問詞，表選擇）

　　　This is the book which I bought yesterday.（關係代名詞，代替先前曾提及的事或物）

7. For question number 7, please look at picture G.

Question number 7: Why is the girl crying?

(A) She can't find her way home.

(B) She is hungry.

(C) She lost money.

(D) She hurt herself while walking.

問題：這女孩為何在哭？

選項：(A) 她找不到回家的路。

　　　(B) 她餓了。

　　　(C) 她把錢弄丟了。

　　　(D) 她在走路時傷了自己。

8. For question number 8, please look at picture H.

Question number 8: When does the store open? And when does it close?

(A) It opens at 7: 30 a .m and closes at 4 p.m.

(B) It opens at 8 a .m. and closes at 3:30 p.m.

(C) It opens at 11 a .m. and closes at 8 p.m.

(D) It opens at 7 a .m. and closes at 4:30 p.m.

問題：商店何時開始營業？何時關門？

選項：(A) 早上七點半營業，下午四點關門。

　　　(B) 早上八點營業，下午三點半關門。

　　　(C) 早上十一點營業，晚上八點關門。

　　　(D) 早上七點營業，下午四點半關門。

提示："when" 可以同時當疑問詞，關係代名詞及關係副詞：

　　　When are you leaving？（疑問詞）

　　　This is the time when each of us should work together.（代名詞）

　　　This is the time when (=at which) he will come.（副詞）

9. For question number 9, please look at picture I.

Question number 9: Does the boy have a hat on?

(A) Yes, he does. He has a hat on.

(B) No, he doesn't. He has a cap on.

(C) Yes, but his hat is worn out.

(D) No, he doesn't. He has earmuffs on.

問題：這男孩帶著一頂有帽簷的帽子嗎？

選項：(A) 是的，他帶著一頂有帽簷的帽子。

　　　(B) 不，他沒有。他帶著一頂棒球帽。

　　　(C) 是的，但他的帽子已經磨破了。

　　　(D) 不，他沒有。他帶著一付耳罩。

提示：就如同「帽子」可能會是 "hat" 也可能是 "cap" 一樣，英文中有一些容易混淆的字。如：beard/mustache/whisker（鬍鬚）、will（助動詞；將…）/will（名詞；意志，決心，天意，遺囑）、borrow from/lend to（從…借來；借給…）等。如果不仔細區分，在答題上會造成很多不必要的損失。

10. For question number 10, please look at picture J.

Question number 10: Which description best describe the picture?

(A) The man is trying hard to catch the plane.

(B) The man is trying hard to stay away from the plane.

(C) The man is taking a walk in the park.

(D) The plane is going to take off.

問題：下列敘述中何者能最恰當地描述圖示？

選項：(A) 這位男士嘗試去趕上飛機。

(B) 這位男士嘗試去躲避飛機。

(C) 這位男士正在公園散步。

(D) 飛機正要起飛。

11. For question number 11, please look at picture K.

Question number 11: What does the woman do for a living?

(A) She is a postwoman.

(B) She is a garbage collector.

(C) She is a school teacher.

(D) She is a model.

問題：這位女士的工作是什麼？

選項：(A) 她是位郵差。

(B) 她是位垃圾收集員。

(C) 她是位學校老師。

(D) 她是位模特兒。

12. For question number 12, please look at picture L.

Question number 12: What are they doing?

(A) They are fighting against each other.

(B) They are talking to each other.

(C) They are greeting each other.

(D) They are bidding farewell to each other.

問題：他們正在做什麼？

選項：(A) 他們正在相互廝殺。

(B) 他們正在相互交談。

(C) 他們正在相互寒喧。

(D) 他們正在相互道別。

13. For question number 13, please look at picture M.

Question number 13: What is the woman selling?

(A) She is selling noodles.

(B) She is selling hot dogs.

(C) She is selling ice cream.

(D) She is selling flowers.

問題：這女人正在賣什麼？

選項：(A) 她正在賣麵條。

(B) 她正在賣熱狗。

(C) 她正在賣冰淇淋。

(D) 她正在賣鮮花。

14. For question number 14, please look at picture N.

Question number 14: Who is the man on the right of the picture?

(A) He is the bride.

(B) He is the groom.

(C) He is the best man.

(D) He is the father of the bride.

問題：圖示中右方的男人是誰？

選項：(A) 他是新娘。

(B) 他是新郎。

(C) 他是伴郎。

(D) 他是新娘的父親。

答案：B

提示：(1)疑問詞 "who" 問「關係」：

"Who is he?"

"He is my father."

"what" 問「職業、身份、地位」：

"What is he?"

"He is my school principal."

(2)關係代名詞 "who" 的用法有下列幾種：

He is the man who came to see us last night.（主格）

He is the man whom we saw last night.（受格）

He is the man whose father is a teacher.（所有格）

(3) bridegroom（新郎）、bride（新娘）、best man（伴郎）、bridesmaid（伴娘）

15. For question number 15, please look at picture O.

Question number 15: What holiday is it?

(A) It's Halloween.

(B) It's Christmas.

(C) It's New Year.

(D) It's Independence Day.

問題：圖示中的節日為何？

選項：(A) 萬聖節。

　　　(B) 耶誕節。

　　　(C) 新年。

　　　(D) 美國獨立紀念日。

第二部份：問答

16. Question number 16: How's the world treating you?

(A) It treats me unfairly.

(B) It's terrible!

(C) How are you?

(D) I have been traveled around the world.

問題：你最近如何？

選項：(A) 它待我很不公平

　　　(B) 糟透了！

　　　(C) 你好嗎？

　　　(D) 我曾經環遊世界。

提示：傳統英文課本中的寒喧語不外乎 "How are you?" 或 "How do you do?"，但在實際的英語會話中，寒喧語很可能是："What's up?"、"How's going?"、"How goes it with you?"、"How have

you been?"、"How are things with you?"、"How's everything with you?" 等。所以了解口語表達遠比制式回答來的有用。在選項中，A 只是一單純的敘述，而非回答。只有 B 是針對題目作答，表示最近生活過得並不如意。

17. Question number 17: We seem to keep running into each other.

(A) Yeah! It's a small world, isn't it?

(B) Let me know when you'll be here next time.

(C) We should stop doing that!

(D) Something is bound to happen.

問題：我們好像總是不期而遇。

選項：(A) 是呀！這世界還真小。

　　　(B) 下次你要來這時先讓我知道。

　　　(C) 我們該停止這種做法。

　　　(D) 有事要發生嘍！

答案：A

提示：本題乍看之下，會讓人覺得它是個敘述句，但實際上它想表達的是「世界上人如此多，為何我總是碰到你？」所以，「世界真小」這個回答不僅說明了原因同時也化解了些許的尷尬！

18. Question number 18: Have you ever met Bob before?

(A) I don't think I have the pleasure.

(B) Whom are you talking about?

(C) It doesn't ring a bell.

(D) Do I have to?

問題：你見過鮑伯嗎？

選項：(A) 我沒見過。

　　　(B) 我們在說誰呀？

　　　(C) 我記不起來。

　　　(D) 我一定要嗎？

答案：A

提示：(1)助動詞開始的問句，照理說要用 "yes"

或 "no" 回答，但 "I don't think..." 也間接的代表了否定，所以答案選 A。

⑵ have/has + ever/never + gone to... :
表動作：

Has he gone to Japan?

（他去日本了嗎？）

have/has + ever/never + been to... :

表經驗：

Have you ever been to Japan?

（你曾去過日本嗎？）

⑶若問題為 "Do you know Bob?" 則 C 是正確答案。

19. Question number 19: Give me a call when you have time, will you?

(A) Not a chance.

(B) You bet I would.

(C) We'll see.

(D) I don't think so.

問題：你有時間的話，給我通電話，好嗎？

選項：(A) 門兒都沒有！

(B) 我一定會。

(C) 再說吧。

(D) 我不這麼認為。

答案：B

提示："bet" 本為「打賭」，既然敢賭，就代表「有把握」，所以答案 B 是最佳的選擇。

20. Question number 20: How was the game last night?

(A) Wish you were there.

(B) I used to play games on weekends.

(C) It's the worst I have ever seen.

(D) All my family like to play computer games .

問題：昨晚的比賽如何？

選項：(A) 真希望你在場。

(B) 我習慣在週末玩遊戲。

(C) 那是我所看過中最爛的一場。

(D) 我所有的家人都喜歡玩電腦遊戲。

答案：C

21. Question number 21: How can I ever thank you?

(A) Don't mention it.

(B) Buy me a present.

(C) Try to return me a favor next time.

(D) You could if you try.

問題：我該如何謝你呢？

選項：(A) 別放在心上。

(B) 買個禮物給我。

(C) 下次再回報我。

(D) 如過你盡力你會想到的。

提示：本題的真正意思並不是要詢問如何回報他人的協助，而是表示感激之意。B 選項 "Don't mention it." 是對方對他人的答謝所做的貼心回應。回應他人道謝的用語還有："You are welcome."、"My pleasure."、"Not at all."、"It was nothing, really."、"No problem."、"No sweat."

22. Question number 22: I am sorry but you lost me.

(A) You can give me your address again.

(B) You want me to give you a map?

(C) There is an information desk over there.

(D) You want me to repeat it again?

問題：對不起，但我聽不懂。

選項：(A) 你可以再給我一次你的住址。

(B) 你要我給你一份地圖嗎？

(C) 那裡有詢問台。

(D) 要我再說一遍嗎？

提示：聽不懂或沒聽清楚時還可以用下列語句："Excuse me?"、"I don't quite catch that."、"What was that?"、"Come again?"、"I'm afraid I had trouble understanding it."

23. Question number 23: What time do you have?

    (A) My watch says 11:30.

    (B) I have the slightest idea.

    (C) It's way pass your bed time.

    (D) I am already late for my work.

    問題：現在幾點？

    選項：(A) 根據我的手錶，現在是十一點半。

    　　　(B) 我一點概念都沒有。

    　　　(C) 早就過了你睡覺時間了。

    　　　(D) 我上班已經遲到了。

    提示："What time do you have?" 意思是「現在幾點。」問時間的說法還有："Do you have the time?"、"What time is it?"、"Do you know what time it is?"
    回答的方法則有："It's twelve noon/midnight."、"It's twelve o'clock sharp.（十二點整）"、"It's ten after/past twelve.（十二點十分）"、"It's ten to/till twelve.（十一點五十分）"、"It's almost twelve."、"It's just after twelve."、"It's a little past twelve."、"It's not quite twelve."、" It's three hours ahead/behind.（時差）"

24. Question number 24: Don't you hate all this rain?

    (A) How unfortunate!

    (B) Couldn't be better!

    (C) Things could be worse.

    (D) There will be heavy rain tomorrow.

    問題：這雨還真讓人討厭！

    選項：(A) 真不幸！

    　　　(B) 再好不過了！

    　　　(C) 事情可能會變的更糟。

    　　　(D) 明天會有豪雨。

    提示：C 選項表現出沮喪絕望的心情，類似的說法還有："I feel so low."、"I am feeling depressed lately."、"It's depressing."、"Nothing seems to go right."、"I feel so empty."、"I don't feel like doing anything."

25. Question number 25: That's a lovely necklace you have.

    (A) You're welcome.

    (B) The fake one would be cheaper.

    (C) Well, thank you. That's a present for my birthday.

    (D) The necklaces and earrings are all on sale now.

    問題：你的項鍊真可愛。

    選項：(A) 不客氣。

    　　　(B) 假的項鍊比較便宜。

    　　　(C) 謝謝你。那是我的生日禮物。

    　　　(D) 項鍊和耳環現在都在特價。

26. Question number 26 ：Are you losing your mind?

    (A) On the contrary, I know exactly what I am doing.

    (B) Yes. Do you know where I can find it?

    (C) No. I am just looking.

    (D) Yes, but I have no choice.

    問題：你瘋了嗎？

    選項：(A) 恰好相反。我非常清楚自己在做什麼。

    　　　(B) 是的。你知道我在那裡可找到它？

    　　　(C) 不是。我只是看看。

    　　　(D) 是的，但我別無選擇。

    提示：英文中有許多表達都有「昏了頭」、「迷失方向」、「不懂」的意思：
    I am sorry, but what you said lost me.
    I am sorry, but what you said did not ring a bell.

27. Question number 27: The fax machine is out of paper.

    (A) I bought a new one at home.

(B) I'll see if I can get some.

(C) I'll call the serviceman.

(D) The machine doesn't work.

問題：傳真機沒有紙了。

選項：(A) 我在家裡買了一個新的。

　　　(B) 我去看看能否找些。

　　　(C) 我去打電話給維修人員。

　　　(D) 這個機器沒辦法運轉了。

28. Question number 28: Why are you transferring to another school?

(A) I can't wait to go to the new school.

(B) It was absolutely the best place.

(C) We decide to transfer him to a new office.

(D) I am not happy with the environment here.

問題：你為何要轉到另一個學校去？

選項：(A) 我迫不及待要去新的學校。

　　　(B) 它真的是一個很棒的地方。

　　　(C) 我們決定把他調到新的辦公室。

　　　(D) 我不喜歡這裡的環境。

提示："why" 可以當疑問詞及關係副詞：

Why were you late for school today?（疑問詞）

This is the reason why (=for which) he was absent yesterday.（關係副詞）

29. Question number 29: We are currently out of this item.

(A) When will the next shipment come in?

(B) When is it due?

(C) When will you have more?

(D) The new product has come on to the market.

問題：這項貨品目前缺貨。

選項：(A) 下批貨品何時到？

　　　(B) 何時到期？

　　　(C) 何時你會有更多的貨品？

(D) 新產品已經上市了。

提示：答案 C 似乎也是個可能的答案，但我們通常會將這個表達用在已擁有部分貨品但希望能有更多數量時，而不適用在缺貨而查詢何時會有新貨到達。

30. Question number 30: What's that smell?

(A) There is something wrong with my nose.

(B) I don't like the smell of the flowers.

(C) I think something is burning.

(D) Mm...the soup smells delicious.

問題：什麼味道啊？

選項：(A) 我的鼻子有問題。

　　　(B) 我不喜歡這種花的味道。

　　　(C) 我想有東西在燃燒。

　　　(D) 這湯聞起來好香。

第三部份：簡短對話

31. Question number 31:

M: What does John's new girlfriend look like?

W: I have no idea. But I overheard that she is a beauty.

M: How come some other guys have all the luck?

W: Are you telling me that you feel sorry we go steady?

Question: What's the relationship between the man and the woman?

(A) Husband and wife.

(B) Father and daughter.

(C) Boyfriend and girlfriend.

(D) Classmates.

男：約翰新女友長相如何？

女：我不知道。不過我聽說她是個美人。

男：為何他男人總是運氣較好！

女：你覺得和我穩定交往有點可惜嗎？

問題：這對男女之間的關係為何？

選項：(A) 先生太太。

(B) 父親女兒。

(C) 男女朋友。

(D) 同學。

提示：「go steady」意思是「穩定交往」，通常代表男女朋友之間的關係，所以對話中的女生聽到她的男朋友稱讚其他女生便醋勁大發，因此選男女朋友才是正確答案。

32. Question number 32:

W: My new colleague is terrible!

M: Why did you say that?

W: He never comes to work on time and he is always full of excuses.

M: Why don't you say something to your boss?

W: I can't. He is my boss' son-in-law.

Question: Why is the woman feeling upset?

(A) She is happy with her co-worker.

(B) She is in bad terms with her co-worker.

(C) The man is her boss' son-in-law.

(D) The man is having a crush on her.

女：我的新同事糟糕透了！

男：為何你會這樣說？

女：他從沒準時上班而且他總是理由一大堆。

男：為何不向老闆反應？

女：不行。他是老闆的女婿。

問題：為何這位女士覺得沮喪？

選項：(A) 因她和同事相處愉快。

(B) 因她和同事相處不愉快。

(C) 因這男人是她老闆的女婿。

(D) 因這男人暗戀她。

提示：「term」為單數時解為「任期、專門名詞、學期」，若為複數形時則為「條件」。"in terms of（就…而言）"、"in good/bad terms with（關係良好/惡劣）"、"come to terms with（達成協議）"

33. Question number 33:

M: Did you start working again?

W: Yes. It's hard to make both ends meet on my husband's small income.

M: Then, what about your kid? Who's taking care of him?

W: My mother is; she is kind enough to step in and help me out.

Question: What information can we draw from this conversation?

(A) The woman used to work before she gave birth to her son.

(B) The woman is in the job market for the first time.

(C) The woman is trying to find a job.

(D) The man is trying to give the woman a job.

男：你又開始工作了嗎？

女：是的。靠我先生有限的薪水想要量入為出有些困難。

男：那你的孩子呢？誰在照顧他？

女：我母親；多虧她體貼的伸出援手幫我的忙。

問題：根據上述的對話，我們可以做出何種結論？

選項：(A) 這位女士在生產前就已經有過工作經驗。

(B) 這位女士首次進入職場。

(C) 這位女士試著找份工作。

(D) 這位男士試著提供這位女士一份工作。

34. Question number 34:

M: This river looks very polluted.

W: I know. The city has just started making efforts to clean it up.

M: I wonder what the result will be.

W: I guess we can only wait and see.

Question: Are the man and the woman confident that the city will do a good job?

(A) They are not sure.

(B) They are certain.

(C) They are positive about it.

(D) They are angry with it.

男：這條河看起來污染很嚴重。

女：是啊。市政府剛開始要努力整頓它。

男：不知結果會如何。

女：我們只有靜觀其變了。

問題：這對男女對市政府把事做好有信心嗎？

選項：(A) 他們沒把握。

　　　(B) 他們有把握。

　　　(C) 他們對這件事有信心。

　　　(D) 他們對此感到生氣。

提示：本題應屬所謂的「推測」或「推理」；根據題中的文字來做合乎邏輯的猜臆。關鍵字在於 "wonder" 解釋成「懷疑、不知道」，例：

I wondered if James would recognized me after so many years.

（不知道詹姆士在那麼多年後還能不能認出我。）

35. Question number 35:

M: How do you like your new school?

W: I don't like it a bit. My classmates just make fun of my accent constantly.

M: What are you going to do about that?

W: I can only try and try really hard to improve myself.

M: Or, you could just ignore it.

W: That will be hard to do!

Question: What will the woman do?

(A) Quit her school.

(B) Give up learning completely.

(C) Try really hard to improve herself.

(D) Try really hard to ignore other students.

男：你的新學校如何？

女：我一點都不喜歡。我的同學總是拿我的口音

開玩笑。

男：你要如何處理那個問題呢？

女：我只能努力再努力來改進自己。

男：或者你可以試著不理這件事。

女：那還真困難！

問題：這位女生會如何做？

選項：(A) 不再去學校。

　　　(B) 完全放棄學習。

　　　(C) 努力嘗試改進自己。

　　　(D) 努力嘗試不理其他學生。

提示："how" 和 "when" 及 "why" 一樣。可當疑問詞也可當關係副詞：

How are you today?（疑問詞）

Tell me how (=by which) you did it.

（關係副詞）

36. Question number 36:

W: Do you want to watch the weather report?

M: No. It makes no difference to me whether it rains or not. I am going to stay home anyway.

W: Come on. Cheer up! It's not the end of the world you can't go out.

M: I wish I had studied harder. In that case, I won't be grounded by my father.

Question: Why can't the man go out?

(A) He was grounded by his father.

(B) It's going to rain.

(C) He doesn't feel like to.

(D) He is going to stay home and catch some sleep.

女：你想不想看氣象報告？

男：不想。下不下雨對我而言毫無影響。反正我要待在家裡。

女：別這樣。開心點。你不能外出也不是世界末日。

男：我真希望我能多用功些。如此一來，我就不

10

會被父親禁足了。

問題：為何這位男生無法外出？

選項：(A) 因為他被父親禁足。

　　　(B) 因為會下雨。

　　　(C) 因為他不想出去。

　　　(D) 他要待在家中補眠。

提示：「看」在英文中可能有不同的字，除了 "watch TV"、"see a movie"、"read a book" 外，還有 "behold（目不轉睛的看）"、"view（因調查而觀看）"、"gaze（因吃驚、高興或興趣而熱心地看）"、"glare（因敵意、怒氣而注視）"。因此，確實了解每個英語字彙的意義，有助於了解文意。

37. Question number 37:

M: Were there many people at the concert last night?

W: Yes, we had to make our way through the crowd.

M: What if something happened, I mean, what if a fire broke out?

W: In that case, we could only keep our fingers crossed!

Question: Did a fire break out at the concert last night?

(A) Yes, but the firefighters put it out.

(B) Yes, a fire did break out in the concert last night.

(C) Yes, and everyone's fingers had been crossed.

(D) No, it was only his imagination.

男：昨晚的演唱會人很多嗎？

女：是的。我們必須穿過人群才能進入。

男：如果發生了什麼事，我是說，如果著火了怎麼辦？

女：那麼，我們只好自求多福了！

問題：昨晚的演唱會發生大火了嗎？

選項：(A) 是的，但消防員把火撲滅了。

　　　(B) 是的，昨晚的演唱的確發生大火。

　　　(C) 是的，而且每個人都交叉手指。

　　　(D) 沒有，這只不過是他的想像。

38. Question number 38:

W: I can't make out the meaning of this novel. It's hard for me.

M: Who wrote it?

W: I believe it was Charles Dickens.

M: What's it about?

W: I can't tell, basically, it was about good times and bad times and so on.

Question: What does the word "time" mean in this conversation?

(A) It means days, months, years, and so on.

(B) It means the minutes and seconds.

(C) It means the period of time that people are in.

(D) It means the days, the months, and the years when people were born.

女：我弄不懂這本小說的意思；對我而言，它太難了。

男：誰寫的？

女：我相信是狄更生。

男：是關於什麼？

女：我沒法分辨。基本上是和好的時代和壞的時代等等有關。

問題：本段對話中的 "time" 是指什麼？

選項：(A) 泛指年月日等等。

　　　(B) 泛指分秒。

　　　(C) 泛指當時人們所處的時代。

　　　(D) 泛指人們出生的年月日。

提示："time"（時間、期間、時刻）、"times"（時代、日期）。

39. Question number 39:

M: How was the meeting?

W: I'm afraid we didn't make any progress.

M: Why is that?

W: Because everyone in the meeting was too busy at finger-pointing.

Question: What really happened at the meeting?

(A) Everyone was busy using power point.

(B) Everyone was busy blaming each other.

(C) Everyone was busy snapping his fingers.

(D) Everyone was busy playing games with his fingers.

男：會議進行的如何？

女：我怕我們沒有任何進展。

男：為何如此？

女：因為與會者都忙著在相互指責。

問題：會議中到底發生什麼事？

選項：(A) 每個人都忙著用電腦做簡報。

(B) 每個人都忙著相互指責。

(C) 每人都忙著彈指發出劈啪聲。

(D) 每個人都忙著用手指玩電動遊戲。

40. Question number 40:

W: Is there any room left in your car?

M: No, but we'll try to make room for you if you want.

W: Well, that's very sweet of you. Thank you.

M: Hey, that's what friends are for.

Question: Which of the following has the similar meaning to the last sentence?

(A) A friend in need is a friend indeed.

(B) A dog is man's best friend.

(C) With a friend like him, who needs enemies.

(D) One for all and all for one.

女：你車上還有空位嗎？

男：沒有。但如果你願意，我們可以騰出個位子來。

女：你真夠意思。謝謝你。

男：要朋友是幹麼的！

問題：下列敘述中，那種說法和對話中的最後一句意思相近？

選項：(A) 患難見真情。

(B) 狗是人類最好的朋友。

(C) 有友如此，誰需要敵人。

(D) 我為人人，人人為我。

提示：就如同中文的使用一樣，英文中的俗語、俚語、格言、寓言、典故等的使用都會賦予詞句新的意思。如在本練習中第三十三題的 "to make both ends meet（量入為出）"，及本題中的(A)「患難見真情」和(D)的「人人為我，我為人人」都是最好的說明。

41. Question number 41:

M: I am going to my French class. See you.

W: How about your Japanese and computer classes?

M: I am taking all three classes at the same time.

W: You can't do that! Don't bite more than you can chew.

Question: How does the woman feel about the man's taking three classes at the same time?

(A) She thinks that's unbelievable.

(B) She thinks that's very courageous of him.

(C) She thinks that's impossible for him to do a good job.

(D) She thinks that's stupid.

男：我要去上法文課了。待會見。

女：那你的日文課和電腦課呢？

男：我同時選三門課。

女：你不能這麼做；貪多必失。

問題：這位女子對這位男士同時選三門課的感覺如何？

選項：(A) 她覺得不可思議。

(B) 她覺得他很勇敢。

(C) 她覺得他不能把事做好。

(D) 她覺得這件事很蠢。

42. Question number 42:

W: It's just not my day today!

M: Why do you say that?

W: I won the lotto but I also got a ticket for double-parking when I ran to the store to get my lotto.

M: I guess that's what they say you can't have your cake and eat it too.

Question: What's the ticket the woman is talking about?

(A) A traffic ticket for double-parking.

(B) A traffic ticket for turning right on red light.

(C) A traffic ticket for buying the lotto.

(D) A traffic ticket for not fastening seat belt.

女：我今天可真倒楣！

男：你為何會如此說？

女：我贏了樂透，但我也因為到店裡買樂透彩券並排停車而被開罰單。

男：我想這就是所謂魚與熊掌不可兼得這句話的意思吧。

問題：這位女士口中的罰單是什麼？

選項：(A) 併排停車的交通罰單。

(B) 紅燈右轉的交通罰單。

(C) 購買樂透彩券的交通罰單。

(D) 未繫安全帶的交通罰單。

43. Question number 43:

M: You know I am half Japanese and half Indian.

W: You are pulling my leg, aren't you?

M: No, I am dead serious about this.

W: That's a first for you.

Question: Do you think the woman believe

what the man has told her?

(A) Yes, she believes in the man completely.

(B) Yes, but with some reservations.

(C) No, she doesn't believe a word of what he said.

(D) No, and she made sure that the man knew it too.

男：你知道我有一半日本人和一半印度人的血統嗎？

女：你在開我玩笑，對吧？

男：不，我可是十分正經。

女：你正經，那倒是第一次。

問題：你覺得這位女子相信男士所說的嗎？

選項：(A) 是的，她完全相信。

(B) 是的，但語多保留。

(C) 不，她一點都不信。

(D) 不，她同時確定男士知道她對他的不信任。

提示："with some reservations（語多保留）"、"with little reservation （或有些許疑問）"、"with no reservation（全力支持）"。

44. Question number 44:

W: Are you still angry with me?

M: No, I just need some time by myself.

W: Why? I thought you were not angry with me.

M: I know, but I just want to be left alone for a while.

Question: Why is the man acting like this?

(A) He doesn't want to talk to the woman.

(B) He doesn't want to come near to the woman.

(C) He is still angry with the woman.

(D) He is thinking about something else.

女：你還生我的氣嗎？

男：沒有。我只是需要獨處的時間。

女：為什麼？我以為你不生我的氣了。

男：我知道，但我就是希望一段時間不被打擾。

問題：為何男子有如此表現？

選項：(A) 他不想和女子說話。

(B) 他不想靠近女子。

(C) 他仍在生女子的氣。

(D) 他在想其他的事。

提示："I just need some time by myself" 這就是所謂的「委婉」用語，用衝擊力較低的字眼來形容心中的想法。有時因避諱也會如此用。例：He is gone!/He passed away. = He is dead.

45. Question number 45:

M: Where did you go last night?

W: I went out with some friends of mine.

M: What did you do?

W: Are you checking on me?

Question: Do you think the woman is happy with all these questions?

(A) No, she is about to lose her temper with all these questions.

(B) No, she is disappointed with all these questions.

(C) Yes, and she answered all these questions.

(D) Yes, she is quite happy with all these questions.

男：你昨晚去哪了？

女：我和我的一些朋友出去。

男：你做那些事？

女：幹麼？你在調查我嗎？

問題：你覺得女子對這些問題感到高興嗎？

選項：(A) 不，她快要失控生氣了。

(B) 不，她因這些問題而感到沮喪。

(C) 是的，而且她還回答所有問題。

(D) 是的，她對這些問題感到相當高興。

Test ❷

第一部份：看圖辨義

1. For question number 1, please look at picture A.

   Question number 1: Are these sleeves too long?

   (A) Yes, they are. They are too long for me.

   (B) No, they aren't. They are too short for me.

   (C) No, they aren't. They are just fine.

   (D) Yes, they are just perfect for me.

   問題：這袖子太長了嗎？

   選項：(A) 是的，它們對我而言太長了。

   　　　(B) 不，它們對我而言太短了。

   　　　(C) 不，它們對我而言剛好。

   　　　(D) 是的，它們對我而言剛好。

2. For question number 2, please look at picture B.

   Question number 2: Where is the bank?

   (A) It is around the corner.

   (B) It is next to the post office.

   (C) It is further down the street.

   (D) It is opposite to the post office.

   問題：銀行在哪裡？

   選項：(A) 在轉角。

   　　　(B) 在郵局旁邊。

   　　　(C) 在街道的盡頭。

   　　　(D) 在郵局對面。

3. For question number 3, please look at picture C.

   Question number 3: Where can one get the prescription filled when one is not feeling well?

   (A) In a convenience store.

   (B) In a pharmacy.

   (C) In a restaurant.

   (D) In a theater.

   問題：當一個人不舒服時可以在哪裡配藥？

   選項：(A) 在便利商店。

   　　　(B) 在藥局。

   　　　(C) 在餐廳。

   　　　(D) 在電影院。

   提示：(1)中英文在使用動詞時，會有些不同的習慣，不可因中文的習慣去判斷英文動詞的選擇。例如：

   　　　"have the film developed（洗照片）"、"apply the make-up（敷）"、"wear cosmetic（塗抹）"、"prepare the meal（備餐）"、"do lunch（一起吃午餐）"、"kill time（打發時間）"

   　　　(2)"where" 也可能是疑問詞和關係副詞：

   　　　Where are you going now?（疑問詞）

   　　　This is the place where (=in which) he was born.（關係副詞）

4. For question number 4, please look at picture D.

   Question number 4: What time does the clock say?

   (A) Ten to three.

   (B) A quarter after two.

   (C) Two thirty.

   (D) A quarter to two.

   問題：時鐘顯示幾點了？

   選項：(A) 兩點五十分。

   　　　(B) 兩點十五分。

   　　　(C) 兩點半。

   　　　(D) 一點四十五分。

5. For question number 5, please look at picture E.

   Question number 5: What's the weather forecast for Taipei?

   (A) Partly cloudy.

   (B) Sunny and hot.

(C) Cold and wet.

(D) Foggy.

問題：台北市的氣象預報為何？

選項：(A) 多雲。

(B) 晴朗且熱。

(C) 冷且溼。

(D) 多霧。

6. For question number 6, please look at picture F.

Question number 6: What do you think the man in the picture needs most?

(A) A television.

(B) Money.

(C) Water.

(D) A camera.

問題：圖中男子最需要的為何？

選項：(A) 電視。

(B) 錢。

(C) 水。

(D) 照相機。

7. For question number 7, please look at picture G.

Question number 7: What kind of holiday are these people celebrating?

(A) The Chinese New Year.

(B) Halloween.

(C) The Lantern Festival.

(D) Christmas.

問題：這些人在慶祝何種節日？

選項：(A) 中國新年。

(B) 萬聖節。

(C) 元宵節。

(D) 耶誕節。

8. For question number 8, please look at picture H.

Question number 8: What does this man do for a living?

(A) He is a bus driver.

(B) He is a cashier.

(C) He is a butcher.

(D) He is a teacher.

問題：這男人賴何維生？

選項：(A) 他是公車駕駛。

(B) 他是收銀員。

(C) 他是肉販。

(D) 他是老師。

提示：題目雖問「賴何維生」，實際上也就是問何種職業。

9. For question number 9, please look at picture I.

Question number 9: What kind of food is not shown in the shop window?

(A) A ham.

(B) A grape wine.

(C) A cheese.

(D) A hamburger.

問題：哪一樣食物沒有在櫥窗中展示？

選項：(A) 火腿。

(B) 葡萄酒。

(C) 起士。

(D) 漢堡。

10. For question number 10, please look at picture J.

Question number 10: Why is the girl dipping her foot into the pool?

(A) She is trying to find out the temperature of the water.

(B) She is trying to see if anyone could hear her.

(C) She is trying to find out the answer to the question.

(D) She is trying to know how much it costs.

問題：這女孩為何把腳伸入游泳池中？

選項：(A) 她想知道水溫。

(B) 她想知道是否有人聽到她的聲音。

(C) 她想知道問題的答案。

(D) 她想知道它要多少錢。

11. For question number 11, please look at picture K.

Question number 11: What is the girl doing while the boy is rowing the boat?

(A) She is encouraging the boy.

(B) She is listening to the radio.

(C) She is looking around.

(D) She is taking a nap.

問題：當男孩在划船時，女孩正在做什麼？

選項：(A) 她在替男孩加油打氣。

　　　(B) 她在聽收音機。

　　　(C) 她在四處張望。

　　　(D) 她在睡覺。

提示："while" 或 "when" 解釋為「當」；通常代表兩個動作同時發生，動作需時較短者用過去簡單式，較長者則用過去進行式：

He called while I was eating my dinner last night.

I was eating my dinner when he called last night.

12. For question number 12, please look at picture L.

Question number 12: Where is the boy?

(A) The boy is standing next to the door.

(B) The boy is standing away from the door.

(C) The boy is standing at the door.

(D) The boy is standing against the door.

問題：男孩在哪裡？

選項：(A) 男孩站在門邊。

　　　(B) 男孩站在離門很遠的地方。

　　　(C) 男孩站在門口。

　　　(D) 男孩倚門而立。

提示："next to the door（緊臨門邊）"、"at the door（在門口）"、"against the door（倚

門而立）"。

13. For question number 13, please look at picture M.

Question number 13: What is the girl doing?

(A) She is logging on to the computer.

(B) She is plugging in the computer.

(C) She is signing up on the net.

(D) She is moving the computer.

問題：女孩正在做什麼？

選項：(A) 她正在登錄電腦。

　　　(B) 她正在插電腦插頭。

　　　(C) 她正在線上報名。

　　　(D) 她正在移動電腦。

14. For question number 14, please look at picture N.

Question number 14: It's now ten o'clock in the morning. What class does Mary have next period?

(A) Math.

(B) History.

(C) Geography.

(D) English.

問題：現在是上午十點。瑪莉下節課是哪個科目？

選項：(A) 數學。

　　　(B) 歷史。

　　　(C) 地理。

　　　(D) 英文。

15. For question number 15, please look at picture O.

Question number 15: Where are these two people?

(A) They are in an MRT station.

(B) They are at a bus stop.

(C) They are in the train station.

(D) They are in a ferry building.

問題：這兩人在哪裡？

選項：(A) 他們在捷運站。

(B) 他們在公車站。

(C) 他們在火車站。

(D) 他們在渡船大樓。

第二部份：問答

16. Question number 16: How much hotter can it be?

(A) I don't know, but I do know that it's only August now.

(B) It should cool off pretty soon.

(C) Thanks to global warming.

(D) Yesterday was better.

問題：天氣還能變的多熱呢？

選項：(A) 我不知道，但我知道現在才八月呢。

(B) 應該很快就會變涼快了。

(C) 多虧了全球暖化。

(D) 昨天還比較好。

提示：外國人習以問題來回答問題：

Why can't we go as planned?

（為什麼我們不能如期出發？）

You tell me?（你說呢？）

或，以「間接」的方式來回答：

What is he?（他是做什麼的？）

He is nothing but a thief.（除了賊外，他麼都不是。）

17. Question number 17: Could you turn up the air conditioner?

(A) I am freezing.

(B) Sure. No Problem.

(C) What for?

(D) Are you too cold?

問題：你能把冷氣機開強一點嗎？

選項：(A) 我都凍僵了。

(B) 當然。沒問題。

(C) 為什麼？

(D) 你會感到太冷嗎？

18. Question number 18: Our school principal,

Mr. Smith, passed away the other day.

(A) I don't know what to say.

(B) My heart goes with you.

(C) He is bad news.

(D) You can say that again.

問題：我們學校校長史密斯先生前幾天過世了。

選項：(A) 我不知該說些什麼。

(B) 我和你感受一樣。

(C) 他真是個麻煩。

(D) 你說的沒錯。

19. Question number 19: Let's do something this weekend.

(A) Sorry, but life is short.

(B) OK. What about tomorrow?

(C) Sure. What do you have in mind?

(D) It's a piece of cake.

問題：我們這個週末一起做些什麼吧。

選項：(A) 對不起，人生苦短。

(B) 好啊，明天如何？

(C) 好啊。你有什麼計畫？

(D) 那太簡單了。

20. Question number 20: How about having dinner together after work on Saturday night?

(A) That's not a good day for me.

(B) Something suddenly came up.

(C) How about a cup of tea?

(D) When on Saturday?

問題：周六下班後一起吃晚餐如何？

選項：(A) 我那天不方便。

(B) 突然有事發生。

(C) 來一杯茶如何？

(D) 周六什麼時間？

21. Question number 21: I am waiting for you in front of the theater.

(A) I'll be probably about fifteen minutes late.

(B) The movie theater is around the corner.

(C) It starts at five o'clock.

(D) What's the name of the movie?

問題：我正在電影院前等你。

選項：(A) 我可能會遲到十五分鐘。

　　　(B) 電影院就在轉角。

　　　(C) 它五點開始。

　　　(D) 電影的名字是什麼？

22. Question number 22: I'd like to invite you over for dinner next week.

(A) I had good time last weekend.

(B) Please show me the way.

(C) The food there is great.

(D) Did you talk to your parents first?

問題：下禮拜我想請你到我家吃晚餐。

選項：(A) 上禮拜我玩的很愉快。

　　　(B) 請告訴我怎麼走。

　　　(C) 那裡的食物很棒。

　　　(D) 你先問過你父母親了嗎？

23. Question number 23: Sorry to keep you waiting.

(A) It's OK. Traffic is usually bad during this hour.

(B) That's a lousy excuse!

(C) Perhaps you need more exercise.

(D) You should at least have a good reason.

問題：對不起讓你久等了。

選項：(A) 沒關係。這個時間的交通通常很糟糕。

　　　(B) 這真是爛透了的藉口。

　　　(C) 也許你需要多一點運動。

　　　(D) 你至少該有個好理由。

24. Question number 24: How's the dinner?

(A) Who cooked the meal?

(B) Oh, I'm surviving.

(C) Medium-rare, please.

(D) It's delicious

問題：晚餐還好吧？

選項：(A) 誰準備餐點的？

　　　(B) 噢，還算可以。

　　　(C) 我要五分熟。

　　　(D) 美味可口。

25. Question number 25: May I have a word with you?

(A) I just can't figure him out.

(B) Sure. What's about?

(C) I didn't mean it.

(D) I don't feel like to go with you.

問題：我能和你說句話嗎？

選項：(A) 我就是看不透他。

　　　(B) 當然。有什麼事？

　　　(C) 我不是故意的。

　　　(D) 我不想和你一起去。

提示：在使用問句時，"can" 通常代表「能力、體力」，而 "may" 則用來「徵詢他人的同意」。例：

Can you help me move this box?

（你可以幫我搬這個箱子嗎？）

May I have a word with you if you have time?（如果你有時間的話，我可以和你說句話嗎？）

26. Question number 26: When do you open?

(A) We never close.

(B) I'll give you a lift home if you like.

(C) The business hours are from 11 a.m. to 10 p.m.

(D) There is a nice restaurant over there.

問題：你們何時開門？

選項：(A) 我們從不關門。

　　　(B) 如果你需要的話，我可以順道載你回家。

　　　(C) 營業時間是上午十一點到晚上十點。

　　　(D) 那邊有一間不錯的餐廳。

27. Question number 27: I'd like to open a savings account.

(A) Sure. Here are the application forms.

(B) Do you have enough money?

(C) I am sorry, but we are fully booked.

(D) It is open at two o'clock in the afternoon.

問題：我想開個活期儲蓄戶頭。

選項：(A) 好啊。這是申請表格。

　　　(B) 你有足夠的錢嗎？

　　　(C) 對不起，但我們已經客滿了。

　　　(D) 它每天下午兩點開門。

28. Question number 28: I hate my haircut! Any suggestions?

(A) How about trimming a bit on the sides?

(B) The shampoo is especially for greasy hair.

(C) I don't like my new hairstyle.

(D) It is half price now.

問題：我恨死我的髮型！有任何建議嗎？

選項：(A) 在兩邊修一下如何？

　　　(B) 這款洗髮精適用於油性髮質的人。

　　　(C) 我不喜歡我的新髮型。

　　　(D) 現在是半價。

29. Question number 29: Is there garlic in it? I don't really like the taste.

(A) The garlic has a strong flavor.

(B) Yes, but I can have that exchanged right away.

(C) That's too much!

(D) It is free after eight o'clock.

問題：這裡頭有大蒜嗎？我實在不是很喜歡它的味道。

選項：(A) 大蒜有一種很強烈的味道。

　　　(B) 有，但我可以馬上換過來。

　　　(C) 太多了！

　　　(D) 八點以後免費。

30. Question number 30: How would you like your steak cooked?

(A) Medium rare, please.

(B) The meat is still raw.

(C) How about some salad on the side?

(D) Can I have another drink?

問題：你的牛排要如何烹飪？

選項：(A) 我想要四分熟。

　　　(B) 肉還是生的。

　　　(C) 要不要在旁邊搭配些沙拉？

　　　(D) 我能再要一杯飲料嗎？

提示：烘烤煎炸食物時有幾種選擇："rare（全生）"、"medium rare（三四分熟）"、"medium（五分熟）"、"well-done（全熟）"、"overcooked（太老）"、"undercooked（尚未煮熟）"。

第三部份：簡短對話

31. Question number 31:

M: What time does your plane take off?

W: In an hour, 12:30.

M: Does that mean you won't have time for the last-minute shopping?

W: I can always make time for that!

Question: Do you think the woman will still try to buy something?

(A) Yes, she will.

(B) No, she won't.

(C) It's hard to tell.

(D) I love it.

男：你的飛機何時起飛？

女：再一個小時，十二點三十分。

男：那是否代表你不會有時間做購物的最後衝刺？

女：我總是能為買東西挪出時間來。

問題：你覺得這位女士還是會試著買些東西嗎？

選項：(A) 會的，她會。

　　　(B) 不，她不會。

　　　(C) 很難判斷。

　　　(D) 我喜歡。

提示：(1) in + 時間：在…之內；通常和

"within" 意思相近：

I will be back in three days.

（我在三天之內就會回來。）

(2) by + 時間：在…之前

You have to hand in your report by this Friday.

（你必須在星期五之前交報告）

32. Question number 32:

W: I think we can get to our hotel in about two hours.

M: I don't think so; we have to take the traffic into consideration.

W: Are you telling me that there might be a chance that we get stuck in a traffic jam?

M: It's rush hour now.

Question: Which of the following hours is when the conversation is least likely to happen?

(A) 7 to 9 a.m.

(B) 5 to 8 p.m.

(C) 11 am to 1 p.m.

(D) 11 pm to 12 midnight.

女：我想我們可以在兩個小時內到達旅館。

男：我不以為然。我們得把交通狀況列入考慮。

女：你是在告訴我，我們可能陷在車陣中？

男：現在可是尖峰時刻。

問題：這段對話最不可能發生在下列哪個時間？

選項：(A) 上午七點到九點

(B) 下午五點到八點

(C) 上午十一點到下午一點

(D) 晚上十一點到凌晨

提示：(1)英語中有許多與 hour 相關的用語：
"rush hour,"（尖峰時刻）"office hour,"（上班時間）"late hours,"（晚睡晚起）"small hours"（三更半夜）

(2)本題的重點在 "least likely（最不可能）"。比較級或最高級的使用並不只

有 "more" 或 "most"，有時 "less" 或 "least" 也是其代表。

33. Question number 33:

M: I can't believe that they towed my car away.

W: Where did you park it?

M: I parked my car in the loading and unloading zone.

W: No wonder. Don't you know you can only park there after 8 p.m.?

M: I know, but I thought I could just get by without being caught.

Question: Which of the following statements can best describe the man?

(A) The man was playing things by the book.

(B) The man was taking his chances.

(C) The man was pretty sure that he would be lucky.

(D) The man had no idea what the loading and unloading zone mean.

男：我不敢相信他們把我的車拖走了。

女：你把車停在哪裡？

男：我把車停在裝貨卸貨區。

女：難怪，難道你不知道裝卸區只有在晚上八點以後才開放停車？

男：我知道。我只不過以為我可以投機而不被抓到。

問題：下列敘述何者最能形容這男子的做法？

選項：(A) 這男子依法行事。

(B) 這男子想試試他的運氣。

(C) 這男子覺得他的運氣很好。

(D) 這男子不知道裝貨卸貨區代表的是什麼。

34. Question number 34:

W: What's the matter with you? You look terrible.

M: I feel sick and I have a bad stomachache.

W: Have you eaten anything different recently?

M: Not that I remember, but I did have something really hot last night.

W: That explains everything. You are having diarrhea.

Question: What caused the man to have the stomachache?

(A) Some spoiled food.

(B) Some spicy food.

(C) Some greasy food.

(D) Some plain food.

女：你怎麼了？你看起來糟透了。

男：我不舒服而且我肚子痛。

女：你最近吃了什麼異常的東西嗎？

男：我不記得。但我昨晚吃些很辣的食物。

女：這就對了。你拉肚子了。

問題：造成男子肚子痛的原因為何？

選項：(A) 腐壞的食物。

　　　(B) 辛辣的食物。

　　　(C) 油膩的食物。

　　　(D) 未經調味的食物。

提示："heavy"、"light" 和 "plain" 往往用來形容食物：

I want something light.（清爽）

This chicken tasted plain.（平淡無味）

The soup is too heavy for me.（油膩）

I want a cheeseburger, heavy on mayo.（多加美奶滋）

I want a coffee, light on sugar. （少加糖）

35. Question number 35:

M: Are you ready to order?

W: Not yet, I can't decide what I want.

M: Today's Special looks great.

W: I know, but I am on a diet and that looks too heavy for me.

Question: Why doesn't the woman order Today's Special?

(A) The woman was trying to lose weight.

(B) The woman was trying to gain a few pounds.

(C) The woman was getting a facelift.

(D) The woman was under some special medication.

男：你準備要點餐了嗎？

女：還沒。我不知道我要點什麼。

男：今日特餐看起來不錯。

女：我知道。不過我正在節食，特餐對我而言太油膩了。

問題：女子為何不點今日特餐？

選項：(A) 她正試著減肥。

　　　(B) 她正試著增加體重。

　　　(C) 她正在做拉皮手術。

　　　(D) 她正在接受特別的藥物治療。

36. Question number 36:

W: Tell me why you quit your job.

M: My father is sick and I have to take over his business.

W: I'm sorry to hear that. Is he feeling better now?

M: He is still in the hospital and will probably stay there for a while.

Question: What is the man's father doing now?

(A) He is on medication in the hospital.

(B) He is having a routine physical check-up.

(C) He is working at home.

(D) He is devoting himself to his business.

女：告訴我你為何辭掉工作。

男：我父親生病了而我必須接下他的事業。

女：很遺憾聽到這個消息。他現在好些了嗎？

男：他還在醫院接受藥物治療，而且他很可能要在醫院待一段時間。

問題：這男子的父親在哪裡？

選項：(A) 他在醫院接受治療。

(B) 他正在接受例行身體檢查。

(C) 他在家裡工作。

(D) 他致力於他的事業。

提示：本題對話的第一句為間接問句；試比較下
列兩組句子：

(1) Tell me who he is. （間接問句）

Who is he? （一般問句）

(2) What do you think he will buy? （間
接問句）

What will he buy? （一般問句）

37. Question number 37:

M: I heard that you had spent your summer
doing something unique?

W: Yes. I spent the summer on my brother's
farm.

M: So, how was life there?

W: I milked the cows, fed the chickens, and
did a lot of other things.

M: Sounds like you were having fun there.

W: I did, but I had to get up early every day.

Question: What does the woman think about
the life on the farm?

(A) Easy and pleasant.

(B) Enjoyable but challenging.

(C) Difficult and boring.

(D) Carefree and happy.

男：我聽說你今年暑假做些不同的事？

女：是的。我把暑假花在我兄弟的農場。

男：那麼，農場的生活如何？

女：我擠牛奶，餵雞，還做了許多其他的事情。

男：聽來你在農場的日子過得挺好玩的。

女：我的確如此，只不過我每天都要很早就起
床。

問題：這女子對農場生活的想法為何？

選項：(A) 輕鬆愉快。

(B) 有趣但有挑戰性。

(C) 困難且無聊。

(D) 無拘無束且快樂。

38. Question number 38:

W: Why don't we take turns driving?

M: All right. You drive first.

W: Why me?

M: Because you started it!

Question: Does the man really like the idea
of taking turns driving?

(A) Yes, he doesn't want to drive anymore.

(B) No, he doesn't have driver's license.

(C) Yes, he has driven for miles and is tired.

(D) No, he just tried to scare the woman
away.

女：我們何不輪流開車？

男：好啊。你先開。

女：為何我先開？

男：因為你建議的。

問題：這男子真的喜歡輪流開車嗎？

選項：(A) 是的，他一點都不想再開車了。

(B) 不，他沒有駕駛執照。

(C) 是的，他已經開了好幾英里而且很疲
憊。

(D) 不，他只是要嚇唬女子而使她打消念
頭。

39. Question number 39:

M: That's a great idea!

W: You think so? It just came to my mind
when I was taking a shower.

M: Really? Maybe I should take showers
more.

W: You are teasing me, aren't you?

Question: Is the man really teasing the
woman?

(A) No, he is not. He is just making jokes on

the woman.

(B) Yes, he is. He is jealous of the woman.

(C) No, he is not, he is just wondering when she will take a shower.

(D) Yes, he is. He hates the woman for coming up with a wonderful idea.

男：這是個好點子！

女：你真的這麼覺的？我在洗澡時想到這個點子。

男：真的？看來我該多洗澡了。

女：你在取笑我，對不對？

問題：這男子真的在取笑女子嗎？

選項：(A) 不，他不是。他只不過是開她玩笑。

　　　(B) 是，他是。他妒忌這女子。

　　　(C) 不，他不是。他只是想知道她什麼時候洗澡。

　　　(D) 是，他是。他恨這女子想出這個好點子。

40. Question number 40:

W: I came across those old photos in the drawer.

M: Look! That's me when I was five.

W: How time flies!

M: You can say that again.

Question: How do the woman and the man feel when looking at the old photos?

(A) They both feel time passes fast.

(B) The woman likes the man better when he was young.

(C) Both of them would like to be kids again.

(D) They both enjoy being grown-ups.

女：我在抽屜裡找到這些舊照片。

男：看！那是我五歲時的照片。

女：時間過的真快！

男：你說的沒錯！

問題：這女子和男子在看照片時的感覺為何？

選項：(A) 他們兩人都覺得時間過的很快。

　　　(B) 他們兩人都覺得男子年輕時較好看。

　　　(C) 他們兩人都希望能再變成孩子。

　　　(D) 他們都喜歡當成人。

41. Question number 41:

M: I heard that you are going to the U.S.

W: I am taking my daughter over for the summer camp.

M: Lucky her! I didn't leave the country until I was thirty.

W: Yes. The youngsters are luckier now than we were then.

Question: Why is the woman going abroad?

(A) She is going abroad for fun.

(B) She is going abroad for business.

(C) She is taking her daughter to the summer camp.

(D) She is joining the summer camp overseas.

男：我聽說你要去美國？

女：我要帶我女兒到那裡參加夏令營。

男：她可真幸運。我一直到三十歲才出國。

女：是啊，現在的年輕人比以前的我們可是幸運多了。

問題：這女子為何出國？

選項：(A) 她出國旅遊。

　　　(B) 她因工作出國。

　　　(C) 她帶女兒參加夏令營。

　　　(D) 她參加海外的夏令營。

42. Question number 42:

W: You look great! What happened to you?

M: I just had a facelift.

W: I didn't know men care about how they look as much as women.

M: Tell me a person who doesn't want to look nice!

Question: What happened to the man?

(A) He just had a plastic surgery.

(B) He just had a heart transplant.

(C) He just had a mole removed.

(D) He just had a spa.

女：你看起來棒透了！怎麼回事？

男：我剛做了拉皮手術。

女：我怎麼不知男人和女人一樣在意他們的長相。

男：告訴我有誰不希望自己看起來漂亮的！

問題：這男子怎麼了？

選項：(A) 他剛做了整形手術。

　　　(B) 他剛做了心臟移植。

　　　(C) 他剛去點痣。

　　　(D) 他剛做完水療。

43. Question number 43:

M: George embarrassed me!

W: Why did you say that?

M: He always makes some stupid remarks in public.

W: Really? I thought he is supposed to be a smart guy.

Question: Why did George embarrassed the man?

(A) Because George always makes a fool of himself by saying something stupid.

(B) Because George acts like a clown in front of everyone.

(C) Because George sings terribly, yet he loves to sing in front of everyone.

(D) Because George loves to show off in front of everyone.

男：喬治讓我感到難堪！

女：你為何如此說？

男：他總喜歡在人前說些傻話。

女：真的？我還以為他是個聰明人呢。

問題：為何喬治使這男子難堪？

選項：(A) 因喬治總是在人前因為說錯話而出盡

洋相。

　　　(B) 因喬治在人前扮小丑。

　　　(C) 因為喬治唱歌很糟糕，但他又喜歡在人前唱歌。

　　　(D) 因為喬治喜歡在人前炫耀自己。

44. Question number 44:

W: Can we have some service here, please?

M: I'll be with you shortly.

W: We have been sitting here for over half an hour and I don't want any more excuses.

M: I am sorry, but a waiter called in sick and we are short of hands.

Question: What's the man trying to explain?

(A) They don't have enough hands.

(B) They are short of waiters.

(C) They are running out of food.

(D) They really don't care that much about the woman and her friend.

女：能有人來招呼我們嗎？

男：我馬上就來。

女：我們已在這坐了半小時，我不要再聽到任何藉口。

男：很抱歉，但有位服務生打電話來通知說他身體不舒服。我們人手不足。

問題：這男子試著解釋什麼？

選項：(A) 他們沒有足夠的手。

　　　(B) 他們人手不足。

　　　(C) 他們食物快用完了。

　　　(D) 他們真的不在乎這位女子和她的朋友。

45. Question number 45:

M: What happened here? Look at the mess!

W: Jean had some of her friends over and they had a small party.

M: Small? You called this a small party? They tore the whole house apart!

W: Calm down. She promised she would clean it up.

Question: What did Jean do?

(A) Jean and her friends had a wild party.

(B) Jean and her friends had a study session.

(C) Jean and her friends had a quiet discussion.

(D) Jean and her friends tore the house apart.

男：發生了什麼事？這裡一片混亂！

女：珍請了她一些朋友過來，他們舉行了一個小派對。

男：小派對？這叫小派對？他們把房子都拆了！

女：冷靜一下。她答應把房子整理乾淨。

問題：珍做了什麼？

選項：(A) 珍和她的朋友舉行了個狂野的派對。

(B) 珍和她的朋友舉行了個讀書會。

(C) 珍和她的朋友舉行了個安靜的討論會。

(D) 珍和她的朋友把房子拆了。

Test ❸

第一部份：看圖辨義

1. For question number 1, please look at picture A.

Question number 1: What time of year is this?

(A) The Chinese New Year.

(B) The Dragon Boat Festival.

(C) The Mid-Autumn Festival.

(D) The Tomb Sweeping Day.

問題：這是一年中的什麼時候？

選項：(A) 農曆春節。

　　　(B) 端午節。

　　　(C) 中秋節。

　　　(D) 掃墓節。

2. For question number 2, please look at picture B.

Question number 2: When is the check-out time for the guests?

(A) At 12 noon.

(B) At 1 p.m.

(C) At 4 p.m.

(D) At 10 a.m.

問題：客人離房結帳的時間為何？

選項：(A) 中午十二點。

　　　(B) 下午一點。

　　　(C) 下午四點。

　　　(D) 上午十點。

3. For question number 3, please look at picture C.

Question number 3: Which statement is correct?

(A) John is shorter than Jenny.

(B) John is the tallest of all.

(C) Jenny is taller than Ann.

(D) Ann is taller than John.

問題：下列敘述何者為真？

選項：(A) 約翰比珍妮高。

　　　(B) 約翰是所有人裡最高的。

　　　(C) 珍妮比安高。

　　　(D) 安比約翰高。

4. For question number 4, please look at picture D.

Question number 4: How does the man feel?

(A) He feels surprised.

(B) He feels embarrassed.

(C) He feels angry.

(D) He feels upset.

問題：這男子的感受如何？

選項：(A) 他覺得驚訝。

　　　(B) 他覺得難堪。

　　　(C) 他覺得生氣。

　　　(D) 他覺得沮喪。

5. For question number 5, please look at picture E.

Question number 5: What item is not needed for this week's grocery shopping?

(A) Milk.

(B) Fruit.

(C) Tissue.

(D) Meat.

問題：哪項物品不在本周購物範圍內？

選項：(A) 牛奶。

　　　(B) 水果。

　　　(C) 面紙。

　　　(D) 肉。

提示：名詞分為可數名詞及不可數名詞；前者又分為普通名詞和集合名詞，後者則分成抽象名詞、物質名詞和專有名詞。不可數名詞沒有複數形，通常不加冠詞 (a, an, the)。而集合名詞雖有單數形和複數形，但表集合體之組成分子時，本身為複數名詞，如 "committee" 除了「委員會」的意思，又有「委員們」之意，在答題時要注意。

6. For question number 6, please look at the picture F.

Question number 6: When will the reception begin?

(A) It begins at six-thirty.

(B) It begins at seven-thirty.

(C) It begins at nine.

(D) It begins at ten.

問題：接待會何時開始？

選項：(A) 六點三十分開始。

　　　(B) 七點三十分開始。

　　　(C) 九點開始。

　　　(D) 十點開始。

7. For question number 7, please look at picture G.

Question number 7: Is the woman doing the laundry?

(A) Yes, she is doing the laundry.

(B) No, she is not. She is dusting the bookshelves.

(C) No, she is not. She is making the bed.

(D) No, she is not. She is sewing the clothes.

問題：這女子在洗衣服嗎？

選項：(A) 不，她不是。她在吸塵。

　　　(B) 不，她不是。她在撣書架上的灰塵。

　　　(C) 不，她不是。她在鋪床。

　　　(D) 不，她不是。她在縫衣服。

8. For question number 8, please look at the picture H.

Question number 8: What do you think the woman is going to make?

(A) She will bake a cake.

(B) She will stir-fry some vegetables.

(C) She will barbeque some ribs.

(D) She will prepare soup.

問題：你覺得這女子要做什麼？

選項：(A) 她可能要烘培一個蛋糕。

　　　(B) 她可能要炒些青菜。

　　　(C) 她可能要烤些肋條。

　　　(D) 她可能要做個湯。

9. For question number 9, please look at picture I.

Question number 9: Which of the following descriptions is NOT correct?

(A) The boy is surfing on the Internet.

(B) The boy is playing a video game.

(C) The boy is memorizing vocabulary.

(D) The boy is looking for some information.

問題：下列何者敘述不正確？

選項：(A) 這男孩在網路上漫遊。

　　　(B) 這男孩在玩電動玩具。

　　　(C) 這男孩在背生字。

　　　(D) 這男孩在找資料。

10. For question number 10, please look at picture J.

Question number 10: Why is the woman seeing a doctor?

(A) She is having a cold.

(B) She is pregnant.

(C) She is depressed.

(D) She is having twins.

問題：這女子為何看醫生？

選項：(A) 她感冒了。

　　　(B) 她懷孕了。

　　　(C) 她有憂鬱症。

　　　(D) 她生雙胞胎。

11. For question number 11, please look at picture K.

Question number 11: What is the man doing?

(A) He is swimming.

(B) He is running on a treadmill.

(C) He is weight-lifting.

(D) He is doing push-ups.

問題：這男子在做什麼？

選項：(A) 他在游泳。

(B) 他在跑步機上跑步。

(C) 他在做舉重運動。

(D) 他在做俯地挺身。

12. For question number 12, please look at picture L.

Question number 12: Where are these men working?

(A) They are working at a construction site.

(B) They are working on a farm.

(C) They are working in a stadium.

(D) They are working in a fast-food restaurant.

問題：這些男子在哪裡工作？

選項：(A) 他們在工地工作。

(B) 他們在農場工作。

(C) 他們在運動場工作。

(D) 他們在速食店工作。

13. For question number 13, please look at picture M.

Question number 13: What's this?

(A) It's a fireworks display.

(B) It's a forest fire.

(C) It's a military parade.

(D) It's a sporting event.

問題：這是什麼？

選項：(A) 煙火展示。

(B) 森林大火。

(C) 閱兵。

(D) 運動活動。

提示：要注意：firework（煙火）和 firecracker（鞭炮）意思不同。

14. For question number 14, please look at picture N.

Question number 14: What place is this?

(A) This is an amusement park.

(B) This is a bookstore.

(C) This is a baseball field.

(D) This is a basketball court.

問題：這是什麼地方？

選項：(A) 這是遊樂園。

(B) 這是書店。

(C) 這是棒球場。

(D) 這是籃球場。

15. For question number 15, please look at picture O.

Question number 15: What is the man doing?

(A) He is taking a bath.

(B) He is taking a shower.

(C) He is washing his face.

(D) He is doing aerobic exercise.

問題：這男子在做什麼？

選項：(A) 他在洗澡。

(B) 他在淋浴。

(C) 他在洗臉。

(D) 他在做有氧運動。

第二部份：問答

16. Question number 16: Do you go to a French restaurant often?

(A) No, I have been there many times..

(B) Yes, I go there on a daily basis.

(C) We went to a downtown restaurant yesterday.

(D) The food is terrible there.

問題：你常去法國餐廳嗎？

選項：(A) 不，我去過那裡好幾次。

(B) 是的，我每天都去。

(C) 我們昨天去一間在市中心的餐廳。

(D) 那裡的食物糟透了。

17. Question number 17: I need a ride tomorrow, or I will be late for my flight.

(A) No problem. I'll pick you up at seven.

(B) Going there by plane is much quicker.

(C) I wish I could go with you.

(D) I ride the bus to work.

問題：我明天需要有人載我一程，否則我會趕不
上我的班機。

選項：(A) 沒問題。我七點來接你。

(B) 搭飛機到那快多了。

(C) 真希望我能和你一起去。

(D) 我搭公車上班。

18. Question number 18: Want to share this with me? This serving is too big for me.

(A) Pass the butter, please.

(B) There's some leftover vegetables.

(C) I can't. I am full already.

(D) Sure. Go ahead.

問題：要不要和我分這個？這裡食物的份量對我
而言太大了。

選項：(A) 請把奶油遞給我。

(B) 那裡有剩下的蔬菜。

(C) 沒辦法，我已經太飽了。

(D) 好啊，盡管拿吧。

19. Question number 19:Why do you look so frustrated?

(A) I know. The test is not so easy.

(B) He is hard to get along with.

(C) Yes, I think yellow color is better for you.

(D) I can't seem to get this idea through to Jack.

問題：為何你看來如此沮喪？

選項：(A) 我知道這個考試並不容易。

(B) 他很難相處。

(C) 是的，我覺得黃色比較適合你。

(D) 我似乎無法讓傑克了解這個點子。

20. Question number 20: What should I do with all these garbage?

(A) You can throw them in the garbage can.

(B) The garbage collector comes every Monday evening.

(C) Sounds great! We have to catch up on many things

(D) I am going on a vacation tomorrow.

問題：我該如何處理這些垃圾？

選項：(A) 你可以把它們丟到垃圾桶。

(B) 收垃圾的人每個星期一晚上會來。

(C) 聽起來不錯。我們有好多事要聊。

(D) 我明天要去度假了。

21. Question number 21: I have to apologize for all the mess.

(A) Don't worry! It's my treat.

(B) You don't have to. It's not your fault.

(C) I would be happy to help you clean the apartment.

(D) That's OK. I don't mind waiting here in line.

問題：我一定對這一團混亂道歉。

選項：(A) 別擔心！這次我請客。

(B) 你不必道歉，又不是你的錯。

(C) 我很樂意幫你打掃公寓。

(D) 沒關係，我不介意在這裡排隊。

22. Question number 22: Which would you prefer, coffee or tea?

(A) I prefer tea to coffee.

(B) Medium rare, please.

(C) The service is terrible here.

(D) Eating less meat makes you healthier.

問題：你要什麼，咖啡或茶？

選項：(A) 我要茶而不要咖啡。

(B) 四分熟，謝謝。

(C) 這裡的服務很差。

(D) 吃少一點肉讓你比較健康。

提示：兩者皆有：both，兩者選一：either/or，
兩者皆無：neither，三者皆有：all，三者

選一：any，三者皆無：none。

23. Question number 23: How did this happen?

(A) I thought she has just bought a new sofa last week.

(B) I'll meet you at the supermarket after dinner.

(C) I have got the flu.

(D) I don't have the slightest idea.

問題：這是怎麼發生的？

選項：(A) 我以為她上禮拜才剛買沙發。

(B) 晚餐後我在超市和你碰面。

(C) 我感冒了。

(D) 我一點都不知道。

24. Question number 24: Why were you late for school today?

(A) I go to school by train.

(B) I got up late and missed my bus.

(C) I was punished for being late again.

(D) The teacher asked me to follow the rules.

問題：你今天為何遲到？

選項：(A) 我坐火車上學。

(B) 我起床晚了又錯過巴士。

(C) 我因為遲到又被處罰了。

(D) 老師要求我遵守規定。

25. Question number 25: Do you know where the nearest bank is?

(A) Sure, no problem.

(B) Yes, I have been there twice.

(C) There is one just around the corner.

(D) The bank lend money at a high interest rate.

問題：你知道最近的銀行在哪嗎？

選項：(A) 當然，沒問題。

(B) 是的，我曾去過那裡兩次。

(C) 在街角就有一家。

(D) 銀行借貸的利息很高。

26. Question number 26: I have been transferred to Tainan.

(A) Really? What about your family?

(B) That serves you right!

(C) I visited old buildings there.

(D) I prefer travelling to Taipei

問題：我被調到台南去了。

選項：(A) 真的？那你家庭怎麼辦？

(B) 你活該！

(C) 我參觀那裡的老舊建築。

(D) 我比較喜歡去台北旅行。

27. Question number 27: Can I have a cup of coffee, please?

(A) No, thanks.

(B) Drinking coffee is not good for your health.

(C) That will be NT$100 dollars.

(D) Sure. How would you like it?

問題：我能要杯咖啡嗎？

選項：(A) 不用了，謝謝！

(B) 喝咖啡對身體不好。

(C) 總共一百元。

(D) 當然。你要怎樣的咖啡？

28. Question number 28: It's harder than you think.

(A) You are having second thought, aren't you?

(B) I failed the test.

(C) Have you tried taking exercis?

(D) Oh, really? I don't mind the challenge.

問題：這比你想像中的還難。

選項：(A) 你在猶豫了，對吧？

(B) 我沒有通過考試。

(C) 你有試過運動嗎？

(D) 噢，真的嗎？我不介意挑戰。

29. Question number 29: Are you getting used to the new school?

(A) Yes, I am. I am used to it already.

(B) It's far away from my home.

(C) We have a new principal this semester.

(D) Yes, he is a friendly person.

問題：你習慣新學校了嗎？

選項：(A) 是的，我已習慣新學校了。

(B) 他離我們家很遠。

(C) 這學期我們有個新校長。

(D) 是的，他是個很友善的人。

提示："used to + V（過去的習慣）"、"be used to + Ving（現有的習慣）"、"get used to + Ving（將有的習慣）"。

30. Question number 30: What's the deadline for the paper?

(A) Wow! I can't believe the deadline is tomorrow.

(B) The paper is due this Friday.

(C) I'm taking a course in chemistry.

(D) Mine is ready.

問題：交報告的期限是何時？

選項：(A) 哇！真不敢相信明天是最後期限。

(B) 報告這個星期五要交。

(C) 我正在修化學課。

(D) 我的已準備好了。

第三部份：簡短對話

31. Question number 31:

W: Good evening. Do you have a reservation?

M: I am afraid we don't. Is there a table available?

W: I only have one table left, and that's near the kitchen.

M: We don't have too much of a choice, do we?

Question: Do you think the man will take the table?

(A) Yes, he will.

(B) Yes, he will but he will insist on switching to another one.

(C) No, he will leave immediately.

(D) No, he will file a complaint to the manager.

女：晚安。請問有訂位嗎？

男：我們沒有。還有任何桌子是空的嗎？

女：我只剩下一張桌子，但它離廚房很近。

男：我們沒有太多的選擇，是吧？

問題：你認為這男子會坐這張桌子嗎？

選項：(A) 是的，他會。

(B) 是的，他會，但他會堅持換到另一張。

(C) 不，他會立即離開。

(D) 不，他會向經理提出抱怨。

32. Question number 32:

M: Can I speak to John, please?

W: He is not in right now. Who's calling?

M: This is Mr. Smith from his school. I need to talk to him about his homework assignment.

W: In that case, can I have him call you back the moment he comes back?

Question: What is the woman offering to do?

(A) She is offering to take the message.

(B) She is offering to have John return the call ASAP.

(C) She is offering to have John run to school right away.

(D) She is offering to have John go to see the caller.

男：我能和約翰講話嗎？

女：他現在不在。請問你是哪位？

男：我是他學校的史密斯先生。我需要和他談談他的家庭作業。

女：那麼，能否等他回來後再告訴他，請他馬上回電話？

問題：這女子提供何種作法？

選項：(A) 她幫他留言。

(B) 她讓約翰立即回電話。

(C) 她讓約翰立即跑到學校。

(D) 她讓約翰去找來電者。

33. Question number 33:

W: I can't make up my mind between these two blouses.

M: Why not take them both?

W: Are you kidding? I have a tight budget.

M: Then, take the less expensive one.

Question: Where would this conversation least likely to happen?

(A) In a department store.

(B) In a duty-free shop.

(C) In a hospital.

(D) In a second-hand store.

女：我無法在這兩件襯衫間作決定。

男：何不兩件都買？

女：你在開玩笑嗎？我預算很緊的。

男：那麼就買較便宜的那件。

問題：這段對話最不可能發生在何處？

選項：(A) 百貨公司。

(B) 免稅商店。

(C) 醫院。

(D) 二手貨店。

34. Question number 34:

M: Are you going to take the job?

W: I really want to since I have been out of a job for some time.

M: So, what are you waiting for?

W: I want to see if they would offer me more money.

Question: What are they talking about?

(A) Finding another job or not.

(B) Turning down the job offer or not.

(C) Going for a job interview or not.

(D) Accepting the job offer or not.

男：你要接受這份工作嗎？

女：我真的很想，因為我已經有一段時間沒工作了。

男：那麼，你還在等什麼？

女：我想看看他們會不會提供更多的薪水。

問題：他們在討論什麼？

選項：(A) 要不要找另一份工作。

(B) 要不要拒絕這份工作。

(C) 要不要去面談。

(D) 要不要接受這份工作。

35. Question number 35:

W: Jack, it's your turn to do the dishes tonight.

M: No, It's not. I did that last night.

W: I picked up the kids and went shopping this afternoon.

M: Next time, let me do those things.

Question: What kind of relationship do the man and the woman have?

(A) Husband and wife.

(B) Mother and son.

(C) Roommates.

(D) Father and daughter.

女：傑克，今晚輪到你洗碗。

男：不。我昨晚做過了。

女：我今天下午接小孩和買東西。

男：下次這些事情讓我做。

問題：這對男女的關係為何？

選項：(A) 夫妻。

(B) 母子。

(C) 室友。

(D) 父女。

提示：本題為「推測」性題目；根據參與對話兩者之間用語的難易度來區分兩者間的關係。若內容詳盡且冗長，通常代表彼此的關係不是很親密；若言簡易賅則暗示彼此關係親密。

36. Question number 36:

M: I hate to go there, especially with all those drillings.

W: But you don't have any choice, do you?

M: I guess you are right, unless I am going to pull it out myself.

W: The only way to stay away from this is to take care of them.

M: I know. I've learned my lesson the hard way.

Question: Where do you think the man is going?

(A) To see a dentist.

(B) To see a plastic surgeon.

(C) To see a construction worker.

(D) To see a psychiatrist.

男：我恨去那地方，特別是又鑽又鑿的。

女：但你別無選擇，不是嗎？

男：我想你是對的，除非我自己把它拔掉。

女：唯一可以遠離那地方的方法就是好好照顧它們。

男：我知道。我可是學到經驗了。

問題：你想這男人要去哪裡？

選項：(A) 牙醫。

(B) 整形醫生。

(C) 建築工人。

(D) 心理醫師。

提示：不少工具書會在 "special" 和 "especially" 之間區分的很細，但兩者其實互為同義字；若一定要區分，不如把注意力放在 "special"、"particular" 及 "specific" 之間：

a special duty

a matter of special importance

He returned late on that particular day.

The book was written for specific

purpose.

37. Question number 37:

W: What's the purpose of your visit here?

M: I am here to see some of my friends and do some sight-seeing as well.

W: How long you plan to stay here?

M: I am leaving on Monday, two weeks from now.

W: Enjoy your stay here.

M: Thank you. I will.

Question: Where does this conversation happen?

(A) At the immigration check point in an airport.

(B) At the reception desk in a hotel.

(C) At the information center in downtown city.

(D) In a welcome party.

女：你來訪的目的為何？

男：我來見些朋友以及觀光。

女：你打算在這裡待多久？

男：我兩周後的星期一離開。

女：享受你在此的時間。

男：謝謝你，我會的。

問題：這段對話在哪發生？

選項：(A) 機場移民檢查。

(B) 旅館接待櫃檯。

(C) 市中心詢問中心。

(D) 歡迎酒會。

38. Question number 38:

M: What do you think of your new boss?

W: He is getting on my nerves simply by looking at him.

M: Me too. He looks so serious.

W: Looks like the good time is over for all of us.

Question: Which of the following

statements is correct?

(A) The new boss is an easy-going man.

(B) The new boss has a very pleasant personality.

(C) The new boss does everything by the book.

(D) The new boss is hard on everyone.

男：你覺得我們的新老闆如何？

女：光看著他就讓我生氣。

男：我也是。他看起來好嚴肅。

女：看來我們的好日子不多了。

問題：以下敘述何者正確？

選項：(A) 新老闆是個很容易相處的人。

　　　(B) 新老闆有個讓人喜歡的特質。

　　　(C) 新老闆凡事照章行事。

　　　(D) 新老闆對每個人都很嚴厲。

39. Question number 39:

W: Don't forget to include Patrick and his wife.

M: I almost did. Thanks for reminding me.

W: They were the first couple to say hello to us when we moved in.

M: How can I forget that, especially when the cake they brought was the only thing we had that day.

W: We got to have them over.

Question: What are the woman and the man doing?

(A) They are planning a trip.

(B) They are planning a party.

(C) They are planning a meeting.

(D) They are planning a school reunion.

女：別忘了派翠克和他太太。

男：我差點忘了。謝謝你提醒我。

女：他們是我們搬進來時第一對來打招呼的夫婦。

男：我怎能忘記，尤其是他們帶來的蛋糕是我們

那天唯一吃的東西。

女：我們一定要邀請他們。

問題：這對男女在計劃何事？

選項：(A) 他們在計劃旅行。

　　　(B) 他們在計劃聚會。

　　　(C) 他們在計劃會議。

　　　(D) 他們在計劃同學會。

40. Question number 40:

M: I went to visit Mary in the hospital.

W: What happened to her?

M: She fell while skiing and broke her arm.

W: How awful! Is she OK now?

M: She would be out of the hospital in a couple of weeks.

Question: What went wrong with Mary?

(A) She fell and broke her arm while skiing.

(B) She fell and broke her arm while watching other skiing.

(C) She fell and broke her arm while someone ran into her.

(D) She fell and broke her arm while climbing ladder.

男：我去醫院看瑪莉。

女：她怎麼了？

男：她在滑雪時跌倒並摔斷手臂。

女：多可憐！她現在好些了嗎？

男：她該在兩周後出院。

問題：瑪莉出了什麼事？

選項：(A) 她在滑雪時跌倒並摔斷手臂。

　　　(B) 她在看他人滑雪時摔倒並跌斷手臂。

　　　(C) 別人撞到她，讓她跌倒並摔斷手臂。

　　　(D) 她爬樓梯時跌倒並摔斷手臂。

41. Question number 41:

W: How about some more dessert?

M: I really love to have some, but I can't.

W: Why? You don't like it?

M: No, I am too full.

Question: Why can't the man have more dessert?

(A) He is just being polite.

(B) He is too full to have any.

(C) He doesn't really like it.

(D) He is on a diet.

女：再來些甜點？

男：我真的想要，但我不行。

女：為什麼？你不喜歡嗎？

男：不，我太飽了。

問題：為何這男子不多吃些甜點？

選項：(A) 他只是客氣。

(B) 他因太飽而吃不下。

(C) 他並不是真的喜歡甜點。

(D) 他在節食。

42. Question number 42:

M: Do you like to take a walk in the park?

W: Yes, I do. I enjoy walking in the park on weekends.

M: Me, too. But I hate to walk alone.

W: Really?

Question: What does the man have in mind?

(A) He is thinking of asking the woman out for a drink.

(B) He doesn't really like to walk in the park.

(C) He only walks with women.

(D) He doesn't like to walk alone.

男：你喜歡到公園散步嗎？

女：是的，我喜歡。我喜歡週末到公園散步。

男：我也是，但我不喜歡一個人散步。

女：真的？

問題：這男子心中在想什麼？

選項：(A) 他想邀請女子去喝一杯。

(B) 他並不真的喜歡在公園散步。

(C) 他只喜歡和女子散步。

(D) 他不喜歡一個人散步。

43. Question number 43:

W: Can I tell you a secret?

M: Sure. My lips are sealed.

W: Mary broke up with her boyfriend last week.

M: That's too bad.

Question: What does the man mean when he said, "My lips are sealed?"

(A) He can't speak.

(B) He will tell the first person he meets.

(C) He will keep secrets.

(D) He doesn't really want to know anything.

女：我能告訴你個秘密嗎？

男：當然。我的嘴已貼了封條了。

女：瑪莉上個星期和她男友分手了。

男：真可惜。

問題：當男子說他的嘴被封住了，他的意思為何？

選項：(A) 他沒辦法說話。

(B) 他會告訴他碰到的第一個人。

(C) 他會保守秘密。

(D) 他並不真想知道任何事。

44. Question number 44:

M: Do you see any supermarket around?

W: I thought I saw one just across the street.

M: Where?

W: It's over there.

Question: Where is the supermarket located?

(A) It's no where to be found.

(B) Right next to where they stand.

(C) Across the street from where they stand.

(D) They have no idea.

男：你有沒有在附近看到任何超級市場？

女：我以為我在附近看到一家。

男：哪裡？

女：就在那裡。

問題：超級市場在哪裡？

45. Question number 45:

W: Are you done with your homework?

M: It will be another twenty minutes. Why?

W: I need you to run some errands for me.

M: But I have a date with my friends afterwards.

Question: What does the woman want from the man?

(A) She wants to have a chat with him.

(B) She wants him to do something for her.

(C) She needs him to help her take care of her child.

(D) She is just asking.

女：你做完功課了嗎？

男：還要二十分鐘。幹嘛？

女：我要你幫我跑腿。

男：但我做完功課後和朋友有約。

問題：這女子需要男子作什麼？

選項：(A) 她要和他聊天。

       (B) 她要他替她做些事。

       (C) 她要他幫她照顧小孩。

       (D) 她只是問問。

Test ❹
第一部份：看圖辨義

1. For question number 1, please look at picture A.

Question number 1: If Mary wants to go to the park, which direction should she head for?

(A) She should head for the east.

(B) She should head for the west.

(C) She should head for the south.

(D) She should head for the north.

問題：如果瑪莉要去公園，她該往那個方向走？

選項：(A) 瑪莉應該往東行。

(B) 瑪莉應該往西行。

(C) 瑪莉應該往南行。

(D) 瑪莉應該往北行。

2. For question number 2, please look at picture B.

Question number 2: Where in this building will you have the best view of the city?

(A) The department store on the 3rd floor.

(B) The Supermarket on B1.

(C) The Parking Lot on B5.

(D) The Observatory on the 91st floor.

問題：你在這棟建築物的什麼位置可以擁有最佳的城市展望視野？

選項：(A) 3 樓的百貨公司。

(B) 地下 1 樓的超級市場。

(C) 地下 5 樓的停車場。

(D) 91 樓的觀景台。

3. For question number 3, please look at picture C.

Question number 3: Why does Mary look so angry?

(A) She is mad at someone.

(B) There is a lot of garbage in the room.

(C) Someone throws a stone at her.

(D) She breaks up with her boyfriend.

問題：為何瑪莉看來很生氣？

選項：(A) 她在生某人的氣。

(B) 房間裡有很多垃圾。

(C) 有人朝她丟石子。

(D) 她跟男朋友分手了。

4. For question number 4, please look at picture D.

Question number 4: How would you describe the man?

(A) The man dresses himself formally.

(B) The man dresses himself casually.

(C) The man wears jeans.

(D) The man is going to take some exercise.

問題：你會如何形容這男士？

選項：(A) 這男士穿著正式。

(B) 這男士穿著輕便。

(C) 這男士穿著牛仔褲。

(D) 這男士要去運動。

提示：疑問詞 "how" 及 "what" 有時還真不好分！通常 "how" 用來問「狀況」、「方法」、「詢問意見」、「要求說明」、「詢問健康狀況」、「程度」；"what" 則用在「問對方意思」、「目的」、「行業」、「地位」、「國籍」。兩者都可用在感嘆句。

5. For question number 5, please look at picture E.

Question number 5: Where is the scene in the picture most likely to happen?

(A) In an Emergency Room.

(B) In an Examination Room.

(C) In a Waiting Room.

(D) In an Operating Room.

問題：這個圖片中的情景最有可能發生在下列那個地方？

選項：(A) 急診室。

(B) 診間。

(C) 候診室。

(D) 手術室。

提示："most likely（最可能）"、"least likely（最不可能）"。英文的使用該是雙行道，例如：

He is taller than me. ⟷ I am shorter than him.

A is superior to B. ⟷ B is inferior to A.

I prefer tea to coffee.=I like tea better than coffee. ⟷ I like coffee less.

千萬不可將語法和用法拘泥在一定的範圍內或一定的形式結構上。

6. For question number 6, please look at picture F.

Question number 6: What's the woman's profession?

(A) She is a cashier in a supermarket.

(B) She is a manager in a store.

(C) She is a cleaning lady in a restaurant.

(D) She is a nurse in a hospital.

問題：這女子的職業為何？

選項：(A) 她是超級市場的結帳員。

(B) 她是商店經理。

(C) 她是餐廳的打掃工人。

(D) 她是醫院護士。

提示：問「職業」有不同的說法："What line of work are you in?" 或 "What's your area of expertise?" 當然，"What are you?" 則是最直接了當的用法。而市場商店的用詞則有："convenience store（便利商店）"、"mom-and-pop store（雜貨舖）"、"shopping mall（購物中心）"、"shopping gallery/arcade（精品街）"、"hypermarket（大賣場）"、"megastore（超級大賣場）"。

7. For question number 7, please look at picture G.

Question number 7: When will the flight for Hong Kong leave?

(A) It leaves at 10:30 a.m.

(B) It leaves at 12:30 p.m.

(C) It leaves at 1:30 p.m.

(D) It leaves at 2:00 p.m.

問題：往香港的班機何時起飛？

選項：(A) 十點半起飛。

(B) 十二點半起飛。

(C) 一點半起飛。

(D) 兩點起飛。

8. For question number 8, please look at picture H

Question number 8: Is the gas tank almost empty?

(A) No, it is not. It's about one quarter full.

(B) No, it is not. It's about half full.

(C) No, it is not. It's full.

(D) Yes, it's almost empty.

問題：汽車油箱是不是幾乎要空了？

選項：(A) 不，它還有四分之一。

(B) 不，它還有一半。

(C) 不，它是滿的。

(D) 是的，它幾乎空了。

9. For question number 9, please look at picture I.

Question number 9: What are the boys and girls doing?

(A) They are eating together.

(B) They are playing together.

(C) They are studying together.

(D) They are dancing together.

問題：這些男孩和女孩正在做什麼？

選項：(A) 他們在一起吃東西。

(B) 他們在一起遊戲。

(C) 他們在一起讀書。

(D) 他們在一起跳舞。

10. For question number 10, please look at picture J.

Question number 10: What subject is the boy working on?

(A) He is working on History.

(B) He is working on Math.

(C) He is working on English.

(D) He is working on Biology.

問題：這男孩正在讀哪個科目？

選項：(A) 他正在讀歷史。

　　　(B) 他正在讀數學。

　　　(C) 他正在讀英文。

　　　(D) 他正在讀生物。

11. For question number 11, please look at picture K.

Question number 11: What are these men doing?

(A) They are talking.

(B) They are swimming.

(C) They are dancing.

(D) They are singing.

問題：這些男人正在做什麼？

選項：(A) 他們在說話。

　　　(B) 他們在游泳。

　　　(C) 他們在跳舞。

　　　(D) 他們在唱歌。

12. For question number 12, please look at picture L.

Question number 12: What's happening here?

(A) People are watching a musical.

(B) People are going to a concert.

(C) People are watching a movie.

(D) People are listening to a lecture.

問題：這裡發生了什麼事？

選項：(A) 人們在欣賞音樂劇。

(B) 人們要去參加演唱會。

(C) 人們在看電影。

(D) 人們在聽演講。

提示：音樂劇或舞台劇通常在 "theater" 中演出；演奏會則在 "concert hall"；演講討論則在 "auditorium" ；電影通常在 "movie theater" 或 "cinema"。

13. For question number 13, please look at picture M.

Question number 13: What kind of activity is this?

(A) It's a track and field contest.

(B) It's a basketball game.

(C) It's a football match.

(D) It's a golf game.

問題：這是何種活動？

選項：(A) 田徑賽。

　　　(B) 籃球賽。

　　　(C) 足球賽。

　　　(D) 高爾夫球賽。

提示：運動項目的場地：

　　　field：田徑、足球 (soccer)、美式足球 (American football)

　　　court：籃球、排球、壁球 (squash)

　　　course：高爾夫球

14. For question number 14, please look at picture N.

Question number 14: What do people do with these things?

(A) They use these to write and send letters.

(B) They use these to take notes.

(C) They use these to write diaries.

(D) They use these to draw pictures.

問題：人們用這些東西做什麼？

選項：(A) 用來寫信及寄信。

　　　(B) 用來記筆記。

　　　(C) 用來寫日記。

(D) 用來畫畫。

15. For question number 15, please look at picture O.

Question number 15: What is the boy doing?

(A) He is chasing the dogs.

(B) He is flying a kite.

(C) He is sending an email.

(D) He is flying an airplane.

問題：這男孩在做什麼？

選項：(A) 他在追狗。

　　　(B) 他在放風箏。

　　　(C) 他在寄電子郵件。

　　　(D) 他在開飛機。

第二部份：問答

16. Question number 16: What kind of course do you take?

(A) Business English and Elementary Japanese.

(B) I know you like me.

(C) I only go there once a week.

(D) I am trying to be smarter.

問題：你選修了什麼課程？

選項：(A) 商用英文和初級日文。

　　　(B) 我知道你喜歡我。

　　　(C) 我一星期去一次。

　　　(D) 我試著變得聰明些。

提示："take courses（選課）"、"drop courses（退選）"、"take leave of absence（休學）"、"drop out（輟學）"。

17. Question number 17: What year are you?

(A) I am a senior.

(B) I was born in 1981.

(C) It's been four year since I moved here.

(D) I am eighteen years old.

問題：你是幾年級學生？

選項：(A) 我是大四學生。

(B) 我在 1981 年出生。

(C) 我搬來這裡已經四年了。

(D) 我十八歲。

提示：本題中的 "year" 是指「年級」而非「年齡」或「年份」，可比較以下的意義：

What year is this wine?（這是哪一年份的紅酒？）

How many years of working experience do you have?（你有幾年的工作經驗？）

此外，「大一學生」是 "freshmen"，「大二學生」是 "sophomore"，「大三學生」是 "junior"，「大四學生」是 "senior"。

18. Question number 18: Where do you work?

(A) No, I am between jobs.

(B) I am a good doctor.

(C) I work in Sanmin Bookstore.

(D) I love my job.

問題：你在哪裡工作？

選項：(A) 不，我在待業中。

　　　(B) 我是一個好醫生。

　　　(C) 我在三民書店工作。

　　　(D) 我熱愛我的工作。

提示：本題問工作地點而非從事何種工作；疑問詞的分辨是本題的關鍵。

"between jobs（待業）" 以及類似的用語如 "go-between（中間人）"、"a teacher-would-be（未來老師的人選）"、"a teacher-to-be（即將要當老師的人）"、"a teacher-want-to-be（想當老師的人）" 等，這些字都是基於實際需要而有的「另類表達」，不妨稍加注意。

19. Question number 19: Are you as busy as ever?

(A) Fine, thank you.

(B) Yes, it's a peak season.

(C) Well, nothing much.

(D) Good for you!

問題：你像以往一樣忙碌嗎？

選項：(A) 很好，謝謝你。

　　　(B) 是的。現在是旺季。

　　　(C) 沒什麼特別的。

　　　(D) 真替你感到高興！

提示：It's a slow season. = The business is slow.（淡季）、It's a peak season.（旺季）。

20. Question number 20: Will you vote for the candidate next month?

(A) I will not vote for you.

(B) I will vote tomorrow.

(C) I need to calm down.

(D) No, I don't like him.

問題：你下個月會把票投給那個候選人嗎？

選項：(A) 我不會投給你。

　　　(B) 我明天會去投票。

　　　(C) 我要冷靜下來。

　　　(D) 不。我不喜歡他。

21. Question number 21: You will come to the picnic this coming Sunday, won't you?

(A) It depends.

(B) I hope not.

(C) Whatever you say.

(D) It looks like rain.

問題：你這個星期天會來參加野餐吧，是嗎？

選項：(A) 不一定。

　　　(B) 我希望不會。

　　　(C) 你怎麼說都可以。

　　　(D) 看起來要下雨了。

提示：附加問句與一般問句相比之下，並沒有特別的回答方式。在思考時可將附加問句轉化成一般問句："Will you come to the picnic this coming Sunday?"，然後依適當的情境加以回答即可。

22. Question number 22: You are the laziest

man I've ever seen!

(A) It's very good.

(B) Tell me more about it.

(C) That's enough!

(D) I'm not listening.

問題：你是我所見過最懶惰的人！

選項：(A) 這很好。

　　　(B) 再告訴我多一點。

　　　(C) 夠了！

　　　(D) 我沒在聽。

23. Question number 23: Do you want to know more about this?

(A) No, I am not interested at all.

(B) No, it is exciting.

(C) Yes, let me tell you more about it.

(D) Yes, I'd like to have some more.

問題：你想了解更多嗎？

選項：(A) 不。我一點都不感興趣。

　　　(B) 不。它很令人興奮。

　　　(C) 好的，讓我多告訴你一些。

　　　(D) 好的，再給我一些。

提示："at all（絲毫不，用於否定涵義）"、"in all（總數）"。

24. Question number 24: I want you to sing at the Christmas party.

(A) Don't ask.

(B) I think you'll be busy then.

(C) Give me a break!

(D) I feel sorry for you.

問題：我要你在耶誕晚會上唱歌。

選項：(A) 別問。

　　　(B) 我想你那時會很忙。

　　　(C) 饒了我吧！

　　　(D) 我為你感到遺憾。

25. Question number 25: Want to go for a swim?

(A) I don't agree with you.

(B) I'd like to do that very much.

(C) Never heard of it.

(D) I don't smoke.

問題：要不要去游泳？

選項：(A) 我不同意你說的話。

(B) 我很想去。

(C) 從來沒聽過。

(D) 我不抽菸。

26. Question number 26: You know smoking is not allowed here.

(A) I am sorry.

(B) It's not possible.

(C) Smoking is bad for you.

(D) You are kidding me.

問題：你知道此地禁止吸煙。

選項：(A) 對不起。

(B) 不可能吧。

(C) 抽菸對你的身體不好。

(D) 你在開玩笑。

27. Question number 27: Do you know the final is coming?

(A) The new movie is coming soon.

(B) Yes, I know, and I am well prepared.

(C) Bless you!

(D) It's just the beginning.

問題：你知道期末考試要到了嗎？

選項：(A) 新的電影快上映了。

(B) 我知道，而且我也準備好了。

(C) 保佑你！

(D) 才剛開始而已。

28. Question number 28: Are you going to finish the project on time?

(A) Nothing is impossible.

(B) You'll have to wait.

(C) I have an idea.

(D) I am a person who gets up very early.

問題：你會準時完成計畫嗎？

選項：(A) 沒什麼不可能的事。

(B) 你必須等。

(C) 我有個點子。

(D) 我很早起床。

29. Question number 29: May I talk to Mr. Smith?

(A) I am talking to Mr. Jones.

(B) Yes, speaking.

(C) Mr. Smith is not talking to you.

(D) Is Mr. Smith there?

問題：請問我可以跟史密斯先生說話嗎？

選項：(A) 我正在跟瓊斯先生說話。

(B) 我就是。

(C) 史密斯先生沒有在跟你說話。

(D) 史密斯先生在那裡嗎？

提示：在電話對談中，she/he is speaking 是「你要找的人正在跟你說話」之意，也就是「我就是」。

30. Question number 30: Do you think we can get another car?

(A) There is a parking lot across the street.

(B) We can't afford that.

(C) How about taking a taxi?

(D) I never take the bus.

問題：你覺得我們可以另外買部車嗎？

選項：(A) 對面有一個停車場。

(B) 我們負擔不起。

(C) 搭計程車如何？

(D) 我從不搭巴士。

第三部份：簡短對話

31. Question number 31:

M: Where does the salad plate go?

W: It goes to the left of the dinner plate.

M: Then, where does the soup spoon go?

W: It goes to the right of the teaspoon.

Question: What are they doing?

(A) They are setting up the dinner table.

(B) They are having a cooking class.

(C) They are eating in a restaurant.

(D) They are buying some plates and spoons.

男：沙拉盤要放在哪裡？

女：放在晚餐餐盤的左邊。

男：那麼，湯匙放哪裡？

女：茶匙的右邊。

問題：他們正在做什麼？

選項：(A) 他們在擺設晚餐餐桌。

(B) 他們在上烹飪課。

(C) 他們在餐廳用餐。

(D) 他們在買一些盤子與湯匙。

提示："set (up) the table" 是「擺設餐桌，準備用餐」之意、"to set someone up" 則是「設計、暗算他人」之意。

32. Question number 32:

W: Do you have the shopping list with you?

M: I have it right here.

W: Did you put the baby powder on it?

M: I didn't. I will put it down right away.

Question: Where are they going?

(A) They are going to the supermarket.

(B) They are going to the toy store.

(C) They are going to the museum.

(D) They are going to the park.

女：你帶購物清單了嗎？

男：在我這邊。

女：你有沒有寫上嬰兒爽身粉？

男：我沒有。我馬上寫上去。

問題：他們要去哪裡？

選項：(A) 他們要去超級市場。

(B) 他們要去玩具店。

(C) 他們要去博物館。

(D) 他們要去公園。

33. Question number 33:

M: Is there a parking garage?

W: Yes, there is. We have a parking garage

in the basement, as well as an indoor swimming pool.

M: What about the laundry?

W: It is on the second floor.

Question: What are these two people talking about?

(A) The woman is thinking of renting a house.

(B) The man wants to rent an apartment.

(C) The man is selling a house.

(D) The man wants to buy a car.

男：這裡有車庫嗎？

女：有。我們在地下室有車庫，還有一個室內游泳池。

男：那洗衣間呢？

女：在二樓。

問題：這兩人在討論什麼？

(A) 這女子想要租一間房子。

(B) 這男子想要租一間公寓。

(C) 這男子在賣房子。

(D) 這男子想要買車。

34. Question number 34:

W: What can I do for you?

M: Can you break this twenty for me?

W: How would you like it?

M: How about one ten, one five and five ones.

Question: Where is this conversation most likely to happen?

(A) In a hospital.

(B) In a school.

(C) In a factory.

(D) In a bank.

女：我能怎麼幫你呢？

男：你能把這張二十元鈔票換成小額的嗎？

女：你想要怎麼換？

男：一張十元，一張五元，和五張一元。

問題：這段對話可能發生在哪個場所？

選項：(A) 醫院。

(B) 學校。

(C) 工廠。

(D) 銀行。

提示："most likely（最可能…）"、"least likely（最不可能…）"。

若最高級當形容詞用，需加定冠詞 "the"；若當副詞用，最高級前則不可加定冠詞。如：

He is the fastest runner of all.

He runs fastest of all.

35. Question number 35:

M: When will you go through with this pile of papers?

W: I don't know. I think I'll have to work late tonight.

M: Then, how about our dinner date?

W: I am sorry, but I will have to take a rain check.

Question: Do you think the man and the woman will go out for dinner as planned?

(A) No, they will probably do that some other time.

(B) No, but the woman writes a check for that.

(C) Yes, because the man is angry.

(D) Yes, they will meet each other in an hour.

男：你何時才能處理完這堆文件？

女：我不知道。我想我今晚要上班到很晚了。

男：那我們的晚餐約會要怎麼辦？

女：對不起，我只好延期了。

問題：你覺得這對男女會依計畫外出晚餐嗎？

選項：(A) 不，他們可能以後再去。

(B) 不，但這女子為此開了張支票。

(C) 會，因為這男子生氣了。

(D) 會。他們會在一小時內碰面。

36. Question number 36:

W: You look worried.

M: Yes, business had gone from bad to worse.

W: Is there anything I can do to help?

M: I don't know. Right now, I can only hope things will turn better eventually.

Question: Does the man have confidence in turning things around?

(A) Yes, he has already turned things around.

(B) Yes, he is confident that things will definitely be better.

(C) No, but he hopes that things will become better eventually.

(D) No, but he will go to the church and pray.

女：你看來有些憂慮。

男：是的。最近生意每況愈下。

女：我能做什麼來幫忙嗎？

男：我不知道。現在，我只能希望情況最後會變的好些。

問題：這男人有把握讓事情好轉嗎？

選項：(A) 是的，他已經讓事情好轉了。

(B) 是的，他有信心事情會變的更好。

(C) 不，但他希望事情最後會變更好。

(D) 不，但他會到教堂祈禱。

37. Question number 37:

M: How's your mother today?

W: She still feels pretty weak.

M: Did you take her to see a doctor?

W: Yes, I did, but the doctor said it would take time and plenty of rest to recover.

Question: What happened to the woman's mother?

(A) She was sick.

(B) She lost her job.

(C) She is going to be a nurse.

(D) She didn't want to go to a doctor.

男：你母親今天好點了嗎？

女：她依然覺得很虛弱。

男：你帶她去看過醫生嗎？

女：去過。但醫生說這需要時間和充分的休息才能恢復。

問題：這個女生的媽媽發生了什麼事？

選項：(A) 她病了。

(B) 她失業了。

(C) 她將要成為護士。

(D) 她不想去看醫生。

38. Question number 38:

M: Linda eats nothing but some fruit every day to keep a good figure.

W: She's going a little too far.

M: What will you do if you were her?

W: I would probably eat healthily and exercise regularly.

Question: How does Linda keep a good figure?

(A) She walk to places where are far away for exercising

(B) She eats healthily and exercise regularly.

(C) She only eats some fruit every day.

(D) She doesn't know what to do.

男：琳達為了保持好身材，什麼都不吃，每天只吃一些水果。

女：她做得有些過分了。

男：要是你，你會怎麼做？

女：我可能會吃得健康而且定時運動。

問題：琳達如何保持好身材？

選項：(A) 她走到很遠的地方，以此作為運動。

(B) 她吃得很健康，並且規律的運動。

(C) 她每天只吃一些水果。

(D) 她不知道該怎麼做。

39. Question number 39:

W: I haven't kept in touch with any of my classmates.

M: Don't you miss them?

W: Yes, I do. But it seems that I'm always too busy to contact them.

M: Come on. That's nothing but an excuse!

Question: What does the man really mean?

(A) If the woman wants, she can still find time to keep in touch with her classmates.

(B) He understands that the woman is too busy for anything.

(C) He believes that the woman does not want to be with her classmates.

(D) He believes that the woman does not miss her classmates at all.

女：我沒和任何同學保持聯絡。

男：你難道不想他們嗎？

女：我想念他們。但我似乎總是太忙而無法跟他們聯絡。

男：少來。那只不過是藉口。

問題：這男子的真正意思為何？

選項：(A) 如果這女子願意，她仍可以找到時間和同學聯絡。

(B) 他了解這女子忙到任何事都不能做。

(C) 他相信這女子並不想和同學在一起。

(D) 他相信這女子一點都不想念她的同學。

40. Question number 40:

M: Would you look over this letter and check if there are any mistakes?

W: I'm all tied up right now, but I can do it tomorrow. Is that OK?

M: But I am in a rush. The letter has to be sent out today.

W: Give me a minute and I'll see what I can do.

Question: Will the woman help the man out?

(A) Perhaps she will, but she needs to make some arrangements first.

(B) Yes, she will help him immediately.

(C) Yes, but the man will have to wait for a long time.

(D) No, she's too busy, so the man will find someone else to help.

男：你能幫我看看這信是否有錯誤嗎？

女：我現在很忙，但我明天能幫你忙。這樣可以嗎？

男：可是我真的很急，這封信今天就要寄出。

女：給我一點時間讓我看看我能怎麼做。

問題：這女子會幫這男子嗎？

選項：(A) 會的，但她要先做些安排。

　　　(B) 會的，她會馬上幫他。

　　　(C) 會的，但男子要等一段很長的時間。

　　　(D) 不會，她太忙了，所以這男子將會找其他人幫忙。

41. Question number 41:

W: What's the rush?

M: I am late for work.

W: Why can't you get up a bit earlier?

M: I've tried, but I can't seem to get enough sleep.

W: You should go to bed before midnight.

Question: What is the man's problem?

(A) He probably goes to bed too late.

(B) He can't sleep well at night.

(C) He has a lot of work to do.

(D) He tries to ask help from the woman.

女：急什麼急啊？

男：我上班要遲到了。

女：你為何不能早起些？

男：我已經試過，但我似乎總是睡眠不足。

問題：這男子的問題為何？

選項：(A) 他很可能太晚睡。

　　　(B) 他晚上睡不好。

(C) 他有很多工作。

(D) 他希望這女子能幫他忙。

42. Question number 42:

M: What's wrong with Judy?

W: She is really mad about something.

M: Oh, in that case, I'd better go and cheer her up.

W: I won't do that if I were you.

Question: What does the woman mean?

(A) She thinks that Judy is not mad at the man.

(B) She encourages the man to talk to Judy.

(C) She will go and cheer Judy up herself.

(D) She thinks Judy might want to be left alone.

男：茱蒂怎麼了？

女：她對某件事非常生氣。

男：喔，這樣的話，我最好去替她打打氣。

女：如果我是你，我就不會如此做。

問題：這女子說的話是什麼意思？

選項：(A) 她認為茱蒂不是在生這男子的氣。

　　　(B) 她鼓勵男子去跟茱蒂講話。

　　　(C) 她會自己去幫茱蒂打氣。

　　　(D) 她覺得茱蒂可能不希望有人打擾。

43. Question number 43:

M: I just got my first credit card and I want to use it today.

W: Does that mean you are going to buy something for me?

M: It's up to you. You can either pick out a dress or have a great dinner.

W: Then, I will settle for a dinner.

Question: Why will the man want to buy something for the woman?

(A) It's her birthday.

(B) She's got a baby.

(C) He's got a new credit card.

(D) She wants to have dinner.

男：我剛拿到我的第一張信用卡，我今天要用用它。

女：這意思是說你要給我買些東西給我嗎？

男：看你了。你可以選一件套裝或是吃一頓大餐。

女：那麼，我就要一份晚餐吧。

問題：為什麼這男子要買東西給這女子？

選項：(A) 今天是她的生日。

(B) 她懷孕了。

(C) 他拿到了新的信用卡。

(D) 她想要吃晚餐。

44. Question number 44:

W: Did you meet the new girl Jean?

M: Yes, I did. Why do you ask?

W: She is not very friendly, isn't she?

M: That's because she is new here and she knows nothing about the environment. I think she's a nice girl.

Question: Who likes the girl more?

(A) The man does.

(B) The woman does.

(C) Both of them like her.

(D) Both of them don't like her.

女：你見過那個新來的，名叫珍的女生嗎？

男：見過。為何這樣問？

女：她並不十分友善，對吧？

男：那是因為她是新來的而且對新環境不了解吧。我覺得她是個不錯的女孩。

問題：誰比較喜歡這新女子？

選項：(A) 這男子。

(B) 這女子。

(C) 兩人都喜歡。

(D) 兩人都不喜歡。

45. Question number 45:

M: How much should I pay for the lunch?

W: Nothing. This is my treat.

M: Well, thanks. May I ask why?

W: It's your birthday today. Don't you remember?

Question: Why does the woman buy the man lunch?

(A) She likes the man.

(B) She has no choice.

(C) It's his birthday today.

(D) They are not friends.

男：我該為這份午餐付多少錢？

女：不用，我請客。

男：喔，謝了。我能問為什麼嗎？

女：今天是你的生日。難道你不記得嗎？

問題：這女子為何請男子吃午飯？

選項：(A) 她喜歡他。

(B) 她別無選擇。

(C) 今天是他的生日。

(D) 他們不是朋友。

Test 5

第一部份：看圖辨義

1. For question number 1, please look at picture A.

   Question number 1: What does the boy have in his hand?

   (A) He is holding an ice cream cone.

   (B) He is holding a bottle of water.

   (C) He is holding a telescope.

   (D) He is holding an MP3 player.

   問題：這男孩手上拿著什麼？

   選項：(A) 他手上拿著一個冰淇淋甜筒。

   　　　(B) 他手上拿著一瓶水。

   　　　(C) 他手上拿著一副望遠鏡。

   　　　(D) 他手上拿著一台 MP3 隨身聽。

2. For question number 2, please look at picture B.

   Question number 2: What does the man wear when going to school?

   (A) An overcoat.

   (B) A bathing suit.

   (C) A sweater.

   (D) A uniform.

   問題：這個男生穿什麼衣服去學校？

   選項：(A) 大衣。

   　　　(B) 泳衣。

   　　　(C) 毛線衣。

   　　　(D) 制服。

3. For question number 3, please look at picture C.

   Question number 3: Which of the following statements is correct?

   (A) This is a loaf of bread.

   (B) This is a jar of jam.

   (C) This is a bottle of milk.

   (D) This is a pack of cigarettes.

   問題：下列敘述何者是正確的？

   選項：(A) 這是一條麵包。

   　　　(B) 這是一罐果醬。

   　　　(C) 這是一罐牛奶。

   　　　(D) 這是一包香菸。

   提示：(1)不論是可數名詞或不可數名詞，當前者用於複數或後者變成可數名詞，都會用到計量單位。例："a flock of birds"、"a herd of cows"、"a pack of wolves"、"a group of people"、"a piece of information"、"a glass of water"、"a pound of flour"。這些單位詞要特別小心。

   　　　(2)當加上形容詞時，形容詞的位置如下："This is a good piece of advice."（○）"This is a piece of good advice."（×）

4. For question number 4, please look at picture D.

   Question number 4: If one wants a pair of running shoes, which floor should one go?

   (A) The 5th floor.

   (B) The 6th floor.

   (C) The 7th floor.

   (D) The 8th floor.

   問題：如果某人要一雙跑步鞋，他該去幾樓？

   選項：(A) 五樓。

   　　　(B) 六樓。

   　　　(C) 七樓。

   　　　(D) 八樓。

   提示：若句子主詞前有 "each"、"every"、"some"、"no"、"all" 等字時，其後要用 "he"、"him" 及 "his"。如：One must do one's best. Everyone must do his best.

5. For question number 5, please look at picture E.

   Question number 5: What is the man doing?

   (A) He is deciding which restaurant to go to.

(B) He is thinking where he should hold the party.

(C) He is thinking how to go to the restaurant.

(D) He is looking for the parking space.

問題：你以為這男人在做什麼？

選項：(A) 他在決定要去那家餐廳。

　　　(B) 他在思考要在哪裡舉行派對。

　　　(C) 他在思考要如何去餐廳。

　　　(D) 他在找停車位。

6. For question number 6, please look at picture F.

Question number 6: Which decription matches the picture?

(A) The boy has short straight hair.

(B) They are wearing short pants

(C) The boy is wearing a skirt.

(D) The girl has long curly hair.

問題：哪一個描述和圖片相符？

選項：(A) 男孩留短直髮。

　　　(B) 他們都穿短褲。

　　　(C) 男孩穿裙子。

　　　(D) 女孩留長長的捲髮。

7. For question number 7, please look at picture G.

Question number 7: How high is the mountain?

(A) The mountain is 785 meters high.

(B) The mountain is 393 meters high.

(C) The mountain is 575 meters high.

(D) The mountain is 875 meters high.

問題：這座山有多高？

選項：(A) 這座山有七百八十五公尺高。

　　　(B) 這座山有三百九十三公尺高。

　　　(C) 這座山有五百七十五公尺高。

　　　(D) 這座山有八百七十五公尺高。

提示：當時間、距離、或價值的複數名詞當主詞

時，其後通常用單數動詞。例如：

Six months is too short to learn English.

Ten miles is too long for me to walk.

Ten dollars is not enough for a good pen.

8. For question number 8, please look at picture H.

Question number 8: How would you describe the woman in this picture?

(A) She has a lot in her mind.

(B) She is a carefree lady.

(C) She is afraid of something.

(D) She is expecting something.

問題：你會如何形容圖片中的女子？

選項：(A) 她心中有許多心事。

　　　(B) 她是為無憂無慮的女子。

　　　(C) 她對某事感到恐懼。

　　　(D) 她在期待某事。

提示："expect（期望）"通常表示對所期盼的結果沒有把握，而"anticipate"則代表期盼某一結果的發生。

As parents, adults usually expect their children to be the best.

I anticipate a happy ending halfway through this novel.

9. For question number 9, please look at picture I.

Question number 9: When is the next train to Tainan?

(A) At 1:30 p.m.

(B) At 1:45 p.m.

(C) At 2:00 p.m.

(D) At 2:15 p.m.

問題：下一班到台南的火車是幾點？

選項：(A) 下午一點半。

　　　(B) 下午一點四十五分。

(C) 下午兩點。

(D) 下午兩點十五分。

10. For question number 10, please look at picture J.

Question number 10: Why was Jack late for school?

(A) The bus he took broke down.

(B) He was stuck in a traffic jam.

(C) He slept late.

(D) The bike he rode broke down.

問題：傑克為何上學遲到？

選項：(A) 他所搭乘的公車拋錨了。

(B) 他遇到塞車。

(C) 他睡過頭了。

(D) 他所騎的單車拋錨了。

11. For question number 11, please look at picture K.

Question number 11: What is this woman doing?

(A) She is brushing her teeth.

(B) She is washing her face.

(C) She is putting on her make-up.

(D) She is doing her daily exercise.

問題：這女子正在做什麼？

選項：(A) 她正在刷牙。

(B) 她正在洗臉。

(C) 她正在化妝。

(D) 她正在做每日的運動。

12. For question number 12, please look at picture L.

Question number 12: What will John have for dinner?

(A) He'll have spaghetti, a pie, and a bottle of beer.

(B) He'll have spaghetti, a piece of toast, and a cup of coffee.

(C) He'll have a steak, a piece of cake and

soup.

(D) He'll have a steak, a piece of toast, and soup.

問題：約翰會吃什麼當作晚餐？

選項：(A) 他會吃義大利麵、一個派和一瓶啤酒。

(B) 他會吃義大利麵 、 一片吐司和一杯咖啡。

(C) 他會吃牛排、一片蛋糕和湯。

(D) 他會吃牛排、一片吐司和湯。

13. For question number 13, please look at picture M.

Question number 13: How would you describe these two people?

(A) They are looking at each other.

(B) They are arguing with each other.

(C) They are talking jokes.

(D) They are having a small talk.

問題：這兩人在做什麼？

選項：(A) 他們互相看著對方。

(B) 他們在相互爭執。

(C) 他們在說笑話。

(D) 他們在聊天。

14. For question number 14, please look at picture N.

Question number 14: Where is this scene most likely to happen?

(A) In a church.

(B) In a cafeteria.

(C) In a classroom.

(D) In a dormitory.

問題：本圖示最可能發生在何處？

選項：(A) 在教堂。

(B) 在自助餐廳。

(C) 在教室。

(D) 在宿舍。

15. For question number 15, please look at picture O.

Question number 15: Why is the baby crying?

(A) Because it is hungry.

(B) Because it misses its mother.

(C) Because it wants to go out.

(D) Because it needs someone to change its diapers.

問題：這嬰兒為何哭？

選項：(A) 因為它餓了。

(B) 因為它想媽媽。

(C) 因為它想出去。

(D) 因為它要人替它換尿布。

提示：名詞一般可分為：

(1)陽性：father、nephew、widower、the sun、the summer、the day，以代名詞 he/his/him 代替。

(2)陰性：mother、niece、widow、the moon、the spring、the night，以代名詞 she/her/her 代替。

(3)通性：student、teacher、parent，依文句中的線索判斷究竟是陰性還是陽性。如：

The student has a dress on; she looks nice on it.

The student had a cap on; he is a baseball player.

但，"infant" 或 "baby" 則慣以 "it" 代替。

(4)無性：stone、desk、tree、building，習以 its/it 代替。

第二部份：問答

16. Question number 16: I wish they could try to solve the problem instead of finger-pointing.

(A) You can say that again!

(B) You are right on the money!

(C) You came up with a wonderful idea.

(D) You are dead wrong about that!

問題：與其相互指責，我寧可他們試著去解決問題。

選項：(A) 你說的對極了！

(B) 你可說中了！

(C) 你想出了個好點子。

(D) 你可是錯到家了！

提示：複合字 (compound word) 的形成方式很多。其中常見的一種是把動詞片語倒裝，變成複合名詞：

stand by = by-standing/bystander（旁觀者）

point finger at = finger-pointing（相互指責）

catch one's eye = eye-catching（吸引人注意的）

to solve the problem = problem-solving（解決問題）

17. Question number 17: What do we need from the supermarket?

(A) We need a Chinese-English dictionary.

(B) We need milk and some bread.

(C) We need some flowers for the living room.

(D) We need to get four chairs and a table.

問題：我們需要從超級市場買哪些東西嗎？

選項：(A) 我們需要一本漢英字典。

(B) 我們需要牛奶和一些麵包。

(C) 我們需要替客廳買些花。

(D) 我們需要四把椅子和一張桌子。

提示：(1)「麵包」、「牛奶」屬不可數名詞，而用來修飾不可數名詞的修飾語有：a lot of、lots of、plenty of、some 等。

(2)few、a few、many、a number of，通常用來修飾可數名詞，而 little、a little、much、a deal of，則以修飾不可數名詞為主。

18. Question number 18: You haven't been very social recently.

(A) I want to buy a new computer.

(B) Dancing classes help improve your social life.

(C) I really need to talk to you now.

(D) I am too busy to have any spare time to socialize.

問題：你最近並不十分善交際。

選項：(A) 我想買部新電腦。

(B) 跳舞課程可以幫你促進社交生活。

(C) 我現在真的需要和你談談。

(D) 我忙到找不出時間交際。

提示："recently" 這個字，若譯成「剛剛」則須與過去簡單式連用；若譯成「最近」則和現在完成式連用。例：

I just talked to him recently.（剛剛）

I haven't seen him recently.（最近）

19. Question number 19: What do you mean you don't have my phone number?

(A) I put your number down in my notebook but I lost it.

(B) May I talk to John, please.

(C) I dial the number, but no one answered it.

(D) You dial a wrong number.

問題：你說你沒有我的電話號碼是什麼意思？

選項：(A) 我把你的電話號碼寫在筆記本上，但我的筆記本丟了。

(B) 我可以和約翰說話嗎？

(C) 我打了這個號碼，但沒人接聽。

(D) 你打錯電話號碼了。

20. Question number 20: How about getting together sometime?

(A) Anyway, time is running out.

(B) I dislike talking this matter here.

(C) OK, how about this weekend?

(D) I prefer cats to dogs.

問題：找個時間聚一聚如何？

選項：(A) 不管怎樣，沒有時間了。

(B) 我不喜歡在此討論這件事。

(C) 好呀！要不要這個周末？

(D) 和狗比起來，我比較喜歡貓。

提示："sometime" 的用法有很多種，下列四個字要特別留意：

I sometimes go to school by bus.（有時）

I will see you sometime in the future.（某時）

I will need some time to think about it.（一些時間）

I have seen her some times on the street in the past ten days.（幾次）

21. Question number 21: There was a Mr. Smith who called while you were out.

(A) Did you take any message?

(B) Who is that handsome guy?

(C) Did he say when?

(D) Too bad, you should have called him.

問題：當你外出時，有位史密斯先生打電話給你。

選項：(A) 你有幫我留話嗎？

(B) 那位帥氣傢伙是誰啊？

(C) 他有說何時嗎？

(D) 真糟糕，你應該打給他的。

提示：若兩動作都發生在過去時間，需時較長者用過去進行式，需時較短者用過去簡單式。試比較：

I was eating dinner when he called me last night.

While I was eating my dinner last night, he called me.

22. Question number 22: When will you be available since I have some questions for you?

(A) I am about to tell you what happened.

(B) It takes me a lot of time to answer the question.

(C) How about this Wednesday?

(D) I will go out wth Sue today.

問題：你何時有空，我有些問題想問你？

選項：(A) 我要告訴你發生了什麼事。

(B) 回答這個問題花了我很多時間。

(C) 這個星期三如何？

(D) 我今天會跟蘇出去。

23. Question number 23: Would you mind turning down the radio?

(A) No, on second thought, I'll buy a new one.

(B) It's making a lot of noise.

(C) Sure. No problem.

(D) I need to turn on the radio now.

問題：你介意把收音機的音量調小聲些嗎？

選項：(A) 不，我改變主意了，我要買一台新的。

(B) 它發出了很多噪音。

(C) 好啊。沒問題。

(D) 我現在需要打開收音機

24. Question number 24: Are you going to the Book Fair next week?

(A) What for? I am not going anywhere.

(B) Really? When did it happen?

(C) I don't like books anyway.

(D) Yes, I was going to ask you about that myself.

問題：你下周要去書展嗎？

選項：(A) 幹嘛？我哪裡都不去。

(B) 真的？何時發生的？

(C) 反正我不喜歡書。

(D) 是的，我正想問你這件事。

25. Question number 25: What do you think about the movie?

(A) It's not as good as I think.

(B) It has so many big stars.

(C) It's a musical, isn't it?

(D) It has beautiful scenery.

問題：你覺得這部電影如何？

選項：(A) 它並沒有想像中的好。

(B) 電影裡有好多大明星。

(C) 它是部音樂片，不是嗎。

(D) 電影裡有漂亮的景色。

提示：四個答案似乎都說得過去，但題目是問看法而不是描述電影，所以 A 是最合適的答案。

26. Question number 26: Can I help you with something?

(A) I am just going to check out

(B) Well, I am looking for a birthday present.

(C) I will pack this present before his birthday.

(D) I am just leaving.

問題：我能幫你忙嗎？

選項：(A) 我正要去結帳

(B) 嗯，我想找件生日禮物。

(C) 在他生日之前我會包裝這個禮物

(D) 我剛要離開。

27. Question number 27: Where can I find the cough medicine?

(A) The second shelf to your right.

(B) You can got the prescription filled here.

(C) You need to to take the cough medicine right now.

(D) Why don't you try the new medicine?

問題：咳嗽藥在哪裡？

選項：(A) 你右邊的第二個架子上。

(B) 你可以在此拿到處方。

(C) 你需要馬上服用咳嗽藥。

(D) 何不試試新的藥？

28. Question number 28: We'd like to change to another room if you have one.

(A) You have to check out at noon.

(B) We close at eleven o'clock.

(C) May I know what's the trouble?

(D) The manager is off today.

問題：如果你還有其他房間的話，我們想換一間。

選項：(A) 你必須在中午前退房。

(B) 我們十一點關門。

(C) 我可以知道出了什麼事嗎？

(D) 經理今天休假。

29. Question number 29: Where do you think you are going?

(A) To my room if that's OK with you.

(B) I don't think so.

(C) I'm going to take a shower first.

(D) To the park.

問題：你以為你要去哪？

選項：(A) 到我房間，如果你沒意見的話。

(B) 我不這麼認為。

(C) 我要先去洗個澡。

(D) 去公園。

提示：本題不該視為一般的問句，所以也不能依照字面的意思選答案，而說者在說的時候往往有另一層意思。

(1)一般問句

"Where are you going?"

（你要去那裡？）

"I am going to the park."

（我要去公園。）

(2)特殊情境（此問句本身的語氣不同於一般問句）

"Where do you think you are going?"

你要去那裡？（說者想表達的是：你自以為自己是誰呀！）

"To my room if you don't mind."

你不介意的話，去我自己的房間（其實

是：你又算老幾？還想管我！）

30. Question number 30: Are you with me in this matter?

(A) Sorry, I can't. I have an exam tomorrow.

(B) I am always on your side!

(C) As a matter of fact, I don't like it.

(D) I receive high salary. I can't complain.

問題：在這件事上你和我立場一致嗎？

選項：(A) 抱歉，我不行，我明天有考試。

(B) 我永遠站在你這邊。

(C) 事實上，我不喜歡它。

(D) 我的薪水很高，沒什麼好抱怨的了！

第三部份：簡短對話

31. Question number 31:

W: Would you turn on the TV? There's a program I want to watch.

M: What channel is it on?

W: I think it's on Channel 24.

M: You mean the Movie Channel, right?

Question: What program do you think the woman wants to watch?

(A) It will probably be a movie.

(B) It will probably be a TV cooking show.

(C) It will probably be a football game.

(D) It will probably be a variety show.

女：你能打開電視嗎？有個節目我想看。

男：那個頻道？

女：我想是第二十四頻道吧。

男：電影頻道，對吧？

問題：你覺得這女子想看何種節目？

選項：(A) 可能是電影。

(B) 可能是烹飪節目。

(C) 可能是美式足球比賽。

(D) 可能是綜藝節目。

32. Question number 32:

M: Look who's here!

W: Mr. Smith! What a small world!

M: I am really glad to see you again.

W: It's been almost ten years since we last met in 1998.

Question: How long is it that the man and the woman haven't seen each other?

(A) Since 1989.

(B) About ten years.

(C) About two years.

(D) About twenty meters.

男：看看是誰在這裡！

女：史密斯先生！這個世界真小！

男：我真的很高興再見到你。

女：自從 1998 年見到你現在都快十年了。

問題：這對男女有多久沒見面了？

選項：(A) 從 1989 年以來。

(B) 快十年。

(C) 快兩年。

(D) 快二十公尺。

33. Question number 33:

W: Do you know who that American is, David?

M: The one talking to the principal over there?

W: Yes, that's him.

M: He is an exchange scholar from the States.

Question: What is the American?

(A) He is a teacher.

(B) He is a writer.

(C) He is a painter.

(D) He is a musician.

女：你知道哪美國人是誰嗎，大衛？

男：那個正在和校長說話的人嗎？

女：是的，就是他。

男：他是從美國來的交換學者。

問題：這位男子是做什麼的？

選項：(A) 他是位老師。

(B) 他是位作家。

(C) 他是位畫家。

(D) 他是位音樂家。

34. Question number 34:

M: What's the easiest way to get to the airport?

W: I would say by taxi.

M: But that would cost me a bundle, right?

W: But that also saves you the trouble.

Question: What are they talking about?

(A) Taking taxi to the airport is the cheapest way.

(B) Taking taxi to the airport is the easiest way.

(C) Taking taxi to the airport is the most expensive way.

(D) Taking taxi to the airport is the quickest way.

男：到機場最容易的方法為何？

女：搭計程車。

男：但那會花我一大筆錢，對吧？

女：可是那樣也替你省下不少麻煩。

問題：他們在討論什麼？

選項：(A) 搭計程車到機場是最便宜的方法。

(B) 搭計程車到機場是最容易的方法。

(C) 搭計程車到機場是最昂貴的方法。

(D) 搭計程車到機場是最快的方法。

35. Question number 35:

W: I'd like to get some souvenirs but I have a tight budget. Where would you recommend?

M: There's a shopping center in a suburb, and you could find some street vendors around some tourist attractions as well.

W: What's the difference?

M: You probably get a better quality in the mall but you will definitely get a better deal from those venders.

Question: Where do you think the woman will end up going?

(A) The shopping center.

(B) The street vendors.

(C) The convenient store.

(D) The toys store.

女：我想買些紀念品，但我的預算有限。你會推薦我去哪？

男：在郊區有間購物中心，同時你可以在觀光景點附近找到一些小販。

女：兩者的差別在哪？

男：在購物中心你能買到品質較好的東西，但從路邊小販那，你一定會找到更便宜的價錢。

問題：你覺得這女子最後會到哪裡去？

選項：(A) 購物中心。

(B) 路邊小販。

(C) 便利商店。

(D) 玩具店

36. Question number 36:

M: Cheer up! It's only a game.

W: But my team lost their chance of getting into the championship series.

M: They can always come back next year.

W: But it will be a disappointment for all the fans this year!

Question: What are they talking about?

(A) A social gathering.

(B) A TV game show.

(C) An academic competition.

(D) A sport event.

男：振作點！只不過是一場比賽。

女：但我的隊伍喪失了進軍冠軍賽的機會。

男：他們明年還是可以重新來過啊。

女：但今年對所有球迷而言會是失望的一年。

問題：他們在說些麼？

選項：(A) 一種社交聚會。

(B) 一種電視遊戲比賽。

(C) 一種學術競賽。

(D) 一種運動比賽。

37. Question number 37:

W: Jack, could you finish it up for me?

M: What's the rush?

W: Something just came up and I have to take care of that immediately.

M: Leave it to me.

Question: Will the man help the woman out?

(A) Yes, but with some conditions.

(B) No, he will not.

(C) Yes, he will.

(D) No, he has his own problem to worry about.

女：傑克，你幫我將這事收個尾嗎？

男：你在急什麼？

女：有件事臨時發生而我必須馬上處理它。

男：交給我吧。

問題：這男子會幫這女子嗎？

選項：(A) 會的，但他有些條件。

(B) 不，他不會。

(C) 會的，他會。

(D) 不，他自己也有問題要處理。

38. Question number 38:

M: It's the garbage collection today.

W: Did you sort out all the trash?

M: No, I didn't. I thought trash is trash.

W: Haven't you heard of reuse, reduce, and recycle?

Question: What is the woman trying to persuade the man to do?

(A) To put the papers in the trash.

(B) To take out the garbage when he goes.

(C) To separate everything according to their weight.

(D) To separate garbage according to their categories.

男：今天是收集垃圾的日子。

女：你把垃圾分類了嗎？

男：我沒有。垃圾就是垃圾。

女：你從沒聽過「反覆使用，減少使用，和回收」嗎？

問題：這位女生試著說服男生什麼？

選項：(A) 把報紙丟到垃圾桶裡。

(B) 在他離開時帶走垃圾。

(C) 將所有東西依重量分開。

(D) 將垃圾依類別分開。

39. Question number 39:

W: I just dropped by to say goodbye.

M: What time are you leaving?

W: I am going to try to catch the ten o'clock flight.

M: Take care and give my best regards to your parents.

Question: When is the woman leaving?

(A) She will try to leave at ten.

(B) She is leaving at ten thirty.

(C) She won't leave for a while.

(D) She is not leaving at all.

女：我只是來跟你說聲再見。

男：你何時離開？

女：我要試著趕上十點的那班飛機。

男：好好照顧自己並代我向你父母致意。

問題：這女子何時離開？

選項：(A) 她試著趕上十點的班機。

(B) 她將在十點半離開。

(C) 她暫時將不會離開。

(D) 她根本不會離開。

40. Question number 40:

M: Jean, my bus is leaving. I'd better hit the road.

W: Have a nice trip. Drop a line after you

get there.

M: I sure will. Thank you. So long.

W: Goodbye and take care.

Question: What does the woman ask the man to do?

(A) To call her when he arrives.

(B) To send her an e-mail when he gets there.

(C) To write her when he gets to the destination.

(D) To buy her a thread when he sees the special one.

男：珍，我的車要離開了。我得上路了。

女：一路順風。到了之後記得寫信給我。

男：我一定會。謝謝你。再見。

女：再會，好好照顧自己。

問題：這女子要求這男子做什麼？

選項：(A) 到了之後打電話給她。

(B) 到達目的地後寄電子郵件給她。

(C) 到達目的地後寫信給她。

(D) 看到特別的線幫她買一條。

41. Question number 41:

W: How did you do in your test?

M: I blew it!

W: How did that happen? I thought you were well prepared.

M: I thought that, too. But I guessed I wasn't that ready.

Question: What happened to the man?

(A) He was well prepared.

(B) He wasn't quite well prepared as he thought he would be.

(C) He wasn't sure.

(D) He just didn't study at all.

女：你試考的如何？

男：我弄砸了！

女：怎麼會這樣？我以為你已經準備好了。

男：我也是這麼認為。但我猜我還是準備的不夠好。

問題：這男子到底發生了什麼事？

選項：(A) 他做好萬全準備。

(B) 他並不如自己想的準備妥當。

(C) 他也不知道。

(D) 他根本沒讀書。

42. Question number 42:

M: What do you think about Mary's going steady with John?

W: I think they are made for each other.

M: Does that mean you believe something nice will come out of their relationship?

W: I surely hope so!

Question: What does the woman believe?

(A) That Mary and John might get married someday.

(B) That Mary and John will split up soon.

(C) That Mary and John remains to be good friends forever.

(D) That Mary and John will have bad days in the future.

男：你對瑪莉和約翰穩定交往有什麼看法？

女：我覺得他們是天生一對。

男：那是不是說你相信他們會有好結果？

女：我衷心期盼！

問題：你覺得這女子相信什麼？

選項：(A) 瑪莉和約翰未來會結婚。

(B) 瑪莉和約翰將來會分手。

(C) 瑪莉和約翰將永遠是好朋友。

(D) 瑪莉和約翰未來日子會很苦。

43. Question number 43:

W: Hello, San Min Bookstore.

M: Hi, I want to know how to get to your bookstore.

W: OK, you may take MRT to Zhongshan Junior High School Station. It's just next to the station.

M: Well, it's very convenient for me to get there. Thank you. I'll get there later.

Question: What is the woman trying to tell the man?

(A) To take bus to the bookstore.

(B) He dials a wrong number.

(C) To take MRT to the bookstore.

(D) The bookstore opens at nine o'clock.

女：您好，三民書局。

男：您好，我想知道要怎麼去你們的書店？

女：好的，您可以搭捷運到中山國中站。書店就在旁邊。

男：好的，要到那裡對我來說非常方便。謝謝你，我待會就過去。

問題：這位女士試著想告訴男士什麼？

選項：(A) 搭公車到書局。

(B) 他打錯電話。

(C) 搭捷運到書局。

(D) 書局早上九點開門。

44. Question number 44:

M: Blood is thicker than water, you know.

W: But, sometimes, it is too close for comfort.

M: Still, one can't live without one's family.

W: If only the family can learn when to let go.

Question: What are these two talking about?

(A) They are having different views on family.

(B) They are having a pleasant discussion on family.

(C) They are having a conversation on how important the family is.

(D) They are having a quarrel about family.

男：你知道嗎，血濃於水？

女：但有時人會因沒有距離而感到不自在。

男：儘管如此，人還是無法脫離家庭而生活。

女：但願家人知道何時該放手就好了。

問題：這兩人在討論什麼？

選項：(A) 他們對家庭有不同的看法。

(B) 他們對家庭進行了愉快的討論。

(C) 他們正在討論家庭的重要性。

(D) 他們對家庭起了爭吵。

45. Question number 45:

W: Do I need to have an appointment before I can see the doctor?

M: It would be better for you to do so.

W: But the pain is killing me!

M: Only if you had brushed your teeth more often!

Question: What kind of doctor is the woman going to see?

(A) A physician.

(B) A surgeon.

(C) A psychiatrist.

(D) A dentist.

女：我一定要先預約才能去看這位醫生嗎？

男：這樣做對你而言會比較好。

女：但我真的痛死了！

男：如果你多刷牙就沒事了。

問題：這女子要去看哪種醫生？

選項：(A) 內科醫生。

(B) 外科醫生。

(C) 心理諮商師。

(D) 牙醫。

第一部份：看圖辨義

1. For question number 1, please look at picture A.

   Question number 1: Which of the following vegetables is not shown in the picture?

   (A) A tomato.

   (B) A carrot.

   (C) A potato.

   (D) A cabbage.

   問題：下列哪種蔬菜沒有在圖片裡？

   選項：(A) 番茄。

   　　　(B) 紅蘿蔔。

   　　　(C) 馬鈴薯。

   　　　(D) 包心菜。

2. For question number 2, please look at picture B.

   Question number 2: What are these people doing?

   (A) They are competing in a sport event.

   (B) They are listening to a speech.

   (C) They are discussing a problem.

   (D) They are having a beach party.

   問題：這些人正在做什麼？

   選項：(A) 他們正在參加一項運動競賽。

   　　　(B) 他們正在聽一場演講。

   　　　(C) 他們正在討論一個問題。

   　　　(D) 他們正在舉行一個海灘派對。

3. For question number 3, please look at picture C.

   Question number 3: What is this man doing?

   (A) He is building brick walls.

   (B) He is cooking rice.

   (C) He is designing a poster.

   (D) He is repairing wooden furniture.

   問題：這男子在做什麼？

   選項：(A) 他在鋪磚牆。

   　　　(B) 他在煮飯。

   　　　(C) 他在設計海報。

   　　　(D) 他在修補木頭家具。

4. For question number 4, please look at picture D.

   Question number 4: What's wrong with the man?

   (A) He is having a headache.

   (B) He is having a stomachache.

   (C) He is having a toothache.

   (D) He is coughing.

   問題：這個男人怎麼了？

   選項：(A) 他頭痛。

   　　　(B) 他胃痛。

   　　　(C) 他牙痛。

   　　　(D) 他在咳嗽。

5. For question number 5, please look at picture E.

   Question number 5: It's raining hard outside, and the wind is blowing wild. What does John need most if he has to go out?

   (A) A shopping bag.

   (B) A pair of sunglasses.

   (C) An umbrella.

   (D) A sweater.

   題目：外面下著大雨刮著強風，如果約翰要出門，他最需要的是什麼？

   選項：(A) 一個購物袋。

   　　　(B) 一副太陽眼鏡。

   　　　(C) 一把雨傘。

   　　　(D) 一件毛衣。

6. For question number 6, please look at picture F.

   Question number 6: Where do you think this scene is most likely to happen?

   (A) In a hospital.

(B) At a hotel.

(C) In a restaurant.

(D) In a movie theater.

問題：下列情景最可發生在何處？

選項：(A) 醫院。

　　　(B) 旅館。

　　　(C) 餐廳。

　　　(D) 電影院。

7. For question number 7, please look at picture G.

Question number 7: What is the woman doing?

(A) She is asking for the check.

(B) She is serving a customer.

(C) She is ordering a meal.

(D) She is looking at the menu.

問題：這女人在做什麼？

選項：(A) 她在要帳單。

　　　(B) 她在服務一個客人。

　　　(C) 她在點餐。

　　　(D) 她在看菜單。

8. For question number 8, please look at picture H.

Question number 8: How long does it take for John to go to Taichung by bus?

(A) 30 minutes.

(B) 5 hours.

(C) 2 hours.

(D) 4 hours.

問題：約翰搭巴士到台中需要多少時間？

選項：(A) 三十分鐘。

　　　(B) 五個小時。

　　　(C) 兩個小時。

　　　(D) 四個小時。

9. For question number 9, please look at picture I.

Question number 9: What is the customer complaining about?

(A) The soup is cold.

(B) There's a fly in the soup.

(C) The fish has gone bad.

(D) He was served a wrong meal.

問題：這男人在抱怨什麼？

選項：(A) 湯冷掉了。

　　　(B) 湯裡有一隻蒼蠅。

　　　(C) 魚壞掉了。

　　　(D) 餐點送錯了。

10. For question number 10, please look at picture J.

Question number 10: What is the occasion in this picture?

(A) A wedding reception.

(B) A funeral service.

(C) A graduation ceremony.

(D) A farewell party.

問題：圖中為何種場合？

選項：(A) 結婚宴會。

　　　(B) 葬禮儀式。

　　　(C) 畢業典禮。

　　　(D) 餞行宴會。

11. For questions number 11 and 12, please look at picture K.

Question number 11: Look at the price tag of each item. How much are they?

(A) The milk powder costs two thousand dollars.

(B) The strawberry yogurt costs thirty-three dollars.

(C) The cheese costs three hundred and forty-eight dollars.

(D) The ham costs three hundred and seventeen dollars.

問題：請看每件物品的價格標籤。他們的價格為何？

選項：(A) 奶粉價值兩千元。

(B) 草莓優格價值三十三元。

(C) 起司價值三百四十八元。

(D) 火腿價值三百一十七元。

提示："cost" 通常與金錢連用，而 "take" 則以時間為主：

It cost me one hundred dollars for this book.

It took me three hours to finish my homework.

"spend" 若和 "in" 連用則加 Ving；若與 "on" 連用則加 N：

He enjoys spending time in playing video games.

He enjoys spending money on books.

12. Question number 12: Compare the price. Which of the following statements matches the picture?

(A) The cheese is more expensive than the ham.

(B) The yogurt is the cheapest.

(C) The milk powder is much cheaper than the ham.

(D) They are of the same price.

問題：試比較價錢。以下敘述何者與圖片相符？

選項：(A) 起司比火腿貴。

(B) 優格是最便宜的。

(C) 奶粉比火腿便宜。

(D) 他們價錢相同。

提示：嚴格來說，"expensive（昂貴）" 的相反詞應為 "inexpensive"；"cheap" 有時帶著「價廉物不美」、「小氣」的涵意。

This store is famous for its inexpensive products.

Jack is really cheap; he took his girl to the McDonald's for her birthday dinner.

13. For question number 13, please look at picture L.

Question number 13: What kind of TV program is it in the picture?

(A) A cooking show.

(B) A singing contest.

(C) A game show.

(D) A talk show.

問題：下列圖示為何種電視節目？

選項：(A) 烹飪節目。

(B) 歌唱比賽。

(C) 競賽節目。

(D) 訪談節目。

14. For question number 14, please look at picture M.

Question number 14: What is the man doing?

(A) He is washing the floor.

(B) He is picking up the trash.

(C) He is washing the dishes.

(D) He is sweeping the floor.

問題：這男子正在做什麼？

選項：(A) 他在洗地板。

(B) 他在撿垃圾。

(C) 他在洗碗。

(D) 他在掃地。

15. For question number 15, please look at picture N.

Question number 15: What is this poster for?

(A) It's a poster for a drama club.

(B) It's a poster for a dance performance.

(C) It's a poster for a movie.

(D) It's a poster for a political campaign.

問題：這是張何種性質的海報？

選項：(A) 戲劇社的海報。

(B) 舞蹈表演的海報。

(C) 電影海報。

(D) 政治競選的海報。

第二部份：問答

16. Question number 16: Mary loves sweets; she has a sweet tooth.

(A) She just went to a dentist last week.

(B) Yeah, she loves to eat anything that is sweet.

(C) Actually, she is a very sweet girl.

(D) As I know, she is really into making candies.

問題：瑪莉喜歡甜食，她長著一顆「甜齒」。

選項：(A) 她上禮拜才剛去看牙醫。

(B) 是啊，她喜歡任何甜的東西。

(C) 事實上，她是個甜美的女孩。

(D) 就我所知，她非常喜歡做糖果。

17. Question number 17: Want to split the last piece of cake with me?

(A) Honestly, I don't have enough money.

(B) Sorry, I didn't order this.

(C) I'd like something sweet.

(D) I can't. I am too full.

問題：要跟我平分這最後一塊蛋糕嗎？

選項：(A) 老實說，我錢帶不夠。

(B) 抱歉，我沒有點這個。

(C) 我想要些甜的東西。

(D) 不行。我太飽了。

18. Question number 18: It's going to be a big decision to work abroad!

(A) That's why I need some time to sleep on it.

(B) That's why I need to take a shower.

(C) That's why I need to take a nap.

(D) That's why I need to come back to Taiwan.

問題：到國外工作將是個大決定！

選項：(A) 這也是為什麼我需要時間想一下。

(B) 這也是為什麼我要洗個澡。

(C) 這也是為什麼我要小睡一下。

(D) 這也是為什麼我要回到台灣。

提示："to sleep on it"「睡一下，明天再說」是典型的口語表達；意思是把問題如枕頭般放在頭底下，先睡一覺，明天再解決！因此，當某件事需要花時間想一想時，這句話就變成常見的表達。

19. Question number 19: Can you understand what the lecturer was trying to say?

(A) That's beyond my comprehension.

(B) That's out of the question.

(C) That's absolutely ridiculous.

(D) That's terrific!

問題：你能了解講者試著告訴我們的嗎？

選項：(A) 那已經超出我能理解的範圍。

(B) 那是不可能的。

(C) 那實在太荒謬了。

(D) 那真是太棒了！

20. Question number 20: Excuse me, that's not what I ordered.

(A) How would you like your steak?

(B) That would be USD155.

(C) Anything else?

(D) I am sorry. I will have it replaced at once.

問題：不好意思，這不是我點的東西。

選項：(A) 你的牛排要幾分熟呢？

(B) 總共是一百五十五元。

(C) 你還要點些什麼呢？。

(D) 很抱歉。我馬上把它換掉。

21. Question number 21: Would you mind if I smoke?

(A) Smoking is not allowed here.

(B) Mind your own business!

(C) No. Please go outside.

(D) Yes. I'll smoke a cigarette too.

問題：你介意我在此抽煙嗎？

選項：(A) 此處禁菸。

(B) 管好你自己！

(C) 不介意。請你去外面。

(D) 介意。我也要抽一根菸。

22. Question number 22: Do you have any particular hobbies?

(A) I get up early in summer.

(B) I collect stamps.

(C) I want a cup of black coffee.

(D) I love to wear anything red.

問題：你有任何特殊的嗜好嗎？

選項：(A) 我夏天很早起床。

(B) 我收集郵票。

(C) 我要一杯黑咖啡。

(D) 我喜歡穿任何紅色的衣物。

23. Question number 23: I stayed up late last night watching a baseball game on TV.

(A) No wonder you got black and blue all over you.

(B) No wonder you have everything in black and white.

(C) I can see blood in your eyes.

(D) No wonder you got red eyes.

問題：我昨晚因看電視上的棒球比賽而熬夜。

選項：(A) 難怪你青一塊紫一塊。

(B) 難怪你所有的事都白紙黑字的記下來。

(C) 我可以在你眼中見到殺意。

(D) 難怪你滿眼血絲。

24. Question number 24: He passed away peacefully last week.

(A) At least he didn't suffer.

(B) I am glad to hear that.

(C) I wonder when he'll be back.

(D) He died from a serious car accident.

問題：他上星期平靜的過世了。

(A) 至少他沒受苦。

(B) 我很高興聽到這個消息。

(C) 我不知道他什麼時候回來。

(D) 他死於一場嚴重的車禍。

提示：(1)「死」在英文中是個禁忌 "taboo"，所以西方人會用其他詞彙如："kick the bucket"、"gone to meet his maker" 來替代。

(2) "die of" 通常指因「疾病、飢餓」而死去，"die from" 則指因「外傷、偶然」原因而死。

25. Question number 25: The gasoline is running out.

(A) A man is running after me.

(B) We need a mechanic to fix the car.

(C) We need to stop at the nearest gas station.

(D) Get off the car right away!

問題：汽油快要用完了。

(A) 有個男人在後面追趕我。

(B) 我們需要一位技工來修車。

(C) 我們必須在最近的加油站停下來。

(D) 現在馬上下車！

26. Question number 26: How about playing basketball?

(A) Yeah, why not? Baseball is my favorite sport.

(B) Sure. I'll beat you this time.

(C) It's my treat this time.

(D) How about eating Chinese food?

問題：要不要打籃球？

選項：(A) 好啊！有何不可？棒球是我最愛的運動。

(B) 好啊。這次我要贏你。

(C) 這次我請客。

(D) 吃中國菜如何？

27. Question number 27: Which would you prefer, coffee or tea?

(A) The tea is too hot.

(B) What do you have for dessert?

(C) Check, please.

(D) Coffee is fine.

問題：你想要選哪個，咖啡或茶？

選項：(A) 這茶太燙了。

　　　(B) 你們有什麼甜點？

　　　(C) 麻煩你，我要買單。

　　　(D) 我要咖啡。

28. Question number 28: Where are you heading?

(A) I am having a headache.

(B) To the cafeteria. Want to come along?

(C) The ship headed north.

(D) Turn right at the corner and you will see it.

問題：你往那裡去？

選項：(A) 我現在頭好痛。

　　　(B) 去自助餐廳。要一起來嗎？

　　　(C) 這艘船開往北方。

　　　(D) 在轉角右轉你就會看到它了。

29. Question number 29: What happened to you? You look so sad.

(A) My pet cat died last night.

(B) I won the first prize in a speech contest.

(C) Don't worry, be happy.

(D) I'm sorry for your loss.

問題：發生了什麼事？你看來很沮喪。

選項：(A) 我的寵物貓昨晚死了。

　　　(B) 我得了演講比賽第一名。

　　　(C) 不要擔心，快樂一點。

　　　(D) 我很遺憾你的損失。

30. Question number 30: I have a terrible headache. It's killing me!

(A) Let me check for your foot.

(B) You want some pain killers?

(C) I'll call the eye doctor.

(D) Killing yourself is not the only solution.

問題：我的頭很痛，快痛死我了！

選項：(A) 讓我檢查一下你的腳。

　　　(B) 要些止痛藥嗎？

　　　(C) 我會打電話給眼科醫生。

　　　(D) 自殺不是唯一的解決辦法。

第三部份：簡短對話

31. Question number 31:

M: Guess who I ran into this afternoon?

W: Who?

M: Jack. We haven't seen him for a long time.

W: I wonder how he is doing.

Question: What's the conversation about?

(A) An old friend whom they haven't seen for a while.

(B) An old friend whom they have kept constant contact with.

(C) An old friend whom they don't like.

(D) An old friend whom they tried so hard to forget.

男：猜猜今天下午我遇到誰？

女：誰？

男：傑克。我們有好長一段時間沒見到他了。

女：真想知道他近況如何。

問題：這段對話和什麼有關？

選項：(A) 一位他們很久沒見到的老朋友。

　　　(B) 一位他們經常保持聯繫的老朋友。

　　　(C) 一位他們不喜歡的老朋友。

　　　(D) 一位他們努力想忘掉的老朋友。

提示：(1)現在完成式表示剛完成的動作，或由過去某一點時間開始到現在才完成的動作，通常與下列副詞連用：just、yet、already、until now、up to now、recently、lately、for + 一段時間。例：I have just come back from school. Have you seen Tom recently?

　　　(2)若和副詞如 never、ever、once、twice、

several times、before、sometimes、often、seldom 連用時，則表示到目前為止的經驗：

I have never seen a tiger.

They have met each other before.

(3)若與時間或條件子句連用時，可用來代替未來完成式：

I shall call on him when I have finished writing my homework.

If you have done your work, you will get your reward.

32. Question number 32:

W: I don't feel like going anywhere in weather like this.

M: Come on! Today is the last day.

W: You can always rent a video later on.

M: But you will miss all the fun watching it on the big screen.

Question: What are they talking about?

(A) A movie.

(B) A live show.

(C) A game.

(D) A sale

女：我不想在這種天氣出去。

男：拜託！今天是最後一天。

女：你總是可以在以後租錄影帶來看。

男：但你就錯過看大銀幕的樂趣了。

問題：他們在談論什麼？

選項：(A) 電影。

(B) 現場演出。

(C) 比賽。

(D) 大拍賣。

33. Question number 33:

M: The argument went on for hours as neither side would give in.

W: Anything was reached when you left?

M: Yes, they decided to have another meeting to talk about it more.

W: That can't be called as a conclusion, can it?

Question: How would you describe the first meeting?

(A) It's a win-win situation.

(B) It's a no-win situation.

(C) It's a win-loss situation.

(D) It's a loss-loss situation.

男：因為任何一邊都不願意讓步，這個辯論持續了好幾個小時。

女：在你離開時，沒有得到任何結論嗎？

男：有，他們決定召開另外一次會議討論這個問題。

女：這不算是個結論，對吧？

問題：你會如何形容第一個會議？

選項：(A) 這是雙贏的情形。

(B) 這是沒有勝算的情形。

(C) 這是有贏有輸的情形。

(D) 這是雙輸的情形。

34. Question number 34:

W: Jack failed in the exam again.

M: That's too bad. The exam meant so much to him.

W: I know. I wish there was a way I can help him.

M: At least we have to give him credit for trying.

Question: What conclusion can we draw from this conversation?

(A) They are going to give Jack a credit card.

(B) They recognized Jack's efforts in trying to pass the exam.

(C) They felt sorry for Jack since he would never pass the exam.

(D) They will offer after-school lessons for Jack.

女：傑克考試又不及格了。

男：真糟糕。這考試對他而言可是意義重大。

女：我知道。真希望我能有幫助他的方法。

男：至少我們要對他為考試而做的努力給予肯定。

問題：我們可以從這段對話中做出什麼結論？

選項：(A) 他們要給傑克一張信用卡。

(B) 他們肯定傑克為通過考試所做的努力。

(C) 他們對傑克無法通過考試而覺得遺憾。

(D) 他們將提供傑克課後課程。

提示："fail in + N（失敗，失利）"、"fail to + V（未能）"：

John failed in biology last semester.

John failed to show up last night.

35. Question number 35:

M: Wow! That dress sure looks nice on you.

W: Well, thank you. I am glad you like it.

M: Is it very expensive?

W: I got it at a bargain price.

Question: Is the dress really expensive?

(A) No, the woman got it on sale.

(B) Yes, the woman got it at the original price.

(C) Yes, the woman got it at a very high price.

(D) No, the woman paid nothing for the dress.

男：哇！這件洋裝穿在你身上可真漂亮。

女：謝謝你。很高興你喜歡它。

男：它很貴嗎？

女：我是用特價買的。

問題：這件洋裝真的很貴嗎？

選項：(A) 不是，因為這女子是以特價買的。

(B) 是的，因為這女子是以原價買的。

(C) 是的，因為這女子是以非常高的價錢

買的。

(D) 不是，因為這女子是免費得到的。

36. Question number 36:

W: I'd like to return this book and have my money back.

M: What seems to be the problem?

W: No problem at all. It's just that I forgot I already had one at home.

M: In that case, do you have the receipt with you?

Question: What does the woman need to do if she wants to have her money back?

(A) She needs to sign his name on the receipt.

(B) She needs to show the receipt of perchasing the book.

(C) She needs to show both his credit card the the receipt.

(D) She needs to use another credit card to pay the book.

女：我想退還這本書並把錢拿回來。

男：有什麼問題嗎？

女：沒問題。只不過我忘了家裡已經有一本了。

男：這樣的話，你有帶購買的收據嗎。

問題：如果這個女子想要把錢拿回來，她需要做什麼？

選項：(A) 她需要在收據上簽名。

(B) 她需要出示買書的收據。

(C) 她需要出示信用卡跟購買收據。

(D) 她需要用另一張信用卡來付書錢。

37. Question number 37:

M: Want to have dinner with me tonight, Mary?

W: No, I can't. I ran out of money.

M: That's OK. It will be my treat.

W: Then, how about buying me dinner at a five-star restaurant?

Question: Why did Mary turn down the invitation in the first place?

(A) She wanted to save money.

(B) She didn't have any money.

(C) She had little money left.

(D) She didn't want to have dinner with the man.

男：瑪莉，今晚和我一起吃晚餐如何？

女：不行。我的錢花光了。

男：沒關係。我請客。

女：那麼，請我到五星級餐廳吃晚餐如何？

問題：瑪莉為何一開始時拒絕邀請？

選項：(A) 她想要省錢。

　　　(B) 她沒有錢。

　　　(C) 她剩下一點點錢。

　　　(D) 她不想跟這個男子出去。

38. Question number 38:

W: John, what a surprise!

M: I was in the neighborhood, so I decided to drop by to see you.

W: Come in. We have a lot to talk about.

M: Thank you. So, how's everything been going?

Question: Which of the following statements is correct?

(A) John called first before he showed up at the woman's door.

(B) John showed up at the door without telling the woman in advance.

(C) The woman knew that John was going to visit her.

(D) The woman was surprised to see John because she was not ready to see him.

女：約翰，真令人意外！

男：我剛好在附近，所以臨時決定來看看你。

女：請進。我們有好多事要聊。

男：謝謝。那麼，你近況如何？

問題：下列敘述何者正確？

選項：(A) 約翰出現在女子的門前有先打電話。

　　　(B) 約翰沒先事先告訴女子就出現在門口。

　　　(C) 這女子知道約翰要來拜訪她。

　　　(D) 這女子看到約翰很驚訝，因為她還沒準備好要見他。

39. Question number 39:

M: How do you feel being a full-time mother?

W: Being with my children is wonderful. However, I still want to make some money to support my family.

M: What about a part-time job? You don't have to spend much time on work and you can earn extra money.

W: That's a good idea!

Question: What kind of job are they talking about?

(A) A part-time job.

(B) A difficult job.

(C) A highly-paid job.

(D) A temporary job.

男：作為一個全職媽媽，你有什麼感覺？

女：跟我的孩子們在一起很棒。可是，我還是想要賺點錢養家。

男：兼差工作如何呢?你不需要花太多時間在工作上，還可以賺點外快。

女：這主意不錯！

問題：他們所說的是那種工作？

選項：(A) 兼差工作。

　　　(B) 困難的工作。

　　　(C) 高薪的工作。

　　　(D) 暫時的工作。

40. Question number 40:

W: John, I can't answer for your behavior anymore.

M: But why?

W: You will have to learn to grow up and be responsible for yourself.

M: I thought you are supposed to be here and help me all the time.

Question: Between whom is this conversation likely to happen?

(A) A waitress and a customer.

(B) A hostess and a guest.

(C) A mother and a son.

(D) A daughter and a father.

女：約翰，我不能再為你的行為負責了。

男：為什麼？

女：你一定要學會長大並對自己負責。

男：我以為你應該總是在我旁邊幫我。

問題：這段對話最可能發生在誰之間？

選項：(A) 女服務生跟顧客之間。

　　　(B) 女主人跟客人之間。

　　　(C) 母子之間。

　　　(D) 父女之間。

41. Question number 41:

M: How's it going with your preparation for the final exam?

W: I am getting there. By the way, what about the present you promised me if I make progress?

M: I would worry about the exam first if I were you.

W: But you promised me!

M: I'll keep my promise if you keep yours.

Question: What is the man trying to say?

(A) If the woman receives good grades, she will have the present she deserves.

(B) Whether the woman receives good grades or not, she will get the present.

(C) The man doesn't want to keep his promise.

(D) The woman won't get any present whether she receives good grades or not.

男：你期末考準備的如何？

女：漸入佳境。對了，你答應我如果我考好就給我的禮物呢？

男：如果我是你的話，我會先擔心考試。

女：但你答應我的！

男：如果你守信用我就會守信用。

問題：這男人想說什麼？

選項：(A) 如果女子得到好成績，她將會得到她應得的禮物。

　　　(B) 不論這女子成績好壞，她都會得到禮物。

　　　(C) 這男子不想要守信用。

　　　(D) 不論這女子成績好壞，她都不會得到任何禮物。

42. Question number 42:

W: Can I help the next in line, please?

M: I want a cheeseburger, French fries, and a diet coke.

W: Burger with everything on it?

M: Yes, except onion.

Question: What does the man not want to have on his burger?

(A) A tomato.

(B) Cheese.

(C) Onion.

(D) Diet Coke.

女：下一個。

男：我要一個起司漢堡，薯條，和低卡可樂。

女：漢堡上什麼佐料都要加嗎？

男：對，除了洋蔥。

問題：這男子不要在漢堡上加什麼？

選項：(A) 番茄。

　　　(B) 起士。

　　　(C) 洋蔥。

　　　(D) 低卡可樂。

提示：“except” 或 “besides” 都有「除了…之外」的意思；但前者是「排除…之外」，而後者則是「除了…之外，還有…」：

We all failed in the test except Mary and Jane.

（除了瑪莉跟珍之外，其他人都考試不及格。）

Besides Mary and Jane, the rest of us didn't pass the exam

（除了瑪莉跟珍之外，其他人也都沒有通過考試。）

43. Question number 43:

M: I am not going to finish my report on time!

W: But, how are you going to tell Mr. Smith?

M: How about telling him my computer broke down?

W: I thought honesty is always the best policy!

Question: What was the man trying to do?

(A) He was thinking of telling Mr. Smith the truth.

(B) He was thinking of some excuses for not handing in his report on time.

(C) He was thinking of having the woman help him out.

(D) He was thinking of having the woman go to see Mr. Smith with him.

男：我無法準時完成我的報告！

女：那你要如何向史密斯先生說？

男：告訴他我的電腦故障了，如何？

女：我覺得誠實永遠是上策！

問題：這男子想要做什麼？

選項：(A) 他想要跟史密斯先生說實話。

(B) 他在思考無法準時交報告的藉口。

(C) 他想要這女子幫助他。

(D) 他想要這女子和他一起去見史密斯先生。

44. Question number 44:

W: I am sorry, but all those policies are new to me.

M: Don't worry. It takes time for people to fit in.

W: But I don't mean to cause anyone trouble, not to mention losing the job.

M: No one gets fired on the first day at work.

Question: Where is this conversation most likely to happen?

(A) In a classroom.

(B) In a concert hall.

(C) In an online shop.

(D) In an office.

女：我很抱歉，但那些政策對我而言都是陌生的。

男：別擔心。人都需要時間適應。

女：但我不是有意造成任何的麻煩，更別說失去我的工作。

男：沒有人在上班的第一天就被炒魷魚的。

問題：這段對話最可能發生在何處？

選項：(A) 教室。

(B) 音樂廳。

(C) 網路商店。

(D) 辦公室。

45. Question number 45:

W: Can I talk to the person in charge?

M: How may I help you?

W: I want to complain about the guest next door.

M: What happened?

W: They were making funny noises all night long last night.

Question: Where is the conversation likely

to take place?

(A) In a hotel.

(B) In a restaurant.

(C) In a department store.

(D) In a hospital.

女：我能和負責人說話嗎？

男：有什麼我能幫忙的？

女：我要對隔壁房間的客人提出抱怨。

男：發生了什麼事？

女：他們昨晚一整夜都在製造些奇怪的聲音。

問題：這對話最可能發生在何處？

選項：(A) 旅館。

　　　(B) 餐廳。

　　　(C) 百貨公司。

　　　(D) 醫院。

Test ❼

第一部分：看圖辨義

1. For question number 1, please look at picture A.

Question number 1: Which of the following statement can best describe the man in the picture?

(A) He feels very hot.

(B) He is very angry.

(C) He burns something on his head.

(D) He sets fire on his head.

問題：下列何者敘述最能描述途中男人的狀況？

選項：(A) 他覺得很熱。

(B) 他很生氣。

(C) 他在頭上燒東西。

(D) 他在頭上縱火。

2. For question number 2, please look at picture B.

Question number 2: What are these people doing?

(A) They are doing exercises.

(B) They are watching TV.

(C) They are playing baseball.

(D) They are reading novels.

問題：這些人正在做什麼？

選項：(A) 他們在做運動。

(B) 他們在看電視。

(C) 他們在打棒球。

(D) 他們在讀小說。

3. For questions number 3 and 4, please look at picture C.

Question number 3: What do you think the man is trying to find out?

(A) When the scale will be ringing.

(B) How much he weighs.

(C) What the scale looks like.

(D) Where the scale comes from.

問題：你認為這男子想要知道什麼？

選項：(A) 磅秤什麼時候會響起鈴聲。

(B) 自己的體重。

(C) 磅秤看起來像什麼樣子。

(D) 磅秤是從哪裡來的。

4. Question number 4: Why does the man look so worried?

(A) He has failed in the exam.

(B) He has won the lottery.

(C) He has broken up with his girlfriend.

(D) He is overweight.

問題：這男子為何看起來如此憂心？

選項：(A) 他沒通過考試。

(B) 他中了樂透。

(C) 他剛剛與女朋友分手。

(D) 他體重過重。

5. For question number 5, please look at picture D.

Question number 5: How will you describe the picture?

(A) The weather is warm and sunny.

(B) Most people enjoy the nice weather.

(C) It is freezing cold outside.

(D) There is a lot of rain in summer.

問題：你會如何描述這張圖？

選項：(A) 天氣很溫暖，陽光普照。

(B) 大部分的人都在享受這種好天氣。

(C) 外面冷得要命。

(D) 夏天雨很多。

6. For question number 6, please look at picture E.

Question number 6: What's ten divided by two?

(A) Five

(B) Twenty

(C) Twelve

(D) Eight

問題：十除二時，答案是

選項：(A) 五。

　　　(B) 二十。

　　　(C) 十二。

　　　(D) 八。

提示：「加」：plus、add、and：

　　　　Two and two are four.

　　　　Two added to two makes four.

　　　　= Add two and two and you get four.

　　　「減」：subtract、minus、deduct：

　　　　You get three if you subtract two from five.

　　　「乘」：multiply、time：

　　　　Five multiplied by three is fifteen.

　　　「除」：divide：

　　　　Six divided by two is/gives/equals three.

7. For question number 7, please look at picture F.

Question number 7: What is the woman doing?

(A) She is sorting out the garbage.

(B) She is looking for some food.

(C) She is feeding her cat.

(D) She is burning the waste.

問題：圖中女子在做什麼？

選項：(A) 她在做垃圾分類。

　　　(B) 她在找尋食物。

　　　(C) 她在餵貓。

　　　(D) 她在燒垃圾。

8. For question number 8, please look at picture G.

Question number 8: What causes the man and the woman to have an argument?

(A) A traffic accident.

(B) They don't have money.

(C) Neither of them wants to do the dishes.

(D) The man wants to go out.

問題：造成這對男女爭執的原因為何？

選項：(A) 交通事故。

　　　(B) 他們沒有錢。

　　　(C) 兩個人都不想洗碗。

　　　(D) 男子想要出去。

9. For question number 9, please look at picture H.

Question number 9: What's the matter with the boy?

(A) He is having a fever.

(B) He is drinking soda.

(C) He is doing his homework.

(D) He is listening to music.

問題：這男孩怎麼了？

選項：(A) 他正在發燒。

　　　(B) 他在喝汽水。

　　　(C) 他在做功課。

　　　(D) 他在聽音樂。

10. For question number 10, please look at picture I.

Question number 10: It's 2 p.m. now. When will the next "King Kong" movie be showing?

(A) 11: 30

(B) 1:00

(C) 3:30

(D) 7:30

問題：現在是下午兩點鐘。下一場「金剛」電影什麼時候會放映？

選項：(A) 十一點半。

　　　(B) 一點。

　　　(C) 三點半。

　　　(D) 七點半。

11. For question number 11, please look at

picture J.

Question number 11: What might these people be doing now?

(A) They are surfing the Internet.

(B) They are seeing movies.

(C) They are hiking in the mountains.

(D) They are doing scientific tests.

問題：這些人在做什麼？

選項：(A) 他們在上網。

(B) 他們在看電影。

(C) 他們在山裡面健行。

(D) 他們在作科學試驗。

提示："surf" 及 "browse" 這兩個字因電腦的普及，已在英語字彙中據一席之地；前者泛指在網際網路中往來，而後者則有瀏覽的意思。

12. For question number 12, please look at picture K.

Question number 12: What are they doing?

(A) They are playing American football.

(B) They are playing soccer.

(C) They are playing computer games.

(D) They are playing chess.

問題：他們在做什麼？

選項：(A) 他們在玩美式足球。

(B) 他們在踢足球。

(C) 他們在玩電腦遊戲。

(D) 他們在下棋。

13. For question number 13, please look at picture L.

Question number 13: Which of the following statements is true?

(A) The boy is helping his mother look after his sister.

(B) The boy is helping his mother clean the room.

(C) The boy is helping his mother paint the wall.

(D) The boy is helping his mother do the dishes.

問題：下列敘述何者為真？

選項：(A) 男孩在幫她母親照顧妹妹。

(B) 男孩在幫她母親打掃房間。

(C) 男孩在幫她母親粉刷牆壁。

(D) 男孩在幫他母親洗碗盤。

14. For question number 14, please look at picture M.

Question number 14: What can you do with these things?

(A) Putting the jigsaw puzzle together.

(B) Sending a fax.

(C) Doing the cut and paste.

(D) Taking notes.

問題：你可以用這些東西來做什麼？

選項：(A) 拼圖。

(B) 傳真。

(C) 剪貼。

(D) 做筆記。

15. For question number 15, please look at picture N.

Question number 15: Where is the baby?

(A) In a cradle.

(B) On the bed.

(C) On its mother's back.

(D) In a car.

問題：嬰兒在那裡？

選項：(A) 搖籃裡。

(B) 床上。

(C) 媽媽的背上。

(D) 車子裡。

第二部份：問答

16. Question number 16: Do you want to know what happened next?

(A) I am all ears.

(B) I am all eyes.

(C) I am all hearts.

(D) I am all by myself.

問題：你想知道接著發生了什麼嗎？

選項：(A) 我洗耳恭聽。

(B) 我正在看。

(C) 我很專心。

(D) 我獨自一人。

17. Question number 17: Look! The cat by the window is looking at us.

(A) Don't do that again!

(B) That's my grandmother.

(C) Hey! What are you doing now?

(D) Wow! It's so beautiful!

問題：看！窗邊的那隻貓正在看著我們。

選項：(A) 別再這樣做了！

(B) 那是我的祖母。

(C) 嘿！你在做什麼？

(D) 哇！牠好漂亮！

18. Question number 18: Men are stronger than women physically.

(A) I'm not that strong.

(B) I don't agree with that.

(C) Have you been there before?

(D) That would be fine.

問題：男人生理上較女人來的強壯。

選項：(A) 我沒有那麼壯。

(B) 這點我不同意。

(C) 你有去過嗎？

(D) 那樣很好。

19. Question number 19: Who is the person in charge of the operation here?

(A) We are all students.

(B) I'm a doctor, and she's a nurse.

(C) Yes, sir.

(D) That's Mr. Smith. He is the manager here.

問題：誰是這裡的作業負責人？

選項：(A) 我們都是學生。

(B) 我是醫生，她是護士。

(C) 是的。

(D) 是史密斯先生。他是這裡的經理。

20. Question number 20: Our proposal was approved.

(A) I am really glad about the news.

(B) That's a bad idea.

(C) I hope thing will turn out to be better.

(D) Let's pray everything will be just fine.

問題：我們的企劃通過了。

選項：(A) 我對這消息感到很高興。

(B) 這是個壞主意。

(C) 我希望事情會變的更好。

(D) 讓我們祈禱事情會一帆風順。

21. Question number 21: Would you like some milk?

(A) Why do you like ice cream?

(B) Yes, sure. Coke is my favorite.

(C) No, I only drink milk.

(D) No, thanks. Just water will be fine.

問題：要不要來一些牛奶？

選項：(A) 你為什麼喜歡冰淇淋？

(B) 當然好啊。我最喜歡可樂了。

(C) 不，我只喝牛奶。

(D) 不，謝了。只要水就好。

22. Question number 22: Look at John. He's been sitting there all morning.

(A) What's wrong with him?

(B) He must be falling in love with the chair.

(C) He is looking for his cat everywhere.

(D) Maybe we should call him Jerry.

問題：你看約翰。他一整個早上都坐在那邊。

選項：(A) 他怎麼了？

(B) 他一定是愛上那張椅子了。

(C) 他正到處找他的貓。

(D) 也許我們該叫他傑瑞。

23. Question number 23: Excuse me. I think you're sitting in my seat.

(A) Are you sure? My name is Jason.

(B) Really? I'll sit here all night.

(C) Oops, I'm sorry.

(D) You can't do this to me!

問題：抱歉，我想你佔了我的座位。

選項：(A) 你確定嗎？我叫傑森耶。

(B) 真的嗎？我要在這邊坐上整晚。

(C) 噢，我很抱歉。

(D) 你不能這樣對我！

24. Question number 24: Who usually makes the decisions in your family?

(A) Let's find out.

(B) My father does.

(C) You're the boss.

(D) We usually eat out.

問題：在你家中做決定的人通常是誰？

選項：(A) 讓我們找出來。

(B) 是我爸爸。

(C) 聽你的。

(D) 我們通常都外出用餐。

25. Question number 25: I heard Mike is a good basketball player.

(A) That's why he is so crazy.

(B) That's why he is so clever.

(C) That's why he is so popular.

(D) That's why he is so weak.

問題：我聽說麥可是個優秀的籃球員。

選項：(A) 這也是他為何如此瘋狂的原因。

(B) 這也是他為何如此聰明的原因。

(C) 這也是他為何如此受歡迎的原因。

(D) 這也是他為何如此虛弱的原因。

26. Question number 26: Oh, no. We're running out of gas.

(A) Finally!

(B) Great, now I can watch TV.

(C) It's just about time to have dinner.

(D) Is there any gas station nearby?

問題：噢，慘了。沒油了。

選項：(A) 終於！

(B) 太好了，我現在可以看電視了。

(C) 剛好該吃晚餐了。

(D) 附近有加油站嗎？

27. Question number 27: When will the breakfast be served?

(A) Do you have the time?

(B) How many people in your party?

(C) From 6:30 to 10:00 a.m.

(D) It's a Japanese restaurant.

問題：早餐何時開始？

選項：(A) 你知道現在幾點嗎？

(B) 你們總共有幾人？

(C) 早上六點半到十點。

(D) 那是日式餐廳。

28. Question number 28: Can I pay with my credit card?

(A) Sure, we only take cash.

(B) No problem.

(C) That's a question!

(D) It's your own business.

問題：我可以用信用卡付帳嗎？

選項：(A) 當然可以，我們只收現金。

(B) 沒問題。

(C) 那是一個問題。

(D) 那是你家的事。

29. Question number 29: Why did you spend so much money on the business trip?

(A) I can give you the list of all expenses.

(B) Yes, it's very cheap.

(C) Seven hundred and thirty thousand dollars..

(D) That's a good trip.

問題：為什麼你這次出差花了這麼多錢？

選項：(A) 我可以列出開銷細項給你。

(B) 是的，很便宜。

(C) 七十三萬。

(D) 那是個很棒的旅行。

30. Question number 30: Does anyone know anything about first aid? Someone has fainted.

(A) Stay away from me! I am afraid of blood.

(B) I know CPR. Let me try.

(C) Who is that guy?

(D) Watch out! The car is coming!

問題：誰知道如何急救？有人昏倒了。

選項：(A) 離我遠一點！我怕血。

(B) 我會心肺復甦術。讓我試試看。

(C) 那傢伙是誰？

(D) 小心！車子要來了！

第三部份：簡短對話

31. Question number 31:

M: The election is coming up soon.

W: I watched the debate between two candidates on TV the other day.

M: How did you feel about their performance?

W: To tell you the truth, I didn't like either of them.

Question: What's the woman's opinion about the candidates' performance in the debate?

(A) She liked neither of them

(B) She liked both of them.

(C) She liked one more than the other.

(D) She needed more time to think about it.

男：選舉就快要到了。

女：我那天還在電視上看兩位候選人的辯論。

男：你覺得他們的表現如何？

女：老實說，我兩個都不喜歡。

問題：這女子對候選人在辯論中的表現的看法如何？

選項：(A) 她兩個都不喜歡。

(B) 她兩個都喜歡。

(C) 她喜歡其中一個勝過另一個。

(D) 她需要更多時間來想想。

32. Question number 32:

W: My computer is not working well.

M: Why don't you ask Sam? It's his line of work.

W: Really? I didn't know that.

M: He is definitely a pro in computers.

Question: Why does Sam know a lot about computers?

(A) He speaks French and Germany.

(B) He is a professor.

(C) It is his line of work.

(D) He knows almost everything.

女：我的電腦運作不太順暢。

男：你何不問山姆？電腦是他的本行。

女：是嗎？我不知道呢。

男：他絕對是個電腦高手。

問題：為什麼山姆懂很多關於電腦的事？

選項：(A) 他會說法文和德文。

(B) 他是一個教授。

(C) 那是他的工作領域。

(D) 他幾乎什麼事情都知道。

33. Question number 33:

W: Hello?

M: Hi, I'm Rick Chen, a sales manager from Taipei Bank. Can you give me a few minutes to talk about our new product of financial planning?

W: I'm afraid not. I have work to do.

M: OK, maybe some other time. Thank you, ma'am.

Question: Is the woman willing to talk with

the man right now?

(A) Yes, because she has plenty of time.

(B) Yes, and she is very interested.

(C) No, and she is not home.

(D) No, and she makes an excuse.

女：喂？

男：嗨，我是瑞克‧陳，台北銀行的業務經理。
你能給我幾分鐘的時間，讓我談一下我們最
新理財規劃商品嗎？

女：恐怕不行。我有工作要做。

男：好吧，也許別的時間可以再談。謝謝你，女
士。

問題：這女生現在願意跟這位男生談話嗎？

選項：(A) 是的，因為她時間很多。

(B) 是的，而且她非常有興趣。

(C) 不，而且她不在家。

(D) 不，而且她編了一個理由。

34. Question number 34:

W: You know you are always late for our
date.

M: I promise I'll come on time this time.

W: This is not the first time I've heard you
say so.

M: Trust me one more time.

Question: What's the man's record of being
on time?

(A) Terrible.

(B) Excellent.

(C) So-so.

(D) Perfect.

女：你知道嗎，我們的約會你總是遲到。

男：我答應你這次一定準時。

女：這不是我第一次聽你如此說。

男：再相信我一次。

問題：這男子過去準時的紀錄如何？

選項：(A) 很糟糕。

(B) 非常好。

(C) 平平。

(D) 完美。

35. Question number 35:

M: I think I'll have pizza tonight.

W: As for me, I'll go for fried chicken.

M: I thought you didn't like greasy food.

W: I don't, but I think just one meal doesn't
really matter.

Question: What is true about the woman?

(A) She doesn't like pizza.

(B) She always have fried chicken for dinner.

(C) She decides to have pizza.

(D) She usually eats healthy and light.

男：我想我今晚要吃披薩。

女：那我則要炸雞。

男：我以為你不喜歡油膩的食物。

女：我是不喜歡，但我想就一餐而已應該沒關
係。

問題：關於這女生哪個敘述是正確的？

選項：(A) 她不喜歡吃披薩。

(B) 她晚餐總是吃炸雞。

(C) 她決定要吃披薩。

(D) 她通常吃得很健康且清淡。

36. Question number 36:

W: Who is that guy? The young man in
white T-shirt.

M: Oh, that's my brother. He just graduated
from high school.

W: I think I met him before. Is his name
Mark?

M: No, his name is Jonathan.

Question: Which is true about the man's
brother?

(A) He is a high school student.

(B) His name is Mark.

(C) His name is Jonathan.

(D) He is wearing a black T-shirt.

女：那傢伙是誰？穿著白色汗衫的年輕人。

男：喔，那是我弟弟。他剛從高中畢業。

女：我想我曾經見過他。他的名字是馬克嗎？

男：不，他的名字是強納森。

問題：關於這男子的弟弟，哪一項是正確的？

選項：(A) 他是高中生。

(B) 他的名字是馬克。

(C) 他的名字是強納森。

(D) 他穿著黑色汗衫。

37. Question number 37:

M: How was the film?

W: It was too long and very boring.

M: Really? I thought it received some good reviews.

W: Personally, the movie is not my cup of tea.

Question: How does the woman feel about the movie?

(A) It was a good news.

(B) It was long and boring.

(C) It was great.

(D) It was talking about tea.

男：電影如何？

女：它太長了，而且非常無聊。

男：真的嗎？我以為它得到不少好評。

女：就我個人而言，這不是我喜歡的電影。

問題：這女子對這部電影的看法如何？

選項：(A) 它是個好消息。

(B) 它又長又無聊。

(C) 它很棒。

(D) 它是在講有關茶的故事。

38. Question number 38:

W: The bill for the dinner is NT$1,600, tax included.

M: Divided by four of us, that comes to four hundred each.

W: Yes. By the way, where is Jim?

M: He always disappears when it comes to paying the bill.

W: Well, he can run, but he can never hide.

Question: What kind of man is Jim?

(A) He is happy to pay his share when going out with his friends.

(B) He is always trying to get away from paying the bill.

(C) He loves to play hide-and-seek.

(D) He is always short of money.

女：晚餐的帳單含稅總共是新台幣一千六百元。

男：我們四個人均分，每個人四百元。

女：沒錯。對了，吉姆去哪了？

男：只要一到付帳的時候，他總會消失。

女：哼，他躲得了一時，可躲不了一世。

問題：吉姆是怎樣的一個人？

選項：(A) 他和朋友出去時，總是樂意付他的那份帳單。

(B) 他總是會逃避付帳。

(C) 他喜歡玩捉迷藏。

(D) 他總是缺錢。

39. Question number 39:

M: What are you talking about? Don't leave me out.

W: Since Jean is leaving for the States next week, we are thinking of a secret farewell party for her.

M: That's a great idea.

W: Now that you know it, why don't you come and join us to plan the party?

Question: What are they planning?

(A) A talk with Jean.

(B) A performance for Jean.

(C) A trip to the United States with Jean.

(D) A secret farewell party for Jean.

男：你們在說什麼啊？別把我排除在外。

女：因為珍下周就要去美國了，我們在想替她舉辦個秘密的歡送派對。

男：這是個好主意。

女：既然你知道了，何不來跟我們一起計畫這個派對？

問題：他們在計畫什麼？

選項：(A) 一段和珍的對話。

(B) 一場獻給珍的表演。

(C) 一次和珍一起去美國的旅行。

(D) 一個給珍的秘密歡送派對。

提示：英文中有些字詞的意思是固定不變的，例如外來語 "status quo（現狀）"、"now that（既然）"、"only if（若…）"、"if only（若…就好了）"。

40. Question number 40:

W: Hi, good evening. What can I do for you?

M: Is there any seat available for the seven o'clock show?

W: Yes, sure. We still have some good seats.

M: Great. There are two of us, please.

W: OK. That will be $580.

Question: Where does this conversation take place?

(A) A convenience store.

(B) A ticket office.

(C) A police station.

(D) A bus stop.

女：嗨，晚安。我有什麼能為您服務的嗎？

男：七點鐘的表演還有位子嗎？

女：當然。還有一些好位子。

男：太好了。麻煩你，兩位。

女：沒問題。這樣一共是五百八十元。

問題：這段對話發生在什麼地方？

選項：(A) 便利商店。

(B) 售票處。

(C) 派出所。

(D) 公車站。

41. Question number 41:

M: Mary, I lost the photos Amy lent me. What would you do if you were me?

W: Wow, that's bad. She loves those pictures so much that she'll hate you for a long time.

M: I know. I really need your advice.

W: Well, you can first buy her a dinner and a nice gift, and then break the news to her.

Question: Why is the man afraid of Amy?

(A) Because she is very rude.

(B) Because she is a very serious person.

(C) Because she doesn't like the man.

(D) Because she loves those photos very much.

男：瑪莉，我把艾美借給我的照片弄丟了。如果你是我，你會怎麼辦？

女：哇，那遭透了。她是如此地喜愛那些照片，她會因此而恨你很久。

男：我知道。我非常需要你的建議。

女：嗯，你可以先請她吃晚飯，送她一個好禮物，然後再告訴她這個壞消息。

問題：這男子為何怕艾美？

選項：(A) 因為她很粗魯。

(B) 因為她是個很正經的人。

(C) 因為她不喜歡這個男子。

(D) 因為她非常喜愛那些照片。

提示："advice" 是不可數名詞，就如同 "audience"、"information" 等，若要當可數名詞用，一定要加計數單位，例如 a piece of advice/information。

42. Question number 42:

W: I'm thinking of changing my job.

M: Why? I thought you were quite happy with your current one.

W: That's a long story. In short, I don't like my new boss at all.

M: Maybe you should talk to her first.

Question: What's the man's advice to the woman?

(A) To change her boss right away.

(B) To get a new job immediately.

(C) To talk to her boss before making any decision.

(D) To keep quiet.

女：我在考慮換個工作。

男：為什麼？我以為你對目前的工作非常滿意。

女：說來話長。簡而言之，我一點都不喜歡我的新上司。

男：也許你該先和她談談。

問題：這男子給這女子的建議是什麼？

選項：(A) 立刻換掉她的上司。

(B) 馬上找個新工作。

(C) 在做任何決定前先和她的上司談談。

(D) 保持緘默。

43. Question number 43:

M: Hey! There is a scratch on the table. Didn't you notice that?

W: Yes, I did. That's why it's so cheap.

M: What are you going to do about it?

W: A nice tablecloth will do the trick.

Question: Does the woman know about the scratch on the table?

(A) Yes, and she is going to return the table.

(B) Yes, and she has already figured out what she's going to be about it.

(C) No, but she thinks it's pretty cheap.

(D) No, but she'll buy the table and the tablecloth as well.

男：嘿！桌上有一條刮痕。你注意到了嗎？

女：有。這也是為什麼它如此便宜。

男：你要如何解決這問題？

女：一條漂亮的桌布就能發揮功效。

問題：這女子知道桌子上有刮痕的事嗎？

選項：(A) 知道，而且她將退還這張桌子。

(B) 知道，而且她已想出對策。

(C) 不知道，但她認為很便宜。

(D) 不知道，但她將連桌子和桌布一起買。

44. Question number 44:

W: Sir, you can't smoke here. Please put out your cigarette right now.

M: Why? I don't see any sign to tell me this.

W: Here, read the sign.

M: All right. I'll leave.

Question: What might the sign read?

(A) No right turn.

(B) Beware children.

(C) No smoking.

(D) Stop and go.

女：先生，你不可以在這裡吸菸。請立刻把你的菸熄掉。

男：為什麼？我沒有看到任何告示提醒我這件事。

女：這裡，請讀這個告示。

男：好吧。我離開就是。

問題：這告示可能寫些什麼？

選項：(A) 禁止右轉。

(B) 注意兒童。

(C) 禁止吸菸。

(D) 停車再開。

45. Question number 45:

W: Welcome to Sanmin Hotel.

M: We would like to have a twin room.

W: Do you have a reservation, sir?

M: No, we don't.

W: Then, the only one available will be a double room.

Question: Will the situation be different if the man had made a reservation in advance?

(A) No, because he can't afford that.

(B) No, because the hotel doesn't have any twin room.

(C) Yes, because the hotel can make some necessary arrangements.

(D) Yes, because he can move the bed by himself.

女：歡迎來到三民飯店。

男：我們想要一間有兩張單人床的房間。

女：先生，請問你們有預約嗎？

男：沒有。

女：那麼，現有唯一有的是只有一張雙人床的房間。

問題：如果這男子先預約的話，情形會不同嗎？

選項：(A) 不會，因為他負擔不起。

　　　(B) 不會，因為這旅館根本沒有兩張雙人床的房間。

　　　(C) 是的，因為旅館可以做一些必要的安排。

　　　(D) 是的，因為他可以自己移動床。

Test 8

第一部份：看圖辨義

1. For question number 1, please look at picture A.

   Question number 1: What is this picture about?

   (A) A wedding ceremony.

   (B) A reception.

   (C) A graduation ceremony.

   (D) A bachelor's party.

   問題：這張圖片與何種場合有關？

   選項：(A) 結婚典禮。

   　　　(B) 接待酒會。

   　　　(C) 畢業典禮。

   　　　(D) 新郎告別單身派對。

   提示：依西洋習俗，新郎在婚前告別單身而有的狂野聚會稱為 "Bachelor's Party" ；新娘則接受姊妹淘的祝福及結婚禮物，俗稱 "Shower."

2. For question number 2, please look at picture B.

   Question number 2: Who is the person in the picture?

   (A) A teacher.

   (B) An administrator.

   (C) A priest.

   (D) A candidate for an election.

   問題：圖中的人是誰？

   選項：(A) 教師。

   　　　(B) 行政人員。

   　　　(C) 牧師。

   　　　(D) 選舉候選人。

3. For question number 3, please look at picture C.

   Question number 3: What kind of movie is this?

   (A) A war movie.

   (B) A scary movie.

   (C) A comedy movie.

   (D) A cartoon movie.

   問題：這是何種電影？

   選項：(A) 戰爭電影。

   　　　(B) 恐怖電影。

   　　　(C) 喜劇電影。

   　　　(D) 卡通電影。

   提示：「卡通」若用正式的話語則為 "animation"、"animated movie"。

4. For question number 4, please look at picture D.

   Question number 4: How does the woman feel about her meal?

   (A) She thinks it's tasty.

   (B) She thinks it's terrible.

   (C) She is going to take out the food.

   (D) She is not going to pay her bill.

   問題：這女子對這頓飯的感覺如何？

   選項：(A) 她覺得它很美味。

   　　　(B) 她覺得它很糟。

   　　　(C) 她要外帶這些食物。

   　　　(D) 她不會付帳單。

5. For question number 5, please look at picture E.

   Question number 5: While the woman is pushing the cart, what is the man doing?

   (A) He is carrying the baggage with his hands.

   (B) He is throwing the baggage with his hands.

   (C) He is packing the baggage with his hands.

   (D) He is storing the baggage with his hands.

   問題：當女子推行李車時，男子在做什麼？

   選項：(A) 他用雙手拿行李。

   　　　(B) 他用雙手丟行李。

(C) 他用雙手收拾行李。

(D) 他用雙手收藏行李。

6. For question number 6, please look at picture F.

Question number 6: What is the mosquito trying to do?

(A) It is saying good night to John.

(B) It is saying a prayer with John.

(C) It is trying to bite John's nose.

(D) It is trying to sing a song for John.

問題：這隻蚊子想要做什麼？

選項：(A) 它在對約翰說晚安。

(B) 它在和約翰一起禱告。

(C) 它想在約翰鼻子上咬一口。

(D) 它試著唱首歌給約翰聽。

7. For question number 7, please look at picture G.

Question number 7: What is twenty-five percent of one hundred?

(A) Twenty-five

(B) Fifty

(C) Seventy-five

(D) Two hundred

問題：一百的百分之二十五是多少？

選項：(A) 二十五。

(B) 五十。

(C) 七十五。

(D) 兩百。

提示：在以「時間」、「距離」、「價值」、「重量」等為主詞時，其後動詞取單數形動詞：

Six months is too short to learn English.（一段的時間）

Ten miles is too long for me to walk.

Ten dollars is not enough for a pen.

但也有例外情形。例如下列例子：

Six months have passed since I saw her last.（所有的時間）

Millions of dollars were spent on that project.

8. For question number 8, please look at picture H.

Question number 8: Why is the man giving the present to the woman?

(A) Because he loves to eat cake.

(B) Because it's her birthday.

(C) Because she is very sick.

(D) Because the weather is fine.

問題：為何這男子送禮物給這女子？

選項：(A) 因為他喜歡吃蛋糕。

(B) 因為這是她的生日。

(C) 因為她病得很重。

(D) 因為天氣很好。

9. For question number 9, please look at picture I.

Question number 9: How would you describe the closet?

(A) It's neat and tidy.

(B) It's in perfect order.

(C) It's amazingly clean.

(D) It's really messy.

問題：你會如何形容這衣櫥？

選項：(A) 整齊整潔。

(B) 井然有序。

(C) 不可思議的乾淨。

(D) 亂七八糟。

10. For question number 10, please look at picture J.

Question number 10: Where are these people?

(A) In a camp site.

(B) In a parking lot.

(C) At a hotel.

(D) At a gas station.

問題：這些人在哪裡？

選項：(A) 露營區。

　　　(B) 停車場。

　　　(C) 旅館。

　　　(D) 加油站。

11. For question number 11, please look at picture K.

Question number 11: Why was the woman angry at the boy?

(A) Because he was talking in class.

(B) Because he was late in handing in his homework.

(C) Because he fell asleep in class.

(D) Because he didn't show up for class last time.

問題：這女子為何對這男孩生氣？

選項：(A) 因他上課講話。

　　　(B) 因他遲交作業。

　　　(C) 因他在課堂中睡覺。

　　　(D) 因他上次沒來上課。

12. For question number 12, please look at picture L.

Question number 12: What does the woman have in her hand?

(A) A remote control.

(B) A glass of wine.

(C) A bunch of flowers.

(D) A book.

問題：這女子手中拿著什麼？

選項：(A) 遙控器。

　　　(B) 一杯酒。

　　　(C) 一束花。

　　　(D) 一本書。

13. For question number 13, please look at picture M.

Question number 13: What is the weather like?

(A) It's cool and dry.

(B) It's snowy.

(C) It's windy and raining heavily.

(D) It's sunny with scattered clouds.

問題：天氣如何？

選項：(A) 涼爽且乾燥。

　　　(B) 下雪。

　　　(C) 狂風暴雨。

　　　(D) 晴時多雲。

14. For question number 14, please look at picture N.

Question number 14: What are the couple doing?

(A) They are dancing to the music.

(B) They are talking about some secrets.

(C) They are having breakfast.

(D) They are fighting with each other.

問題：這對夫婦在做什麼？

選項：(A) 他們在隨著音樂起舞。

　　　(B) 他們在講秘密。

　　　(C) 他們正在吃早餐。

　　　(D) 他們正在打架。

15. For question number 15, please look at picture O.

Question number 15: What does the man do for a living?

(A) He is a singer.

(B) He is an artist.

(C) He is a police officer.

(D) He is an accountant.

問題：這男子是做什麼的？

選項：(A) 他是歌手。

　　　(B) 他是藝術家。

　　　(C) 他是警員。

　　　(D) 他是會計師。

第二部份：問答

16. Question number 16: I bought a new bicycle just now.

(A) I am sorry to hear that.

(B) Really? What brand is it?

(C) Really? How old is it?

(D) How about taking a taxi?

問題：我剛買了一部新腳踏車。

選項：(A) 我感到很遺憾。

　　　(B) 真的？哪個牌子？

　　　(C) 真的？它用多久了？

　　　(D) 搭計程車如何？

提示："just" 習慣和現在完成式連用；"just now" 則習與過去簡單式或現在進行式連用：

I have just come back from school.

（剛才）

I have reached home just now.

（方才、剛剛）

I am playing tennis just now.（此刻）

17. Question number 17: What do you think about the movie?

(A) It's one of my hobbies.

(B) It will begin at 7:30 p.m.

(C) It's on my desk. You can take it anytime.

(D) It's terrible! I can't believe we came all the way for that.

問題：你覺得電影如何？

選項：(A) 它是我的嗜好之一。

　　　(B) 它將在晚上七點半開始。

　　　(C) 它就在我桌上。你隨時可以拿走。

　　　(D) 爛透了！我真不敢相信我們大老遠跑來看這種電影。

18. Question number 18: What's your excuse for being late this time?

(A) No excuse. I won't let this happen again.

(B) This is the first time I came late.

(C) I know it's too early to have dinner.

(D) Wake me up if you have time.

問題：你這次遲到的理由又是什麼？

選項：(A) 沒有藉口。我下次一定不會讓這種事再發生。

　　　(B) 這是我第一次來這裡遲到。

　　　(C) 我知道現在吃晚餐還太早。

　　　(D) 如果你有時間的話，請叫醒我。

提示：本題作答時關鍵在於 "this time"，言下之意這絕不是第一次。所以答案 A 較為合宜。

19. Question number 19: Which do you like to have, chicken or beef?

(A) I'll have chocolate cake.

(B) I'll have a glass of wine.

(C) I'll have some ice cream.

(D) I'll have the beef.

問題：你要哪個，雞肉或牛肉？

選項：(A) 我要巧克力蛋糕。

　　　(B) 我要一杯酒。

　　　(C) 我要一些冰淇淋。

　　　(D) 我要牛肉。

提示：題目既然是要在兩件東西中選一樣，除非是兩者都不要，否則勢必要依所提供的選項作決定，非所提供的事物絕非正確的選擇。

20. Question number 20: Where are you going after Japan?

(A) I don't like Japan.

(B) I'll probably go to the library.

(C) I'll definitely go there.

(D) I'll probably go to Taiwan.

問題：去過日本之後你要去哪裡？

選項：(A) 我不喜歡日本。

　　　(B) 我可能會去圖書館。

　　　(C) 我一定會去那裡。

　　　(D) 我可能會去台灣。

提示：答案 B 和國家無關，所以不是正確的選擇。A 和 C 皆答非所問，也不能選。

21. Question number 21: I brought you some

desserts.

(A) That's very nice of you.

(B) You are so mean.

(C) What a nice shot!

(D) What are you trying to do?

問題：我帶些甜點來給你。

選項：(A) 你真是好心。

　　　(B) 你真卑鄙。

　　　(C) 這球投得漂亮！

　　　(D) 你想要做什麼？

22. Question number 22: He's the last man I want to work with.

(A) Great, I'll go find him.

(B) Who will help me with the work?

(C) I feel exactly the same.

(D) To work hard is necessary.

問題：我最不想和他一起工作。

選項：(A) 太好了，我去找他。

　　　(B) 誰可以幫我完成這個工作？

　　　(C) 我深有同感。

　　　(D) 努力工作是必要的。

23. Question number 23: You were keeping something from me, weren't you?

(A) No. I lied to you.

(B) Yes. But only because I didn't want you to get hurt.

(C) No. And I'll keep this for good.

(D) Yes. I found it in the backyard.

問題：你有事瞞我，不是嗎？

選項：(A) 不。我騙你。

　　　(B) 是的。但我是因為怕你受到傷害。

　　　(C) 不。而且我會一直保存這個。

　　　(D) 是的。我在後院找到的。

24. Question number 24: How do I get to Grand Central Station?

(A) You can find it everywhere.

(B) He is not my type of person.

(C) The visitor center is over there.

(D) Just turn left at the corner.

問題：我要如何到達中央車站？

選項：(A) 你在任何地方都可以找到。

　　　(B) 他不是我喜歡的類型。

　　　(C) 遊客中心在那邊。

　　　(D) 在街角處左轉即可。

25. Question number 25: How much money do you have?

(A) I could earn NTD 100 a month.

(B) Enough to pay the rent.

(C) I'm five feet and six inches tall.

(D) I don't need any cash.

問題：你有多少錢？

選項：(A) 我一個月賺一百塊美金。

　　　(B) 足夠應付這筆租金。

　　　(C) 我五呎六吋高。

　　　(D) 我不需要任何現金。

26. Question number 26: Are you into hip hop?

(A) No. I am a big fan of Jazz.

(B) Yes, I play video games all the time.

(C) Let's get into the action!

(D) Why don't you hit it hard?

問題：你喜歡嘻哈音樂嗎？

選項：(A) 不。我是爵士迷。

　　　(B) 是的。我總是在玩電動遊戲

　　　(C) 讓我們行動吧！

　　　(D) 你為什麼不盡力呢？

27. Question number 27: What are you doing now?

(A) I am working for my college degree.

(B) I can't tell you why.

(C) I am still a kid.

(D) I will try to get one.

問題：你現在正在做什麼？

選項：(A) 我正在攻讀大學學位。

　　　(B) 我不能告訴你為什麼。

(C) 我還是個孩子。

(D) 我會試著弄到一個。

28. Question number 28: I think she is a warm-hearted woman.

(A) Don't yell at me like that!

(B) Yeah, I saw her steal your money.

(C) She will lose this game.

(D) She is what you think she is.

問題：她是一位熱心親切的女子。

選項：(A) 別對我吼！

(B) 是的，我看見她偷你的錢。

(C) 她將會輸掉比賽。

(D) 她正如你所想像的一樣。

29. Question number 29: Chien-Ming Wang is pitching now.

(A) What's the count?

(B) Are you Mr. Wang?

(C) Where am I?

(D) Do you like peaches?

問題：王建民正在投球。

選項：(A) 球數為何？

(B) 你是王先生嗎？

(C) 這是什麼地方？

(D) 你喜歡桃子嗎？

30. Question number 30: Can you bring me some orange juice?

(A) That will be fine.

(B) I don't like orange juice.

(C) It's up to you.

(D) No problem.

問題：你能幫我帶一些柳橙汁嗎？

選項：(A) 這樣很好。

(B) 我不喜歡柳橙汁。

(C) 隨便你。

(D) 沒問題。

第三部份：簡短對話

31. Question number 31:

W: How do you like your new coat?

M: It's OK, but. what I really want is the latest video game.

W: Hey, don't go too far. It's my present for you.

M: I know, but a video game will be even better.

Question: Who are most probably having this conversation?

(A) A father and her daughter.

(B) A mother and her son.

(C) A boss and his employee.

(D) Two strangers.

女：你喜歡你的新外套嗎？

男：還好 ，不過我真正想要的是最新的電動遊戲。

女：嘿，別太過分了。這是我送給你的禮物。

男：我知道，不過如果是電動遊戲更好。

問題：誰最有可能進行這段對話？

選項：(A) 一對父女。

(B) 一對母子。

(C) 老闆和員工。

(D) 兩個陌生人。

32. Question number 32:

M: Frankly speaking, it's easy to be tricked by instant messages.

W: I know, but it is so convenient.

M: Even if it means someone might take advantage of you?

W: All things considered, yes.

Question: Do you think the woman will stop using instant messages?

(A) No, she will not stop using instant messages.

(B) No, and she will take advantage of others.

(C) Yes, and she will ask others to do the

same.

(D) Yes, unless she knows who is sending her messages.

男：老實說，用即時通很容易會被騙。

女：我知道，但它真的很方便。

男：哪怕是別人可能用它來佔你便宜？

女：考慮所有狀況後，我還是認為它很方便。

問題：你覺得這女子會停止使用即時通嗎？

選項：(A) 不，她不會停止使用即時通。

(B) 不，而且她會去佔其他人的便宜。

(C) 是，而且她會要求其他人也這樣做。

(D) 是，除非她知道誰傳訊息給她。

33. Question number 33:

W: How about some snacks while we are watching the movie?

M: That's a wonderful idea. What are you going to have?

W: I'll have a large Coke, popcorn, a chocolate bar, and a hot dog.

M: Don't you think that's a little bit too much? I thought we just had dinner.

Question: Do you think the man agrees with the woman's order?

(A) Yes, he thinks she is hungry.

(B) Yes, and he wants more.

(C) No, he thinks that she is having too much.

(D) No, he doesn't want her to have anything.

女：要不要在看電影時來點零食？

男：好主意。你要吃些什麼？

女：我要大杯可樂、爆米花、巧克力棒和熱狗。

男：你不覺得那樣有點多嗎？我以為我們才剛吃過晚飯。

問題：你認為這男子同意女子點的東西嗎？

選項：(A) 是，他覺得她餓了。

(B) 是，而且他還要點更多。

(C) 不，他覺得她吃太多了。

(D) 不，他不希望她吃任何東西。

34. Question number 34:

M: Are you feeling OK?

W: No, I am not. I got fed up with the guy living upstairs.

M: What about him?

W: He is always making some noises, day and night.

Question: Why is the woman not happy with her neighbor upstairs?

(A) Because her neighbor doesn't love her.

(B) Because her neighbor is always making noises.

(C) Because her neighbor keeps calling her.

(D) Because her neighbor is cheating on her.

男：你還好嗎？

女：不，我不好。我受夠了我樓上的鄰居。

男：他怎麼了？

女：他不斷在製造噪音，不管白天或晚上。

問題：為何這女子對她樓上鄰居不滿？

選項：(A) 因為她鄰居不愛她。

(B) 因為她鄰居總是製造噪音。

(C) 因為她鄰居一直打電話給她。

(D) 因為她鄰居欺騙她。

35. Question number 35:

W: I don't like my hair. I don't like my look. I don't like anything about me!

M: Look on the bright side. At least you are still alive.

W: With all those, I wish I were dead.

M: Come on! You are not that bad and you know it.

Question: What is the woman talking about?

(A) She wants to kill herself.

(B) She is complaining about herself.

(C) She thinks she is perfect.

(D) She is looking for a way to live.

女：我不喜歡我的髮型；我不喜歡我的長相；我不喜歡所有和我有關的事物。

男：往好處想，至少你還活著。

女：在這種情況下，我情願死掉。

男：別這樣！你並沒那麼糟糕，而且你自己也知道。

問題：這女子在談論什麼？

選項：(A) 她想要自殺。

　　　(B) 她在抱怨她自己。

　　　(C) 她覺得她是完美的。

　　　(D) 她在尋找活下去的方法。

36. Question number 36:

M: Who was the handsome young man you were talking to?

W: It's none of your business.

M: Please tell me!

W: All right. He is the man I am dating now.

Question: Who is that handsome young man?

(A) The woman's new boyfriend.

(B) The woman's father.

(C) The woman's teacher.

(D) The woman's younger brother.

男：和你說話的那個帥氣年輕人是誰？

女：不關你的事。

男：請告訴我！

女：好啦。他是我現正在約會的男子對象。

問題：那個帥氣的年輕人是誰？

選項：(A) 這女子的新男友。

　　　(B) 這女子的父親。

　　　(C) 這女子的老師。

　　　(D) 這女子的弟弟。

37. Question number 37:

W: If you are not watching it, please turn it off.

M: But I like its company.

W: You are wasting money because you need to pay for the electricity.

M: I think I can manage. Thank you.

Question: What is the man probably doing?

(A) Leaving the TV on without watching it.

(B) Buying some things he doesn't need.

(C) Driving his car in the downtown area.

(D) Watching movies without buying his ticket.

女：如果你沒在看的話，請把它關掉。

男：但我喜歡有它陪伴。

女：你在浪費錢，因為你要付電費。

男：我想我還能應付，謝謝你。

問題：這男子可能正在做什麼？

選項：(A) 開著電視但沒在看。

　　　(B) 買一些他不需要的東西。

　　　(C) 在鬧區開車。

　　　(D) 看電影但沒買票。

38. Question number 38:

M: You know Mary can make friends with almost everyone.

W: So?

M: She should be more careful. You never know when bad guys are going to show up.

W: On second thought, you are right.

Question: What do they think of Mary's habits of making friends?

(A) That's something she should be proud of.

(B) That's something she should be more careful about.

(C) That's something she should stop.

(D) That's something she should learn to do.

男：你知道瑪莉跟幾乎所有人都能做朋友。

女：所以呢？

男：她應該更小心點。你永遠不會知道壞人什麼時候會出現。

女：仔細想想，你說的對。

問題：他們對瑪莉交朋友的習慣看法如何？

選項：(A) 那是她該感到驕傲的事。

(B) 那是她該更小心的事。

(C) 那是她該停止的事。

(D) 那是她該學著去做的事。

39. Question number 39:

W: Can you give me some advice?

M: About what?

W: I don't know which one to choose, the red one or the blue one?

M: They both look good on you, but I like the red one better.

Question: What's the man's advice to the woman?

(A) Take the red one.

(B) Take the blue one.

(C) Take them both.

(D) Don't take any of them.

女：能給我些建議嗎？

男：關於哪方面？

女：我不知道要選哪件，紅的還是藍的？

男：這兩件你穿都很漂亮，但我比較喜歡紅的。

問題：男子給女子的建議為何？

選項：(A) 選紅的。

(B) 選藍的。

(C) 兩件都選。

(D) 兩件都不選。

40. Question number 40:

M: Why did you do that?

W: I thought I was doing something right.

M: How could you send the money only because someone asked you to?

W: Don't yell at me! I know I was wrong.

Question: What does the man really mean?

(A) How could the woman be so stupid?

(B) How could the woman send the money

without telling him?

(C) How could the woman force others to do something wrong?

(D) How could the woman be so considerate generous?

男：你為何做那件事？

女：我以為我是在做一件對的事。

男：你怎能因為有人要你寄錢你就真的寄了？

女：別吼我！我知道我錯了。

問題：這男子的真正意思為何？

選項：(A) 這女子怎麼會這麼笨？

(B) 這女子怎麼可以寄錢而不告訴他？

(C) 這女子怎麼可以逼迫他人做錯誤的事？

(D) 這女子怎麼會如此慷慨？

41. Question number 41:

W: Are you done with your homework yet?

M: It will be another twenty minutes.

W: Don't forget to clean up your room afterwards.

M: I can't. I am meeting my friends after I finish my homework.

Question: What will happen next?

(A) The man will finish her homework and then clean up her room.

(B) The woman will ask the man to clean his room.

(C) The woman will clean the man's room herself.

(D) The man will finish his homework and then meet his friends.

女：你做完功課了嗎？

男：還要二十分鐘。

女：之後別忘了把房間清乾淨。

男：不行。做完功課後我要和朋友碰面。

問題：接下來會發生什麼事？

選項：(A) 這男子會做完她的功課然後清理她的

房間。

(B) 這女子會要求男子清理他的房間。

(C) 這女子會自己清理男子的房間。

(D) 這男子會做完他的功課然後和他的朋友碰面。

42. Question number 42:

M: May I help you?

W: Yes, I'm looking for the children's book department.

M: Oh, the children's book department is on the basement floor. You can take the escalator down and it's on your right.

W: Thank you so much.

M: Enjoy.

Question: Where are these two people?

(A) They are in a bank.

(B) They are in a park.

(C) They are in a bookstore.

(D) They are in a train station.

男：有什麼我可以幫忙的嗎？

女：是的，我正在找童書部門。

男：喔，童書部門在地下室。你可以搭手扶梯下去，它就在右手邊。

女：非常感謝你。

男：祝您購物愉快。

問題：他們在什麼地方？

選項：(A) 他們在銀行。

(B) 他們在公園。

(C) 他們在書店。

(D) 他們在車站。

43. Question number 43:

W: What kind of donuts do you want?

M: How about two for each of the chocolate, the strawberry, and the sugar, please.

W: You want some drink to go with them?

M: No thanks.

Question: How many donuts does the man buy?

(A) Three altogether.

(B) Six altogether.

(C) Nine altogether.

(D) Twelve altogether

女：你要哪種甜甜圈？

男：巧克力、草莓、糖霜，每一種各兩個。

女：你要搭配飲料嗎？

男：不，謝了。

問題：這男子總共買了幾個甜甜圈？

選項：(A) 一共三個。

(B) 一共六個。

(C) 一共九個。

(D) 一共十二個。

44. Question number 44:

M: What are you reading?

W: I am practicing my lines. I'll be in the school's play.

M: That's wonderful! When is the play? Need any help?

W: It's two weeks from now and you can help me by reading through these lines with me.

Question: What is the woman going to do in two weeks?

(A) She is going to perform in school's play.

(B) She is going to play in her school's basketball team.

(C) She is going to watch school's play.

(D) She is going to sell tickets for school's play.

男：你在讀什麼？

女：我在練習我的台詞。我要參加學校的戲劇演出。

男：太棒了！何時演出？需要幫忙嗎？

女：兩個星期後，而你可以幫我一起把台詞讀過一遍。

問題：這女子在兩星期後要做什麼？

選項：(A) 她將在學校的戲劇公演裡演出。

(B) 她將在學校的籃球隊裡比賽。

(C) 她將去看學校的戲劇公演。

(D) 她將替學校的戲劇公演賣票。

45. Question number 45:

W: How long have you been with the company?

M: I have been working here for almost ten years.

W: What's your plan for the future?

M: Try to do the job well as much as I could.

W: Great, we'll give you a raise to keep you here.

Question: What will happen to the man?

(A) He will be fired.

(B) He will get more pay.

(C) He will leave the company soon.

(D) He will employ the woman.

女：你在公司工作多久了？

男：我在公司工作將近十年了。

女：你未來的計畫是什麼？

男：盡我最大能力把工作做好。

女：很好，我們會給你加薪把你留下來。

問題：這男子接下來會發生什麼事？

選項：(A) 他會被解僱。

(B) 他會拿到更高的薪水。

(C) 他會很快離開這間公司。

(D) 他會僱用這位女子。

提示：現在完成式 "have/has + p.p." 表示某動作自過去時間開始進行到現在為止；現在完成進行式 "have/has + been + Ving" 則表示動作自過去開始進行到現在並持續到未來：

I have studied English for six years.

(I don't know if I will continue to study)

I have been studying English for six years. (And I'll continue to study)

看完本書之後，還想來點別的嗎？
我們還有…

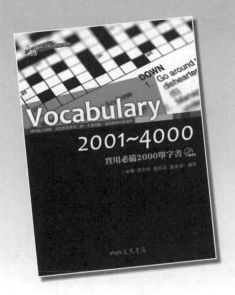

Vocabulary 2001~4000
實用必備2000單字書

丁雍嫻 邢雯桂 盧思嘉 應惠蕙／編著

1. 依據大考中心所公布之詞彙分級表，將其第三、四級有系統地收錄其中。
2. 精心編寫大量例句，讓你精確掌握字的用法。常用片語及同、反義字的補充，豐富實用，讓你輕鬆擴大學習範圍。
3. 每章節均附即時評量，讓你隨時檢驗學習成果。
4. 附線上電子朗讀音檔，讓你加強各單字的唸法，對記憶單字更有莫大的幫助。

Vocabulary 2001~4000
隨身讀

三民英語編輯小組／彙整

1. 最豐富的內容收錄在最迷你的篇幅中，方便攜帶，隨時學習。
2. 依據大考中心所公布之詞彙分級表，將其第三、四級有系統地收錄其中。
3. 補充重要片語及例句，讓你徹底掌握單字用法。
4. 同反義字補充豐富，讓你輕鬆延伸學習範圍。
5. 補充豐富的衍生字，讓你反覆練習強化記憶。

悅讀50

王隆興／編著

- 精選五十篇多元主題的文章，篇篇妙筆生花，精采好讀。
- 命題方向符合各類大考趨勢，讓你熟能生巧，輕取高分。
- 文章程度為大考中心公布之單字表中4000字的範圍，難度相當於全民英檢中級。
- 特聘多位外籍作者親筆撰寫文章，語法用字純正道地。

完全閱讀導引

李文玲／編著

- 第一部份為理論篇，分析閱讀測驗出題方向與作答技巧，幫助你打好根基。
- 第二部分精選四十篇主題多元、趣味性與知識性兼具的文章，幫助你進行閱讀測驗的實戰練習。
- 文章用字符合大考中心公布之單字表中4000字的範圍，且配合全民英檢中級程度。
- 適用於普高、技高學生升學準備或一般讀者強化閱讀能力。

只要本書在手，英檢聽力一次就過！

◆ 內含8回聽力模擬試題，增加實戰經驗。

◆ 提供3種聽力題型的範例分析，精闢解說考試
重心。

◆ 由專業外籍人士錄製MP3朗讀音檔，真實模
擬測驗題目的間隔與速度，讓你提高應試的
熟悉度。

◆ 附電子朗讀音檔，下載方式請見書中說明。